A September Day and Shadow Thriller
WIN OR LOSE

Book Six

AMY SHOJAI

FURRY MUSE
PUBLISHING
P.O. Box 1904
Sherman TX 75091
(903)814-4319
amy@shojai.com

**September & Shadow Pet-centric Thrillers
By Amy Shojai**

LOST AND FOUND

HIDE AND SEEK

SHOW AND TELL

FIGHT OR FLIGHT
Introducing Lia, Tee, and Karma

HIT AND RUN

WIN OR LOSE

Chapter 1 - QUINN

Raised by murderers, on the run since age fifteen, Quinn
Donovan hunted the wicked to redeem her soul. She
relished the recent training that had honed her flaccid
body into lithe strength, sharpened reflexes to whip-
fast, and drilled innovative training until the skills became second
nature—transforming her from prey to hunter. She'd proved
herself four months ago, even before training, but knew she still
had much to learn. Even with bare bones knowledge, the change
offered new-found hope, and the possibility of a future where—
eventually—she'd answer only to herself.

For now, though, she served as a weapon for another to aim
and fire.

As a ghost, nobody would ever hurt her again. She had a new
name, a new body, and a new purpose. No longer hiding in the
shadows, Quinn operated in the light, and those in her sights got
no quarter. She had no problem spilling the blood of bad guys.
Like her bad-ass motorcycle-riding great-granny always said: *An eye
for an eye.*

Quinn touched her newly toned tummy and made room for
Tigger to settle on her lap. He immediately climbed to her
shoulders, draping his large tabby-striped body around her neck,
and kneading with claw-sheathed paws. By rights, she should have

got rid of him. He tied Quinn to her past life, but had saved her sanity. So, like her, she'd changed his name and his appearance. She couldn't trust humans, but the cat never lied. She wouldn't admit it to anyone, but they needed each other. Neither of them had many more lives to spare.

The special phone buzzed. The text messages always came from different numbers. Her stomach fluttered. Another assignment so soon? She completed the most recent one in Mexico in record time by recruiting gullible students on spring break to mule the product over the border. Worked like a charm, and impressed the hell out of her benefactor by creating an ideal new revenue source. Hell, she'd already made all the right connections when she couldn't get what she needed any other way. She smiled. The contacts trusted her. In this business, that meant everything.

But when Quinn checked the text, her smile froze. The cat meowed and immediately head-butted her cheek. Quinn pushed him aside and sprang up with a soft curse. The text had two words:

>*Fix it*

It also contained a picture of a tall heavyset boy, pale dog at his side, sneaking off with a recognizable insulated thermos. Damn!

The cat head-butted her again. Quinn breathed deeply, willing her blood pressure to drop. She texted back a "thumbs up" emoji, gathered the cat into her arms, and buried her face in his short fur.

She'd given the party-hearty kids a chance to do good, instead of just hanging out and puking on the beach. If one boy went sideways, his friends might have followed his lead to line their own pockets. Served her right for going cheap and enlisting amateurs instead of hiring pros. He'd pay, though, for the betrayal.

No time to waste. She used her new skills to run one of the specialized searches on the laptop she'd prepared for just such an emergency. Quinn knew to plan backups and redundancies into everything. That had kept her alive this long, and there'd be less room for error working for the current Organization. As she waited for the report to percolate, Quinn stroked the cat until he had had enough and vaulted to the top of the motel television cabinet. Tigger always wanted to be on the highest perch.

Within minutes, the report spat out the bad news. Of the twenty couriers, sixteen delivered thermoses containing the product to Quinn's dummy recipients in south Texas. Once processed, the drugs continued up the distribution chain per her benefactor's requirement. Quinn's sole responsibility, to get the product across the border, failed. Her boss demanded 100 percent satisfaction. Or suffer the consequences.

Bad enough the delivery never happened. Even worse, the AWOL couriers knew her face and at least part of the enterprise. She'd need to change up her appearance again, and maybe her name, but felt grateful for the warning text. Another failure would earn worse.

How had she so misjudged them? She had to turn this around. *Eye for an eye, tooth for a tooth.* And maybe a bullet for betrayal.

She'd go after the first boy, recover the product, and explain to him the error of his ways. He'd tell her where to find the others, too. She'd learned a lot during her training about how to get answers. With this reprieve, she'd prove her worth once and for all to her boss. She'd **fix it**, all right!

Staring at the disposable phone and the terse text she'd sent quickened Kali's breath. Two words. Enough to rattle the souls of those in her employ. Except this girl, too new to know better, had no clue what she'd set in motion. Her smile widened.

With care, she removed the SIM card. She placed it on a nearby battered butcher-block table stained with unmentionables and used a metal meat mallet to beat it into fragments. She brushed the fragments into a nearby ash tray, already filled to the brim with the remains of the imported cigars she favored. Dropping the phone, she crushed it beneath one elegant stiletto with a satisfying crunch, then kicked the debris into the corner. Her maid service would erase the clutter shortly.

When she beckoned, the man standing watch at the door reached her side in three long strides. He embodied her perfect mate. Much younger than her, biddable, with understated leonine strength she found more appealing than bullish bodyguards. He'd won her favor with his swift execution of each assignment. He never questioned. He followed direction. His stamina and appetite equaled her own. He deserved a reward, a tasty treat, to keep him coming back for more. Kali smiled. She had just the thing, and his fun would also clear the tedious roadblock that threatened her future.

She held out her hand. "Your phone." He handed it over, and she quickly found an online image and showed it to him. "Clarabelle lives in Heartland, Texas. Has all the young studs smitten." She liked that word, rolled it around on her tongue to say it again. "Smitten. She's not shy about sharing her favors. But I want her to be extra nice to one stud in particular, so very nice that young Studly won't say no to a favor. You understand?"

He nodded, eyes gleaming. "The favor?"

"All in due time." She handed back his phone. "Of course, use the Organization's air transport services to expedite the assignment. Make it happen. And once she asks the favor, and he delivers, you can have your fun with her." One of Kali's long, sharp green fingernails drew a line down his bare throat to the open collar of his shirt. "I've had a new identity prepared especially for this assignment. You answer to Mr. Casper Fright. Because you'll be an unfriendly ghost, and anyone who survives this should have nightmares remembering anything about you. Do you like that... Mr. Fright?"

He nodded again, breath quickening. Mr. Fright knew what came next.

"The usual arrangements apply. Success means rewards, and failure—well, you don't want to find out. And after taking care of Clarabelle, if you're still... hungry"—she looked him up and down, smiling at his obvious response—"I'll have more delectables for your exacting tastes."

Much later, after he'd satisfied her—for now—she dismissed Mr. Fright and his insatiable appetite. It made her itch to join him in the titillating up-close work that gave her the ultimate exquisite release, rather than delegating such jobs to inferiors. She couldn't indulge, though. Perhaps after cementing her control by eliminating her rival, she'd reward herself.

"This time, I win and you lose," she whispered. Between Quinn Donovan and Casper Fright, she'd created an unrelenting, indestructible, and unforgiving team to eliminate a certain gadfly named September Day.

Chapter 2-QUINN

Quinn's motorcycle roared up to the dilapidated motel and zoomed into the parking lot. She spotted the kid's lime-green VW crouched in the far corner like a sickly bug, and rolled up beside it. Dismounting in one fluid motion, Quinn took in her surroundings, noting with satisfaction the lack of surveillance cameras. What happened next needed no witnesses.

Even the front office counter looked deserted, at least temporarily. Quinn had no intention of enlisting aid unless absolutely necessary. The fewer people who saw her here, the better. Based on the position of the kid's car, and the lack of other vehicles, she figured one of three rooms held her target.

A dog barked. Bingo! That's right, this kid had the three-legged mutt. She remembered him chastising the rest of the kids for distracting the dog from its "work," whatever that might be.

She checked the pet carrier strapped to the back of her motorcycle. Tigger meowed and pawed the clear plexiglass bubble top. Unlike most cats, Tigger tolerated loud noises. She'd tried pet earmuffs, but he hated those, and she figured his inquisitive nature stood him in good stead. "Hang out for a little. I've got business." The fine weather and cool breeze would keep the cat comfortable until she finished what had to be done.

The dog barked again. She squinted when motion at the

nearest window signaled the animal's presence. When the dog saw
her through the glass, it redoubled barking complaints, so big it
didn't need to paw the glass and bouncing up and down in its
eagerness for attention. Quinn's lip curled. Tigger would never act
so needy. You had to earn Tigger's trust, but after that, he'd protect
you with fierce loyalty. She loved that about the cat.

So much for surprise. She doubted the motel rooms had rear
exits but wouldn't take the chance. Quinn hurried to the door,
glanced around quickly, and then aimed a practiced kick at the
perfect spot just beneath the rickety doorknob.

When the door sprang open, Quinn slipped inside, and
allowed it to rebound and latch behind her. The dim light offered
enough illumination to reveal the boy slumped in a chair, barely
conscious. The dog jumped up and down, nose-poking her and
bumping his big pale chest against her, whining and crying with
urgency.

"Leave me alone, dog. Get back." She noticed a blue leash
slung over a chair. "Okay, settle down, Fido, or whatever you're
called. Let me hook you up." She looped it around the dog's neck
and anchored the animal to the bed's headboard. It moved better
than expected, with only three legs. "I need to talk to your human."

He looked sick. She smelled vomit and nearly stepped in the
mess, and made a face. She recognized the open thermos on the
table beside him, along with a used syringe and vial. The stupid kid
had shot up with her product!

"Hey kid. Kid! Wake up, stay with me there. Kid!" She kneeled
beside him, slapping him gently on both cheeks and then harder
when that had no result. His mouth gaped open, panting in quick,
fruity-smelling breaths. Dammit. "Don't die on me." *At least, not
until you've told me what I need to know.*

He roused, blinking, eyes straining to focus. "Mom? Want
mom…"

"Sure, whatever you want, kiddo. What happened here?
Honey?" She tried to hide the exasperation and inject some
empathy. But, how stupid could he be? "Where are your friends?
The ones with the rest of the, uhm… medicine?"

That's how she'd pitched the project. The kids believed they
"beat the system" when they brought discount medicine from
Mexico back into the states, to supply the less fortunate who
couldn't afford to buy. Sure, that's one way to look at it. Not that

her handlers had any intention of helping anyone but themselves.

His head rolled weakly from side to side as he tried to focus. "Sebastian tol' me...nobody miss a little." His voice slurred making it hard to understand. The dog yelped again. "Lefty's never wrong, hadda take..." He sat in a near trance. One arm moved sluggishly as if pushing through jello to indicate the drugs. He scanned the room, head swiveling molasses slow, searching for sight of his dog. His stomach contracted. "God, it hurts, it hurts!" His eyes rolled upward.

"No, no, no, stay with me. Stay with me. Sebastian told you, huh? Where's Sebastian now? And the others, there are two others never delivered. Hey-hey-hey!" She shook him again. The dog howled.

He focused briefly, blinking hard. "Need a doctor."

"Sure, I already called 911, the ambulance will come anytime." She lied without hesitation. Quinn had practiced the craft on worthier audiences than this poor buffoon. "Where's Sebastian and the others?" He stared. She poked him. "Tell me."

"Sebastian." Incoherent mumblings that made no sense. "Corpus an' sisters ride away away away..." He slumped.

This time, she couldn't rouse him. Quinn efficiently riffled his pockets and pulled out his wallet. Tanner Rudolph, 27 years old. He looked younger. She breathed hard and winced at the dog's repeated cries. He kept pawing at the floor, rooting to shove his big head under the bed. "Oh hush, he had it coming. You deserve somebody smarter." She knew from experience what too much— or too little—of this medicine could do to a person. She'd nearly died, and lost her baby as a result...

No, she wouldn't go there. Quinn shut off that train of thought. Quickly, she went through the rest of Tanner's possessions, collecting everything that easily identified him. He had to have a phone...when the dog whimpered and snuffled under the bed again, Quinn took the hint and collected the boy's phone where it had fallen. The dog tried to grab it. Weird.

She repackaged the drugs, and would see them delivered to satisfy her handlers. As for Tanner Rudolph, the motel staff and then the authorities would find his body quick enough. That gave her an idea, to add even more of a buffer to her timeline...

The dog barked again. He strained against the leash, shifting the heavy bed with him to reach Tanner. The white dog's power and determination overcame any deficit of his missing leg. Lefty licked the boy's slack face, sniffing at his lips, whimpering, levered his nose beneath the limp hand to prompt pets. Then he tipped back his head and howled.

Damn. She couldn't leave him here making such noise. She'd have to do something about the dog after all.

Chapter 3 - SEPTEMBER

S eptember's fingers whitened as they clenched the handle of her coffee mug. Instead of hurling it across the room, she carefully set it on the counter with a soft thunk. "We've already had this conversation, Melinda, and nothing has changed. So make sure you're ready to roll before your dad comes downstairs. He's got a busy day ahead, finalizing the sale of his house. So do I." Her throat ached with the effort to keep her voice light and calm.

The teenager glared, her expression filled with more heat than the scalding coffee. "You and Dad decided. Not me. And not Willie."

"Decided what?" Melinda's younger brother skidded into the room, followed by the scrabbling paws of a white and tan terrier mix.

"Packing us off to Aunt Ethel and Uncle Stanley. For a whole week."

Willie grabbed a piece of toast and broke off a corner for the dog. "I like it there. You're just mad you don't get to camp out at the lake with your friends. A week-long party, and you can't go." He sing-songed the last bit.

Willie hit the target with the unerring aim of an eleven-year-old brother. Melinda flinched. "Shut up, Willie." She tossed her curly red hair, striving for nonchalance, but she couldn't still the slight tremble of her lower lip. She cut her eyes at September. "No reason to tell Dad, since he won't let me go, anyway. Please don't say anything."

September raised her eyebrows. That explained a lot. The girl had turned fourteen last month and had always run with an older crowd. It got her in trouble before, which weighed heavily on her father. Detective Jeff Combs had reason to act overprotective toward his headstrong daughter. As a future step-mom, September felt out of her league with both kids, but especially Melinda.

Willie's dog quickly munched the toast treat and then trotted to the far corner of the kitchen. He stood on his hind legs to scope out the cat's food bowl.

"Willie, please control your dog. We only allow Macy up there, for safety reasons—never dogs. Not even Shadow." At the sound of his name, the big black shepherd pressed against her thigh, and September's hand absently stroked his cheek. "We've talked about this." She kept her voice calm. She didn't want to come off as the "wicked stepmother," especially with the kids' mother so sick. Still, the ship may have already sailed with Melinda.

He shrugged. "Kinsler can't reach Macy's bowl. And besides, he's not a service dog like Shadow, so it's not fair he's gotta follow the same rules. Anyway, the cat thinks it's funny. Don't you, kitty-kitty?" Willie broke off another piece of toast and crossed to offer it to the Maine Coon.

Perched atop the refrigerator, Macy didn't even deign to sniff the buttered offering. He turned his head away, plume-like tail thumping his opinion of Willie's treat. Kinsler jumped up against Willie's thigh, trying to reach the treat, the cat, or both. The boy laughed, held the toast a teasing distance overhead, then grinned when the dog snapped it out of the air.

"That's it, Willie! Take Kinsler outside. Now. I'll call you when your dad's ready to go." September immediately regretted her sharp tone.

In a split second, Willie's face turned from glee to tragedy. His eyes welled. "It's not fair I can't take Kinsler with me. He's my best buddy. You get to keep Shadow with you all the time."

"If Kinsler had Shadow's manners, your Aunt Ethel might not mind him visiting." September wanted to call back the retort, but Willie whirled and headed for the door, Kinsler in tow.

Melinda hissed at September. "Don't you dare yell at my brother. You don't have the right!" Melinda followed the pair into the back garden. The girl didn't have to say *you're not our mom* for it to be heard, loud and clear as any shout.

September stopped herself from chasing the pair to apologize. Too late. Served her right for losing her temper. She couldn't do anything right lately with either of the kids. "Honeymoon's over," she whispered. Both Melinda and Willie had accepted their father's engagement with apparent glee. But then reality set in, especially after visiting their mother these past few weeks in hospice.

Combs now had sole custody since his ex-wife could no longer care for them. The kids' stepfather had been eager to unburden himself, an understandable but totally jerk-worthy reaction in September's opinion. No wonder Melinda and Willie felt untethered, even rejected. Having felt that way for much of her adult life, her heart ached for what they'd gone through, and she wanted to make it up to them. She'd done her best to connect with the pair—with Melinda over girl-talk (not that September felt particularly "girly") and with Willie over training his dog-buddy Kinsler. She had had high hopes they'd become friends.

The second blow was when the kids realized they'd have to move to new schools, away from friends. Combs's tiny house wouldn't fit them all. September's renovated Victorian here on Rabbit Run Road had plenty of space, now the repairs were finished—at least inside. All four of them had agreed to juggle schedules so the kids could finish this year in their familiar schools. Spring break therefore became more precious.

She'd thought the renovations were done until four people had to share the space. They'd added an extra powder room—a teenage girl didn't want to share with her little brother—which meant a delay until the contractors finished. September couldn't wait to have the place to themselves for a week, but felt enormous guilt. What kind of parent wanted to fob off kids on relatives when they could forge stronger bonds?

Shadow yawned loudly and pressed against her thigh. "Maybe I'm not cut out for this," she told him.

"Cut out for what?" Combs asked as he came down the stairs into the kitchen. He looked around the room, then crossed quickly to give her a long kiss. "I'd say you're perfectly suited to this." He wiggled his eyebrows, and she laughed, then pushed him away. He smelled good: spicy aftershave, hair still wet from the shower.

"The kids…" She hesitated. September didn't want to get in between him and his children. Juggling relationships and boundaries between those she loved—and hoped would love her back—still flummoxed her.

"Ah yes, kids. Where are they? I promised to deliver them to Uncle Stan's early this morning. Sign the closing papers on my house at seven—thank goodness, it sold so quickly!—and my shift starts at eight." He poured a coffee into a travel mug, declined the toast but picked up a cheese and jalapeno stuffed burrito she'd warmed in the microwave. "I'll take these to go."

"The kids said their packed bags wait by the front door, but I didn't check." Not when they could see her check, anyway. "They're in the garden. Willie's upset about leaving Kinsler."

"He'll get over it. Aunt Ethel's a cat person, and Kinsler's sort of a mess. Thought you'd help Willie teach him some manners." He took a bite of burrito, chewed.

She bit her lip and looked away. "Better call them in. It rained last night, so it's probably pretty soggy out there." She shrugged. "I'll drop Kinsler at the kennel before my meetings. He'll get a bath before he comes home at the end of the week." The dog had a great time at the kennel, playing with other canine friends.

Both kids trooped through the door into the kitchen, neither looking at September as they wiped their feet. "Kinsler's in the garden, Dad." Willie trailed after his sister to the front door to collect their luggage.

Combs whispered, "I could swing back after dropping off the kids." He leaned in for another kiss. He tasted like sour cream.

She dimpled, but shook her head. "I have the church orchestra rehearsal for the Easter service at eight. And you're cutting it tight for your shift as well."

Combs made a face. "You know, with the dog out of the way, and the kids gone for the week, we could get married. Elope."

"What?"

"Come on, September. I don't need pageant and a bunch of dressed up attendants. We could run down to the JP's office, get married, and spend the rest of the week on a honeymoon. Go wherever we want. Away from here, and job demands." He wiggled his eyebrows again. "We're in the same house, but we never have time to just—just be together."

Oh, didn't she know it! "Honey, I'd love to, but we can't cut the kids out of the big day, they'd never forgive us." *Or me,* she thought. *It'd be my fault.* She hadn't found the right time to ask Melinda and Willie to be part of the wedding party, and wasn't sure they'd accept.

"We'll make it up to them. A family vacation later this summer. Just think of it. This would save headaches, save money, save time. We could start our life together now. No more waiting. And we can still have the reception this summer for family and friends."

"Please, just stop." A headache began building behind her eyes. "We reserved the church, paid musicians, and a deposit for the reception caterer. You put in for time off for our honey—"

"I switched it for this week." He grinned. "Wanted it to be a surprise. Once today's shift finishes at three, I've got four days off. We can pick up the marriage license and…"

"I can't. No! How could you? What were you thinking?" A pulse grew faster in her temple. "You don't just make plans for someone else without telling them." Her face felt hot.

His eyes widened, and he stammered. "Wait, I thought you'd like the surprise." Combs sharpened his tone.

"April and I are doing the Easter concert in Mom's memory. I can't ditch rehearsal. She always dreamed I'd be married in church."

Melinda chose that moment to call out, snarky tone all too familiar, "We're ready whenever y'all finish arguing."

Lips a thin white line, Combs left without another word.

September closed her eyes, her jaw tight, wanting to go after him. She forced herself to wait until the front door opened and closed. Shadow nudged her hand, and she kneeled on the kitchen floor to welcome the black furry body into her arms. Her long dark hair spilled over his neck. He licked tears from her face before she realized they'd appeared.

September wouldn't call Jeff. She knew better than to interrupt Combs at work. He had meant no harm. She knew that. But she needed to explain why keeping to the plan meant so much. It would put a period on that part of her life, so that together they could create a new future together, without the past haunting them.

When the phone rang, September hurried to answer, expecting Combs. With disappointment, she recognized the caller. "Hi, Lia."

"Oh good, glad I caught you before you left to bring Kinsler. We're packed to the gills with spring break." Her cousin Lia owned Corazon Boarding Kennels. "Couldn't have squeezed him in except for that last minute cancellation."

September nodded. "I'll head that way momentarily. We really appreciate the favor. I can keep him here, but—"

"No, that's fine. But since you mentioned it, maybe you can return the favor?" Her tone hinted at delicious mysteries.

"If I can," September answered warily. Impulsive Lia often jumped first without benefit of a parachute.

"Oh, it's nothing bad, September. I really want to do it myself. But I can't get away for the next two weeks, and you've got a week off, so to speak, with no kids or Kinsler..." She again emphasized the doggy favor she'd provided. "So maybe you and Combs could, I don't know, make a day trip of it or something."

Sighing, September massaged the back of her neck. The headache had really taken hold. "Lia, cut to the chase."

"Okay. I got a call from a shelter in Wintergreen, Texas. I'll send you the address. Someone dropped off a dog with no microchip, no collar, and no way to track the owner. Except, it came with your Pets Peeves give-away leash, that blue one with the kennel phone number, so they called me." She paused, and September heard dogs barking in the background. "It's not one of my clients, so best guess, it was one of your behavior consults. Can you look in your records and help find the owner? Or better yet, run down there and get the dog."

Chapter 4 - NIKKI

At eleven years old, a little blood didn't scare Nikki. Spring break meant a whole week helping Doc Eugene with medical treatments, and maybe even surgery at the vet clinic. Bliss!

But sixteen-year-old Hank yearned to go with friends to South Texas. Her brother resented they couldn't afford the trip, especially because he knew about the cash that came regularly in the mail. Mom only spent the *miracle money* on necessities, like rent, and payments on the new-to-them used car she'd need if she got a new job. Dad's old car didn't run so good anymore. Now that Hank had his learner's permit, he got to drive the old car while Dad was away, but only for emergencies. Like taking Nikki to work when Mom couldn't. He resented Nikki's cheerful attitude, resented ferrying Nikki around. She figured that's why they'd ended up here, for a quick kissy-face meet up with Hank's girlfriend.

"Wait here. I'll be back in a minute." He swung out of the car.

"I need to use the facilities." Nikki followed him out and ignored his glare. She stared at the 100+ pumps in the massive service center, as Hank hurried to a van parked in the front row of the Buc-ee's lot. She figured Yolanda or Susie or whatever girl-of-the-month waited in the van, and Hank needed Nikki to zip her lip about the rendezvous. Mom wouldn't be happy Hank brought her along for one of his *romantical* encounters.

She hesitated at the front doors until she saw him climb into the van. She'd heard about the famous spacious bathrooms at Buc-ee's and couldn't miss the opportunity to see them. Her jaw dropped as she pushed inside the massive store. For a moment, she forgot to breathe.

The bustling place, huge by most service station standards, boasted row upon row of offerings. Buc-ee's put other convenience stores to shame. The expected fare of candy bars and common snack food paled in comparison to the deli row of gourmet jerky and sweet puffed corn snacks; plus, there was a place to order breakfast, lunch, or dinner anytime of the day or night. Stuffed toys, including the famous beaver himself—in various sizes—drew Nikki's eyes to the gift shop with Buc-ee themed merch like hats, shirts, home decorating items, and a section devoted to hunters.

On her way to the bathroom, she watched fudge poured onto cold slabs and into Texas-shaped molds. *Maybe on the way out.* Nikki needed to check her wallet, buried deep in her backpack, first.

The bathroom seemed to go on forever. Dozens of stalls, most with a green light over the door showing empty, offered a multitude of choices. Nikki quickly made her toilet, washed her hands, then nodded at the attendant. She figured you could eat off the floor—not that you'd want to.

At the bottom of her backpack, underneath her tablet and a bulky sweater, because the clinic stayed chilly, she found her wallet with the kitty face. Nikki counted her cash. Enough to get some Buc-ee's Nuggets, a package of jerky, and maybe the smallest stuffed beaver toy. Her cat Hope loved stuffed toys, even though she'd started to fade with age. Besides, Doc Eugene had promised a bonus for helping this week.

Nikki took her time. The clinic opened at 6:00 a.m. for surgery drop-offs, but she didn't need to be there until 7:00. Besides, Hank would take as much time as he could with his honey-of-the-week. Nikki made a face. She didn't see it, but girls acted all woo-woo eye-batting swoony around Hank.

Nikki pushed her wallet back into the depths of her bag, added the jerky, and stuck the beaver stuffie on top. She shrugged into the backpack and tore open the nuggets. She'd skipped breakfast. Mom had had no time to fix anything because she had more job interviews today. Mom said she and Hank knew how to wrangle up scrambled eggs and toast if they wanted it. The sweet puffed treat tasted even better than caramel corn, but melted almost without chewing. She munched and smiled on her way back to the car.

Before she made it out the door, Hank grabbed her arm and spun her around, marching Nikki back into the store. "Say nothing." He whispered fiercely. "Don't look back." He pulled her behind an end-cap, and fiddled with her backpack, pulling out the stuffie and tossing it on the ground. His hand left a bloody mark on the toy.

"What's wrong? Hank, you're scaring me." She craned to look over her shoulder at him, but he stayed out of her line of sight.

"Shut up. It's bad. Something terrible. I didn't know…" His voice broke on a half-sob. "Listen, Nikki. I'm in big trouble. You can't tell anyone about this. Promise me." He picked up the beaver toy and stuffed it on top of whatever he'd shoved in her backpack. "Wait for me in the car, okay? Go out like normal. Don't look back." His hands fumbled on her shoulders, tightened, and shook her gently. "Just this once, don't argue, don't question. Please!" He gulped. Then added under his breath, "I don't want you to get hurt, too."

She nodded, blinking rapidly at the terror in his voice. Without turning around, she whispered, "Shouldn't we call the police?"

"God, no!" He shook her harder with the words. He prodded her toward the glass doors. "Normal, Nikki. Get in the car, and I'll come soon as I can, then we'll go home."

"What about my job?" Her lip trembled.

"Forget about the stupid job. I just want us to get out of here alive."

She remembered the bloody handprint on the toy, and gulped, stiffened her spine, and preceded him out the door. A young man with a scruffy beard and reflective aviator sunglasses turned her way. She imagined his glowering look behind the lenses. His lips snarled and he hurried with purpose toward them.

Her brother whispered again. "Change of plans. Nikki, when I say, you run. Run hard and fast. Find a place to hide. It's about to get crazy." His voice crackled. "And don't look back."

"Hank?" She whimpered, and reached behind her to grab at his hand.

He squeezed her fingers. "Don't worry, short-stuff, I'll be fine. Promise." He took a big shaky breath. "Now Nikki, run. Run!"

She ran. Behind her, screams erupted, peppered with staccato shouts of surprise. Nikki wanted to look back, but Hank had scared her so badly she feared looking back might jinx whatever he had planned.

When she sighted the perfect hiding spot across the parking lot, she risked a quick glance back. People milling around the doors hid any details and she couldn't see Hank. Feeling cold on her hand, she looked down, and discovered that clutching Hank's hand had left her own slick with blood. A lot of blood.

Chapter 5 - SHADOW

Shadow stared up into September's face, alert to her every expression. Each eyebrow twitch, brow furrow, and nostril flare spoke volumes. Partnered with her stiff, hunched shoulders, Shadow needed no words to understand: Sad. Worried. Frustrated and stressed. It was a good-dog's job to understand his person and help her feel better.

When she grabbed up the coffee mug, he raced ahead, black tail flagging eagerness for their usual morning romp. That always made him feel better, too, especially when he could make her laugh. He skidded into a sit, his polite request for her to open the back door; at her release, Shadow raced to the garden gate and sat again. Overhead lights painted the area in pools of bright and dark.

The other dog heard and met Shadow on the other side of the gate. But Kinsler didn't sit the way a polite dog should. He wriggled, whined, and yapped, pushing his furry face against the metal grillwork, eager to make contact. Shadow whined and glanced up at September.

She frowned. "He's a mess. Figures."

Black mud stained the much smaller dog's off-white fur from paw to shoulder. But September didn't sound mad. She chuckled, and Shadow's tail swept the pathway clear of leaves as she opened the gate. Kinsler burst out of the entry, circling Shadow and leaping at him. He sat silent, stoic, and maintained his steadfast sit-stay with eyes glued on September's face.

"Good dog, Shadow. Go play. I'll go get a towel. Maybe two towels." She latched the gate and returned to the house.

He launched like a furry rocket, woofing under his breath, bowling over the smaller dog. Kinsler paused only a moment to shake himself and then raced after Shadow. Around and around the pathways they chased, taking turns tagging each other, interweaving games of bitey-face open-mouth tooth fencing. They kicked up fresh-dug dirt until Shadow's paws also held clots of aromatic earth. Shadow carefully inhibited his bites, wanting the game to continue. Better they play here than inside the house, where Kinsler nose-poked Shadow's cat to make him hiss and hide, and tore up a good-dog's bear-toy. Shadow didn't like that. Not at all.

This place belonged to *September*. And September belonged to *Shadow*. They'd been here before anybody else, along with Macy-cat. Together, they shared this house, shared adventures, and shared one heart.

But now many new people crowded the place, and stole September's attention away. That hurt worse than Kinsler ripping bear-toy to pieces. And it made it harder for a good-dog to do his job, keeping September safe from the darkness that still sometimes haunted her sleep—or even her waking moments.

Oh, he knew and accepted the gruff, low-voiced man, but only because September liked Combs very much. He understood people needed other people for some things. But even Combs couldn't keep September safe the way Shadow could.

And why did she need noisy young ones? The older girl made September's eyes rain tears when nobody watched but Shadow. The boy-pup Willie had no meanness but little control, just like Kinsler.

Would September want Shadow to take care of Melinda and Willie, the way he'd taken care of his boy Steven in the before times? He whined, the confusion making him wrinkle his brow. He heard the gate open and shut and knew September had returned to the garden. Maybe she'd come join the game?

Kinsler dove in and grabbed at Shadow's front leg. Shadow growled that he'd had enough. He'd like Kinsler a lot more if the smaller dog showed some respect. At that thought, Shadow turned, tagged the terrier, and Kinsler obligingly rolled in the dirt and showed his tummy.

"Oh, no! Dammit!"

Shadow flinched at September's exclamation. He slicked back his ears. He hadn't hurt the other dog. Not really. Wasn't it his job to teach the other dog manners?

Not in the least put out, Kinsler bounced to his paws, spotted a nearby squirrel hurling curses at them, and raced after it. He barked and jittered around the live oak tree, arguing back at the rodent.

Rather than join in the fun yelling at the squirrel, Shadow cautiously padded to join September at the back of the garden. She stood aghast, staring at a host of uprooted roses. He read the anger on her face and whimpered to beg forgiveness, even though he didn't know what for. He pressed his shoulder against September's calf. But when she saw his muddy paws, September moved away, lips tight in an expression that hurt a good-dog's heart.

Chapter 6 - SEPTEMBER

September hosed off Kinsler's muddy fur, starting at his rear legs and paws, and methodically moving to his front end. She ignored the dog's squeals. The water wasn't cold. He objected to the indignity. And perhaps the loss of fragrant mud he'd perfumed himself with.

No time for a thorough sudsing, if she wanted to drop him off at Lia's before the rehearsal. She didn't mind nose prints on car windows, but drew the line at the clotted mud. The terrier could sprout grass with all the dirt smooshed into his coat.

Not even the aroma of wet dog offended her. But the kids' silence—malicious or not—did. "They knew," she muttered. Maybe they even watched as the terrier uprooted the last of the old garden's glory.

She didn't blame the dog. The word terrier meant "of the earth." Bred to hunt vermin, Kinsler's heritage hard-wired him to dig. Shadow, on the other paw, had no excuse. His antics surprised and disappointed her. As if he read her mind, the big German Shepherd whimpered, cut his eyes sideways, and pressed ears tight to his head.

"Don't give me that face, Shadow. You're next." At least he hadn't rolled in the stuff.

Canine destructiveness arose from owner misunderstanding or miscalculation, not maliciousness; September knew that. Prevention set dogs up for success. Correcting mistakes after the fact rarely proved as effective. So she had nobody to blame but herself. She should have predicted the digging, and maybe Melinda and Willie's silence, too.

Kids mystified her. You could crate dogs to keep them safe and prevent trouble. She sighed. People frowned on crating kids. Her brow wrinkled, and she wondered if she'd ever get the hang of dealing with the kids. So far, she'd made a mess of it. Hell, she couldn't even manage their dog. *Some behavior expert.*

She quickly toweled most of the wet off of Kinsler, then shut the damp dog in the laundry room before returning outside to Shadow. "Stand. Wait." He licked his lips, turning his head away but stood rock solid on the paved path as she hosed off his lower legs. He trembled, and she guessed he wanted to play bite-the-hose. She hadn't invited the game, though, and he knew better than to try. "Shake." She stood back as he dutifully flung off errant wet from his fur. September opened the door and pointed to the floor mat. "Paws." He wiped his front paws and then kicked back paws on the spot. "Good dog, Shadow. I know you didn't mean any harm."

At her tone, his ears came forward, and he pressed his wet face against her thighs. She stooped to gather him in her arms. "Baby-dog, I can't stay mad at you. It's my fault. You just can't let Kinsler lead you astray."

September made a face at her damp, muddy clothes. Shadow waited in the kitchen as she hurried upstairs to change clothes before she strode to her office/music room. September caught up Harmony from the cello stand, slipped the instrument and bow into its canvas case, and grabbed the folder of music. Donning a light jacket, more than enough for the pleasant spring weather, she carried the precious instrument to her car, signaling Shadow to follow.

Once she loaded the cello—it would ride shotgun in the passenger seat, the only place available with the two dogs in the back—September opened the rear door. "Kennel up." Shadow sprang into the back of the car, tail thumping his love of car rides. His wags stopped when she latched the door and returned to the house.

She cracked open the laundry room door, alert in case the

small dog tried to wriggle through the opening. But Kinsler lay in a far corner of the room, in the middle of a pile of dirty clothes. He sat up, one of Willie's stinky athletic socks dangling from his mouth.

"Wanna go for a car ride?" That always prompted tail wags from Shadow. But Kinsler's ears slicked down. His traumatic experience at the hands of a dog-napper had left its mark. Willie hadn't hung Kinsler's halter on the hook, either, and she didn't have time to look for it.

She rummaged in a cupboard to find the small spray bottle, then turned sideways and ignored the dog, letting her hands and arms hang limp. He dropped the sock to come sniff her fingers. Kinsler lowered his head and wagged as she clipped a leash on his collar. She retrieved the dirty sock and spritzed it with the canine pheromone—something that helped reduce canine fear—and waved it several times through the air to dry it before she gave the sock back to him. Kinsler needed the comforting smell more than Willie needed the sock.

"Let's go, brave boy! Go see Shadow, visit Lia. How about that? You love Lia and running through the yard, right?" His ears pricked at the name. All the dogs enjoyed visits to the kennel for play-dates. She wanted to convince him that a car ride was a small price to pay.

After double checking the back door's lock was engaged September grabbed her phone, pocketed it and stuffed the charge cord into her small bag, then headed to the waiting car with Kinsler. Shadow watched from the rear window. His ears flicked when he saw the smaller dog, and he barked once. He turned around and slumped onto the back seat, refusing to look at the terrier when she loaded Kinsler into the dog crate in the rear cargo area.

She slipped into the driver seat and pulled out her phone. She bit her lip. The garden needed more than she could give; time to leave it to the pros. As she pulled out on to the road she called Stonebridge Landscaping, the only option in Heartland. She'd bought a few roses locally, simplified the old garden redesign and planted them herself, all to avoid an awkward meeting with the new owner. If Arnold Stonebridge had no problem dealing with her, then so be it. She left a message, hoping to meet at the house after the music rehearsal.

Twenty minutes later, she pulled up in front of Corazon Boarding Kennels. The two dogs recognized the place. Shadow began paw-dancing on the back seat, while Kinsler's agitated whines grew into excited yaps. "Hold on, boys, give me a minute." She pocketed car keys, swung out of the car, and immediately released Shadow.

In a nearby fenced area under flood lights, a golden-haired girl worked with a black and tan pup. The youngster had inherited Shadow's thick fur and busy tail, and his mother's floppy ears and Rottie build. Magic sat statue still until Lia released him with a quick hand signal. He bounded to the girl, danced around her figure, and then ran to greet his sire, Shadow, with respectful sniffs through the fence.

"Nice control, Lia. Magic's got a solid foundation." September opened the rear car door to access the terrier.

Lia smiled with pride. "He's a natural tracking dog, has great drive, and really gets fired up over sniffing out explosives."

"He'll make a great tactical dog." September pursed her lips. "Where do you want Kinsler? He's still wet, I had to hose him off."

"Digging again, I suppose." She laughed.

Opening the crate, September grabbed the leash to keep the small dog under control. "He and Shadow un-planted some of my roses this morning." She couldn't hide her self-recriminations. Even Lia, a relatively new dog trainer, recognized the innate risk of giving a terrier access to freshly turned dirt.

"Not St. Shadow? Say it isn't so." Lia pointed her mocking tone at the black shepherd, and he reacted with a wide doggy grin others might think was an apology. Lia caught sight of September's expression, and added, "Sorry, that sucks. I know how hard you worked on that. At least he'll be out of your hair for the week, so you can make repairs." She motioned to the nearby gate. "Turn him loose inside the fence. He and the Magical-Pup can wear each other out. Shadow, too."

"Up to Shadow. He's been kind of out of sorts the past few days. I think Kinsler gets on his nerves, too." September walked to the gate, unclipped Kinsler's leash and let him inside. Immediately, Magic left Shadow to join Kinsler in sniff-greetings. "Shadow, want to go play? Ooh look, a squirrel!"

As one, all three dogs' heads came up, and they scanned the area for the varmint. Shadow eagerly pressed forward, asking to join the dogs in the play yard, and September opened the gate again, with a wink at Lia. "Works every time."

"Not nice, September."

"Oh, there'll be a squirrel or three appear soon enough. I lived here with you long enough to know they're thick as ticks in these woods. And probably in your attic. It's squirrel baby season, you know."

Lia grinned as she exited, locking the gate with the dog-proof fastener. She led the way to the office. "I guess you haven't looked up that missing dog?"

September shook her head. "Busy washing dogs and driving over here." For the last few months, she had been recovering from injuries, so had taken few clients. She still conducted the bulk of training here at the kennel, a partnership arrangement that continued after she'd helped fund the kennel renovation. "I keep electronic files now, but I want to grab the paper ones I left here in the file drawers."

"Great, let's look. The shelter put a hold on the dog for three days. But if nobody claims him—or her—you know what'll happen." She opened the door and led the way upstairs. "Can you drive down and pick him up? I would, but like I said, boarding clients plus a few board-and-train, and Magic's police dog basics have me running sixty different directions for the next two or three weeks."

"I can't. I've got Easter music rehearsal, garden repair, and more wedding plans…"

"Eloping?" She grinned, then stammered an apology at September's scowl. "I'm sorry, er, I mean—"

"You in on the big secret, too? Everyone but me?"

Lia wet her lips. "Combs may have mentioned it. That's why I thought picking up the dog might be a fun Good Samaritan thing on your way back. He talked about South Padre Island."

"Oh my lord, no! Not during spring break when it's crawling with kids. I've had my fill of kids!" September bit her lip, wanting to take back the words. "Don't say anything to Combs, Lia. I didn't mean it the way that sounded." Lia had a couple of police officers on speed-dial as mentors and planned to work with the PD once Magic completed his K9 training.

"Lips sealed. Promise."

September followed Lia up the stairs to the apartment space they briefly shared. Only small portions of the original structure remained after renovations from the devastating tornadoes that had struck the kennel, September's house, and all around the county several months before.

What had been the office space in the downstairs portion now held only a short counter with a computer. The remaining open space, with a finished concrete floor, she used for indoor training during inclement weather. Lia had situated all the office materials into what had been September's room. She waved an invitation to search the tall army surplus wooden file cabinet, with wooden rollers that stuck in damp weather.

September yanked hard to open the bottom drawer, shuffled through the hanging folders and pulled out the dozen that represented her past clients. Behavior clients either came once or twice, got help or gave up, or became longtime clients and often friends. These represented the former, one-and-done cases, another reason she hadn't bothered to save them to an electronic copy. "Lia, I really can't run down to Wintergreen. But if I can track down the owner, I'll connect them with the shelter, okay? That's Four Paws, right? I'll let you know what happens." She glanced at the clock on the wall. "I've got cello rehearsal at eight."

"Sure. I understand." Her tone clearly said the opposite. "Can't you take a quick look now?" She paused, and added, "If somebody turned Shadow into the shelter, and I got the call, for sure you'd want me—"

"That's not fair, and you know it. Besides, Shadow's micro-chipped, tattooed, and his notched-ear and furry mug are known throughout Texas and half the country by now. But I get your drift." She covered the exasperation with a short laugh, set the stacked files on the nearby desk. Before she could open the first folder, her phone buzzed. Combs calling to apologize? Or maybe Arnold? "Gotta take this, Lia."

She walked into the other room for privacy, dodging around the shabby, well-loved furniture, before looking at the display and seeing Doc Eugene's name. Had she missed an appointment? Shadow wasn't due for a vet check for another month.

"Hey Doc, what's going on?"

"Nothing, I hope. It's spring break, you know, and it seems every Tom-cat, Dicky-bird, and Hairy-dog needs an emergency appointment. That, and a few boarding clients who couldn't get spots other places."

"Tom, Dick, and Hairy? Lame." But she chuckled. "I'm sort of slammed with busy-ness, too, or I'd offer the help."

"You can still help. I promise it shouldn't take long. See, I have extra help promised, but she's a no show, and isn't answering her phone."

September rolled her eyes. Did everyone think she had time on her hands for errands? "Doc, I've got other appointments today, and right now I'm over at Lia's kennel on my way out. I really can't sub in as a vet tech today. Can't you call the service back—"

"No, that's not it. We'll manage without extra hands. It's Nikki. She's late, and usually she's here champing at the bit, waiting for me to open. Her dad's deployed again, and I can't reach her mom, or her brother. September, I'm worried." He cleared his throat. "You're not all that far from the Larsen's house. Could you just swing by and check to see if she's all right? Please?"

Chapter 7 - NIKKI

Nikki dipped and weaved between vehicles. The big RVs dwarfed her slim figure, some so big she could nearly stand upright beneath the trailers. She whimpered under her breath, worried about Hank, and wiped her bloody hand against one of the massive tires.

She reached the last row and ducked behind an extended-cab pickup. Figuring the distance gave her some cover, Nikki climbed up onto the running board on the passenger side and peered back the way she'd run. A crowd still milled about the entrance; Hank might be part of it, or not, she couldn't tell. Nikki hoped he'd got away from the scraggly bearded man.

Dad's old car parked right next to the store entrance, sat abandoned. She stared, hoping it would rattle to life any second, and race around the massive parking lot to rendezvous with her. Nikki imagined dashing out of hiding at the last minute, Hank stomping the brakes—squealing the tires—so she could grab the door and vault inside. They'd race away like the superheroes she saw on the big screen.

But the car squatted silent and motionless. Where had Hank gone? She scanned the lot for movement, eyes peeled for her big brother's bean-pole height, and white-blond hair. Finally, she spied him limping her way, a Buc-ee's gimme cap camouflaging his neon head. "Nik-keeee! Where are you?" he yelled, panic coloring his voice.

"Here, I'm back here." She waved her hand and yelled again, prepared to hop down and run to meet Hank.

Not far away the sunglasses man heard her, and changed course with a grim smile. She realized he'd waited for just such an opportunity. He redoubled his efforts to catch up with Hank.

"Look out, he's after you!" Nikki screamed.

Hank glanced over one shoulder, saw his pursuer, and tried to run, but tripped. He struggled back to his feet and punched himself free when the heavier man bore down on him. They struggled, and Hank ran with the man in pursuit. A car pulling into the lot nearly hit them, and the sunglass-wearing stranger slapped the hood of the car with a furious expression. He ran on, and soon caught up to Hank, grabbed his arm, and spun him around.

"Where is it? You poached my goods, you no-good son-of-a-"

Nikki squealed, wanting to cover her eyes, but she couldn't look away. In the distance, a siren wailed and drew ever closer. Someone must have called the police. She didn't know whether to be more scared of Hank getting beat up, or getting arrested when they arrived. She winced at each thumping blow that Hank received, hoping he'd duck away or maybe nail the other guy with his own fist. Instead, Hank hollered, fell against a car, and slid down to the ground.

The crowd at the front of Buc-ee's noticed the scuffle had moved, and a few muscled, tattooed motorcycle types strode toward the altercation. Nikki whimpered. They'd for sure break up the fight, but also probably keep Hank here for the police. Boy, was he gonna get it from Mom!

Instead, a lithe figure wearing a tank top, purple paisley do-rag, and form-fitting knee-length leggings raced into view. Nikki wasn't sure where he—or was it a she?—came from, or what such a slight figure could do. She watched, rapt.

"Sebastian, I warned you." The voice, clearly a woman, easily carried. No anger at all, disappointment perhaps, but a matter-of-fact statement that galvanized the man in the sunglasses. He backed away from Hank, with his hands in a warding-off gesture. A blood-stained knife glinted in one hand.

The woman leaped in the air, left foot kicking out in an explosion of movement, catching Sebastian in the throat. He dropped. The knife spun away. Hank scrambled to his feet, turned, and limped away.

Nikki screamed.

Hank yelled as he staggered through the lot. "Nikki, get away, just run!" Hank's voice ended in a ragged scream as he barely dodged clear of the kick-ass girl's pursuit.

The karate lady stopped, pivoted toward Nikki, letting Hank slip away. Nikki hitched her knapsack higher on her shoulders, and the woman glared at her.

Nikki didn't wait to see anything further. She leaped off the perch and, keeping vehicles between her and the new threat, moved toward the far edge of the parking lot. She hazarded climbing onto another running board to try the door. Locked. She trotted to the next truck, also locked. Sobbing, Nikki raced to the last vehicle, an 18-wheeler, and climbed onto the dirt-dusted cab. The door opened under her frantic hands, and she slipped inside.

It smelled of cigarettes and body odor. And safety. Nikki thumbed the lock, but nothing happened. She realized the broken lock that gave her refuge also wouldn't keep the woman, whoever she was, from dragging Nikki out. *God, please keep Hank safe! Don't let him get kicked in the neck, too.*

A ratty faded curtain on a rod separated the driver and passenger front seats from a rear section. Nikki slipped behind the fabric and pulled it back into place. She looked around.

A small kitchenette, another curtain rod with hanging clothes, and a small built-in bed crowded the cab. Nowhere to hide. Nikki whimpered and shrugged off her knapsack. It itched her back and felt like a bullseye somebody could nail with a lethal karate kick or something.

The sirens drew closer and finally stopped, and Nikki guessed the police had arrived. She hoped they caught Sebastian and the evil girl. Hank being arrested at least could keep him safe! She wanted to sneak a peek out the window, but felt sure the girl would see. She had to do what Hank asked. Hide. Wait for him to find her. And not talk to anybody, or he'd get in even bigger trouble.

At the thought, she grappled her knapsack closer, sat on the tiny bed, and opened the flap. Whatever Hank had stuffed inside caused all of this mayhem. Maybe she could give it back to

Sebastian and keep Hank from getting beat up even more. She pulled out the beaver toy, and underneath discovered a paper bag that held three fat plastic thermoses bundled together with tape. Puzzled, she unscrewed the lid of one, but saw only melting ice. She'd have to empty the thermos to really see, and couldn't risk making a mess here in the trucker's domain.

She closed the thermos and pushed the stuffed toy back on top before closing her bag. For now, she had to trust Hank, and keep the mystery contents safe. Nikki risked a quick glance out the curtain, peering through the dirty passenger side window. No girl at all, but a big-bellied trucker with a handlebar mustache lumbered in a beeline toward this very truck.

Nikki squealed, ducked back behind the curtain, and looked frantically for somewhere, anywhere, to shrink into the woodwork. She spied a bit of cloth spilling from the mattress pad on the bed, and tugged it—and the top flipped open. A storage area hid under the bed, with just enough room to squeeze inside. Nikki dropped her backpack into the storage, climbed in beside it, and pulled the top down. Then she held her breath, as she heard the truck door *scree* open and felt the weight shift when the trucker climbed aboard.

The truck roared to life, lurched into gear, and drove away from the Buc-ee's—taking Nikki and the mysterious contraband to destinations unknown.

Chapter 8 - SHADOW

S hadow raced around and around the fenced yard, taking turns playing tag with the other two dogs. Kinsler dodged between massive tree trunks, a flash of light colored fur. But the shepherd-Rottie pup's short black coat made Magic disappear when he hid behind a scrubby stand of saplings. He emerged with a massive stick, holding it aloft with pride, and daring the other dogs to steal it.

Kinsler accepted the invitation, and the pair raced the perimeter of the enclosure. The larger pup kicked up divots of grass and waited for the terrier to catch up. They played tug with the stick, and Shadow watched the two for a long moment before something more intriguing wafted his way.

Squirrel! There, in the branches of the largest tree, far across the field. It smelled of wildness, furry spice.

The other two dogs continued their tug game, oblivious.

As Shadow watched, the rodent scurried across a massive limb and scattered several birds perched on a suspended platform filled with seeds that swung and bounced on a strand high overhead. Shadow froze when it shimmied head first down the strand to reach the container. It hung by rear claws—how did it do that?—while manipulating and gyrating against the container with tiny paws. The lid came off and seeds rained to the ground. With a final squirm, the creature released its grip and fell the short distance, then began shoveling seeds into its mouth.

Shadow trembled, moving one slow paw-step at a time, closer and closer still. He couldn't hold back a whine of excitement, and his mouth watered as he gathered haunches to bound after the elusive creature.

His whine alerted the other two dogs. Without hesitation, Kinsler exploded into a yapping frenzy, chasing the squirrel. Shadow followed a fraction of a second later, but quickly outpaced the smaller dog.

The creature whirled, sprinted the few feet to the tree, and scrabbled up the trunk, chittering insults at the two pursuing dogs. Shadow skidded to a stop when he reached the massive roots, prancing around and around the base while he shouted with excitement at the target far overhead.

Kinsler didn't stop at the trunk. He leaped upward, clawing and scrabbling with his paws, clinging to the rough tree bark. He growled with determination and scrambled another foot higher until his weight overcame him and he slid back to earth. The terrier instead bounced around and around the trunk, screaming with increasing frustration as the squirrel sat calmly washing its whiskers.

Shadow stared at the squirrel, tail waving faster and faster, and cocked his head to examine the massive tree trunk. Kinsler had climbed up the tree, partway. He'd seen Macy-cat scale trees before but never considered trying such a thing himself. September had taught Shadow to climb ladders, and to dig in dirt—just not around roses—and many challenging things, like rescuing September from fire. Sometimes a good-dog needed to learn new things, even when it scared him. Especially when it scared and challenged him. His tail wagged faster. If Macy climbed trees, and Kinsler kind of climbed, and squirrels danced through the branches, why couldn't a good-dog climb, too?

The squirrel stared down at Kinsler's yapping figure and flicked its long, furry tail. Shadow didn't understand squirrel-talk, but thought that might be an insult. Or a dare.

So he turned and trotted a fair distance from the tree. Shadow whirled around and raced back toward it, aiming for the side that leaned away from a good-dog's approach. And when he reached the tree trunk, Shadow leaped as high as he could. He stretched front paws wide to grasp the rough surface. His front dew-claws caught and held, while rear paws pushed him higher, and higher still. Then Shadow reached the lowest, thickest branch of the tree. He hooked one paw over top of the limb to pull himself higher. He balanced easily on the wide crotch of wood, eyed the squirrel that moved higher still, and followed with one paw carefully placed on the stair-step-like lattice of branches.

Kinsler continued barking, now far below Shadow. Things looked different from up high. Wind ruffled Shadow's black fur backward, and he lifted his face into the stream of air, delighted by the stories it told. The squirrel chittered, flicked its tail again, and zoomed further up into the tree, to where limbs bent and danced with the rodent's darting weight.

But Shadow didn't care. The squirrel didn't matter much anymore. He'd conquered the tree, just like Macy! Now he understood why the cat perched on the highest spots. Even the sniffs smelled different up here. He panted, grinning, tail slowly waving with satisfaction.

Then the Magical-Pup screamed.

Chapter 9 - QUINN

Quinn knew her well-placed kick had silenced Sebastian permanently. With the cops on the way, she'd had no choice, and couldn't risk them questioning him. She'd watched long enough to see he no longer had the product, had lost the bounty he'd stolen.

She couldn't abide an inept thief. Granny always said, *Do it right, or not at all.* And that applied to everything. Quinn picked up the knife Sebastian had wielded and her nose wrinkled at the wet stain on the blade. What else had he screwed up?

Nobody had seen her altercation with Sebastian, other than the teenager gimping away across the lot. She eyed the blade, figuring the tow-headed guy for Sebastian's victim. Her gaze took in the young girl across the way with matching pale hair. The boy called her Nikki, but at that distance, Quinn doubted the little girl had seen enough to matter.

Quinn weighed her options: go after and silence the girl who'd already ducked out of sight, or tackle the older kid. If he and Sebastian got into it in a public place, the boy probably knew something about her missing product. Unless Sebastian had the smarts to repackage everything—doubtful—she could still track it easily enough. The Tanner kid had pointed her in the right direction, and once within range, her tracking devices did the rest.

Quinn rubbed her eyes. She'd had to ride all night from south Texas to reach Tanner in Wintergreen, and then another half hour north to track down Sebastian. She didn't begrudge the time spent since she'd soon get square with her employer. The terse *>fix it* haunted her, with the implication of consequences should she fail.

Tigger would need a break soon. He loved riding in the carrier on the back of her bike, but the big feline needed time to stretch his legs and toilet. Sometimes he rode draped across her shoulders, wind slicking back his whiskers, claws gripping her shoulders, and his purr rivaling the groan of her bike. But she couldn't risk it under these circumstances, not while on the job. Lots of people rode similar bikes. Few wore a cat around their neck. She didn't want to be noticed until well away from her tidying-up chore.

A quick glance around oriented Quinn to the flashing cop cars pulling up near the front of the store. If she wanted to hide from them, she'd head that way and blend in with the milling crowd. But she doubted the tow-headed boy had much experience in such things—hell, he'd got sideways with loser-Sebastian—so she did what any freaked-out druggie would do. Quinn headed away from the cops, back toward her bike—parked among a flock of other motorcycles—and scanned the area for clues.

Sure enough, down one row of parked cars she came upon the kid's lost Buc-ee's cap. Dark blood dappled the ground nearby. Sebastian's knife must have scored. A few rows further, closer still to her bike, she heard gasping and muffled sobs from behind a dumpster.

She found him hunched over, eyes squinting against the pain. Quinn sighed and twirled the blade. Sebastian cut the kid, but why? He didn't look savvy enough to get the drop on Sebastian. No, he looked like a football jock, but baby faced and not much older than her. Of course, she felt decades older, and far removed from anything this boy had ever experienced in his protected world.

Her eyes narrowed. "Hey kid. Hey you, get up already." She couldn't see any injury, but that meant nothing. She didn't want him to croak before she found out where he and stupid Sebastian left her product. Each courier carried three specialized thermoses able to stay cool for nearly 50 hours, each filled to the brim with product. Oh, the product wouldn't spoil immediately, but should have been delivered by now. Once she checked that off her list, she'd go after the sisters' thermoses, and finally be square.

And breathe again.

She tapped the knife sharply on the metal dumpster to get his attention. "Get up!" She poked him with her toe.

He shuddered. "Can't. It hurts." He peered up from beneath a fringe of white-blond hair. "That guy, he stuck me with something. The bleeding won't stop. Hurts like hell…"

"The cops are here, bubba." Best-case scenario, he knew nothing, and just got in Sebastian's way. She tested him. "For what you two did, I should turn you over to them." She waited to see what he'd say.

"No! Please, no." He licked his lips. "I did nothing like this before. But when my girlfriend ran out of her medicine, she asked me to help, and…"

Quinn rolled her eyes. "You did it for a girl?" Only suckers let emotions rule their lives. She sighed. It went against the grain to target anyone but bad guys, but he'd admitted his guilt. He knew too much, and he'd seen her. She couldn't let the cops question him. She wiped the bloody knife on his shirt, dropped it into the dumpster, then bent to grab his arm to lever him up. Quinn looped one arm around his waist and draped his other arm over her shoulders. "We need to get you out of here, but then you give me the answers I need." She'd decide what to do with him once he coughed up the details. Maybe she'd get lucky, and he'd croak on his own, like Tanner. *Oh, get over yourself, girlfriend. You'll do what needs to be done. You don't have to like it.*

They made halting progress. Quinn urged him faster when more cop cars rolled into view. With luck, they wouldn't be stopped. All the activity remained closer to the building, but someone would soon locate Sebastian's body. And then the authorities would stop anyone coming or going from the parking lot. "Over here." She helped him onto the bike, handing him her own helmet to cover his beacon-bright hair, and tugged the Buc-ee's cap on her own head. "Hang on tight, bubba." She swung up on the saddle in front of him.

"Hank. My name's Hank."

"Whatever. And one more thing. You got stuck for a reason, and must've stashed the stuff somewhere safe. You'll tell me where, right? Right, Hank?" He had to know his answer meant life or death.

"Yeah. It's somewhere safe, but not for long. And if I tell you, you gotta promise me something, too." He jutted his chin.

Damn, he was more savvy than she'd thought. "You're in no position to bargain. Hang on. If you fall off, I'm not coming back for you. Oh, and if you mess with my cat in the carrier, you die."

Oh, he'd tell all right. Saving her own butt took precedence, so she had to recover his stash before anything else went sideways. Quinn kicked the bike into noisy life, and they roared away from Buc-ee's leaving the cops behind.

Chapter 10 - SEPTEMBER

September disconnected the call from Doc Eugene to rejoin Lia. They both jolted to their feet at an anguished canine wail. September cocked her head. Too high pitched to be Shadow. "Kinsler?"

Lia stretched her mouth wide in a yawning action, flexing her jaw. "That's Magic. More scared than hurt, I think." She ran from the room, leaping down the stairs two and three at a time. September followed more slowly, puzzled by the girl's odd expression. The pair dashed out the front door to reach the exercise yard, the young dog's wails a siren urging them faster.

September paused, scanning the area for Shadow, but didn't see him. Floodlights only stretched so far. Kinsler barked and bounced around a giant live oak tree. *Probably treed a squirrel.*

Lia tore open the gate, leaving it ajar. "Magic! I'm here, come on, boy." She flexed her jaw again in that odd motion. "Let me help you."

The youngster finally appeared from the other side of the yard. When he saw Lia, he screamed again, then ran hell-bent toward her as she dropped to her knees and opened her arms wide.

With surprise, September took in Magic's visage, his jaws stretched wide in the same yawning expression that had stretched the girl's face. She remembered Lia's odd questions about her nearly magical connection with the pup...and shook her head. September didn't buy all that woo-woo animal communication crappiocca. Still, the back of her neck tingled.

"Poor Magic, hush, you're okay, hold still." Lia didn't look at September, but spoke over the youngster's frightened cries. "He's chewed up a stick again. I keep clearing them away, but the wind must've dropped some new ones." The dog pushed hard into Lia's arms, still wailing, jaw stretched wide. "Can you reach to pull it out while I hold him? At least he knows enough to come for help." She put on a cheerful tone, but underneath, she sounded scared.

September nodded. "I don't want to get bit." She waited until Lia put the pup between her knees, facing out, so he couldn't easily escape. September kneeled facing Lia and the pup, waiting as the girl whispered softly into Magic's ears and gently gripped his neck to steady him. "Hold him steady, Lia. Grip him more firmly—"

"He's fine now. I told him… I mean, he understands we'll help take the pain away." Lia blushed but jutted her chin. "Go ahead, he won't move now." She kept one hand on the back of the pup's neck while stroking his throat with the other.

Gingerly, September moved forward to look into the dog's mouth. Even dogs with great temperament bit when in pain. She'd trust Shadow with her life—had repeatedly done just that—but this youngster wasn't his father or his mother. Still a juvenile, with all that implied, she didn't trust the pup.

But he remained steady and frozen in Lia's arms, wails curtailed and dialed down to shivery whimpers. So September dared to look closer and quickly spied the problem.

Like many dogs, Magic loved to chew anything that didn't move faster than him. He'd scored a hefty stick, almost an inch in diameter and bit down hard. His sharp teeth had sheared the wood on both sides, which wedged the remaining portion across the roof of his mouth at the back of his jaw. It kept his mouth propped open in what must be a painful posture. No wonder the pup screamed.

"It's a big stick, Lia." She reached inside Magic's mouth, between his shiny white carnassial molars designed for shearing meat—and fingers. But the stick proved too embedded for her to tug loose, and her attempt only prompted more cries of pain. "Wedged too tight. We need pliers. Or even better, do you have any pruning shears?"

Lia's arms tightened on the pup. "I don't garden. What about cable cutters? I had to repair part of the chain link fence. They're in the toolbox in the laundry room."

September nodded and trotted back to the building, quickly returning with the eight-inch blunt-nosed tool. She again kneeled before the young dog. He trembled, but Lia's light touch held him steady. Taking care the metal didn't hit the pup's teeth, September used them to grasp the center of the stick. The compact beveled jaws needed minimal one-handed pressure to do the job. A sharp *snick* sounded when the cutters cracked through the wood, and the stick came loose.

Magic leaped away when it broke free, shaking his head, bounding and barking with happiness. He raced to join Kinsler. The two dogs gamboled about the trunk the tree, barking and looking into the branches.

"Thanks for your help. Think he'll be okay?" Relief clear in her voice, Lia got to her feet and offered a hand to help September up.

"Probably. But best to get it checked out. There could be splinters, or abrasions." September dropped the cable cutters into her windbreaker pocket.

Lia made a face. "I've got clients dropping off and picking up pets all day long. And I need to get Kinsler settled." She raised her eyebrows, clearly implying a favor deserved a reciprocal boon.

"Guess I could drop Magic off." She'd already agreed to check on Nikki. September suspected Hank had forgotten Nikki needed a ride. She'd take Nikki and Magic to the clinic, then she and Shadow could get back to her own to-do list. At the thought, she looked around for him. "Where's Shadow?"

At his name, a familiar *woof* sounded. The two dogs circling the base of the tree redoubled their own barking, putting paws on the trunk and barking aloft into the branches. September crossed to the tree and looked up, expecting to see one or more teasing squirrels. Shadow looked down from his perch high overhead, tail waving and grinning with a self-satisfied expression.

Lia joined September, mouth gaping at the sight. "Did you teach him that?"

September shook her head. "He figured out the tree on his own."

"I bet he went after a squirrel. The limbs are thick with those pesky tree rats." Lia cocked her head. "Does he know how to get down? One time, my kitten got out and went up a tree, but I had to climb up to retrieve him. I never knew dogs could climb trees."

"They can be taught. And a few breeds, like Catahoulas, and Treeing Walker Coon Hounds, naturally climb trees, usually when they get excited going after prey." Shadow was perched so high, though, she worried he would fall trying to get down. "He probably needs help to find a path down."

Pursing her lips, Lia eyed the tree. "I know your knee still bothers you. Want me to climb up?"

"And have you fall and get hurt, too? No, I've got a better idea." September looked around the enclosure and finally pulled off a long, thin branch from a nearby sapling. "Shadow understands target sticks. This will work, but it won't reach the whole way." She rummaged in her pocket and pulled out her key fob with the laser light. Macy loved chase games with the laser light, but Shadow had never been very interested in it. She hoped he'd pay attention this time.

"This I gotta see." Lia called Magic and Kinsler to her side, clipped a leash on each collar, and led them a distance away to reduce distractions.

Nodding her thanks, September switched on the laser pointer. She'd never taught Shadow the name for the red dot, but he'd seen it from watching Macy. Breaking the behavior into small steps always worked best. So September took several deep breaths to calm herself, decided on the plan, and began with the *show-me* game so Shadow would have context.

"Shadow, this is cat-game." She held up the laser pointer in one hand.

She saw his waving tail slow, as he focused on her words.

September held up her other hand, palm toward the dog so he could see. She turned the laser light against that hand, swirling the light around and around on her palm. "This is red-dot." She knew he saw movement more clearly than static objects and hoped he could detect the light from that distance. Sunrise arrived at 7:30 so the dark actually helped make the laser light more visible. September next pointed the laser light against the trunk of the tree, moving it vertically so that he could follow the light; she stopped when it reached the level of the branch where Shadow stood.

"Baby-dog, *show-me* red-dot." She swirled the red dot on the dark bark of the tree.

He wagged and paw-balanced along the branch to reach the swirling dot, then nose-touched the tree.

"Good boy, good dog!" The target stick only reached seven feet with her arm extended, so she needed to guide Shadow lower—two stair-step branches should do it. September eyed the options and chose the route that looked safest, with the best paw grip. She aimed the laser light back at doggy eye-level, swirled it on the tree bark to catch Shadow's attention. Once he followed the beam, she crept it down to the widest branch immediately below him. "*Show-me* red-dot." She held the light in a steady circular pattern there, waiting for Shadow to gather himself, balance safely, and pick his paw placement. He stepped down gingerly, one paw at a time, but maintained his composure. September moved the light to the next branch and without prompting—now understanding the game—Shadow followed.

Raising the long stick into position, September aimed it at the next branch. "Touch." He readily hopped down, each branch's increase in girth giving Shadow more confidence. With the stick pointing the way, Shadow quickly traversed the rest of the lower branches. At the last one, he gathered himself, bracing his rear paws, and launched himself to land with a solid thump next to September.

"What a smart dog, Shadow! Good dog." He leaped high with excitement, aiming a slurp at September's face, before settling in a sit. His tail swept the grass back and forth.

Kinsler ran up, wriggling his whole body and trying to lick the bigger dog's face. Shadow stiffened, and lifted his lip in a silent snarl; the smaller dog backed away, still wriggling. September frowned, noting the reaction. "Better get Kinsler settled, Lia. I'll collect the files from your office and let you know if I come up with anything. Oh, and I'll drop Magic with Doc Eugene."

The visit to Lia's had already taken too much time. Checking on Nikki and dropping off the pup shouldn't take long, though. The rest of the day should be smooth sailing.

Chapter 11 - KALI

Asmile lit up Kali's face, enhancing the exotic beauty she'd maintained through the years. Her looks hid the ugliness within. She'd inherited both from her parents, the only thing of value she'd claim from the strangers who'd sold her innocence. Good looks made her a winner; the ugly ensured she'd never be a loser again.

She'd clawed her way out of the sewer, separated herself from the dregs of humanity, with no help from anyone. Today, nobody dared speak of her beginnings, not if they wanted to live. Most in the Organization who knew—or suspected—the truth, eagerly embraced the fiction she'd created.

Never knowing her real name, she'd invented one, and she eagerly lived up to her namesake: Kali, goddess of time, of doomsday, and of death. She called the shots, a queen of the damned controlling all she touched.

It had taken decades to reach her current level of power and influence since she became part of the Organization. Those who stood in Kali's way paid dearly. She had a long memory, patience to spare, and considered forgiveness a character flaw. In her youth, she'd indulged in immediate passionate retribution, but with age she'd learned to relish delay, enjoy anticipation, and cherish the planning. Wheels within wheels of planning. Postponing the climax made the release so much sweeter, longer lasting, and more satisfying. She licked her lips.

She'd learned from a master. A brilliant manipulator, controlling hundreds in his empire, Simon Wong ruined her for anything else. Cultivated as an assassin, she used her beauty to get close enough to his enemies to use a silent blade, a tasteless poison, or more exotic techniques. He'd crafted her into his beautiful deadly protege and she'd risen quickly in the Organization.

Far from feeling grateful, she had seethed inside. Why should she perform all the dirty jobs, shoulder all the risk, for him and his cronies to grow their empire? Sure, she'd been born in a crack house, sold by age five, and survived the worst men like him inflicted. She'd waited years to exact vengeance, doing all he asked, but played marionette on her own terms.

When the investigation began into his empire, Simon should have silenced her. She knew everything about his business, including those she'd killed at his behest—or her own whim. By then an old man, bereaved at the loss of his heirs, and trusting her counsel and flattery, he married Kali, thinking to cement his control while preventing his wife from testifying.

But when she married Simon, the bastard had renamed her to suit his needs. He'd dug his own grave. Now, her grasp encompassed the world.

Kaliko Wong.

She'd already arranged Wong's death and enticed Wyatt Teves to assassinate her husband. He'd needed little urging. At the memory, she laughed out loud, imagining Wong's surprise. Afterwards, Kali assumed control and played the part of Simon's vengeful widow. She tracked down enemies and associates from the past who might challenge her and eliminated them.

Only after his death did she learn of an obstacle to her complete control. Simon's loyalists, privy to his darkest secrets, moved against her—and their search for that ultimate leverage grew more dangerous by the day. Her expression soured, perfect purple-stained lips parted, revealing sharp, feral-looking teeth. So she'd remove their leverage. Kill the living evidence.

In this game, the queen had the power of life and death, the ability to move quickly in any direction. She'd previously sent agents after the woman, but none had eliminated her.

Until now.

Quinn had a real chance, a unique association that Kali was using to her advantage. The girl could have been Kali all those years ago, badly bruised but not yet totally defiled. They both experienced unspeakable childhoods, and each wore virtual armor stained with the sins of their survival. The girl had had the balls to ask Kali for help, and paid the demanded price without blinking.

Killing in self defense or revenge counted for little, though. Even a lamb kicked attacking wolves. The girl's true test of allegiance would come soon enough.

Amused, Kali agreed to the girl's innovative operation, then identified and put in place a couple of her own pre-selected couriers. It wouldn't do to be obvious. Despite amateur status, her ultimate quarry had a suspicious nose that sniffed out obvious traps and had the protection of the police. What unfolded must appear natural and coincidental for Kali to win the big prize. Wheels within wheels… She gave Quinn enough rope to get tangled, and soon would throw gas in the mix, then light a match to set off an explosion that would eliminate September Day, and solidify control of Kaliko Wong's future.

Chapter 12 - SEPTEMBER

S eptember glanced in the rear-view mirror. "Just chill, boys. Settle down."

The sun peeked over the horizon, promising a gorgeous spring day. Shadow yawned and woofed under his breath, but sank to a reclining pose in the back seat. Behind him in the cargo area, Magic whined and paced in the tight space.

She shook her head with aggravation, hoping the younger dog didn't get carsick. Shadow loved cars, but not all dogs enjoyed the rides. Youngsters especially seemed prone to quirky tummies, and she didn't know Magic well enough to anticipate. She had a small box of gingersnap cookies in Shadow's go-bag. The ginger settled tummies and doubled as a treat that associated the car with yummies. But with the potential injury to the pup's mouth, September couldn't use them.

Cracking open the rear windows gave the dogs moving air to better orient their balance sense, plus outdoor sniffs to distract them. September set the child-proof lock to keep Shadow from pawing the window open any further. She steadied her cello. It filled the foot well and passenger seat beside her. If Nikki needed a ride to the vet clinic, she'd have to snuggle up in the back beside Shadow. She grinned, knowing both the dog and girl would love that.

The clock on the dashboard taunted her. At the stoplight, September sent a quick text message to the orchestra director, Dr. Parker Belk, as a courtesy. With luck, she'd only be a few minutes late. She'd played the music before and Parker knew she could easily sightread the score.

A text message arrived from Teddy Williams. September grinned. The computer genius had become a grandfather figure to her, and saved her bacon more than once. Now on a well-deserved vacation from his consulting business, Teddy rolled toward South Texas from his last assignment. He planned to meet up with his grandkids who spent spring break on the Gulf. Her eyebrows rose. He'd planned to leave this morning, so...

Quickly, she dialed. As she continued to Nikki's house, Teddy answered her call.

"Hiya, September. You didn't have to call. I know your plans keep you busier than a cat with a cricket."

September laughed. "Yep, I'm on my way to cello rehearsal for Easter, but first I have to drop off Lia's puppy at the vet, and check on Nikki. Later I'm hoping to meet with a gardener. Are you on the road yet?"

"Just left. Have to gas up first, and then me and Nellie Nova will take our time. Meriwether's riding shotgun, supervising. He's curled up on the dash." He added a growl. "I know that's not safe, but ya can't argue with a cat."

She smiled, glad that the big orange and white Maine Coon had settled in so well. "I have a favor to ask. Please say no if it's inconvenient for your plans with the grandkids."

"Go ahead, you know I'll help if I can."

She took a breath, hopeful. "There's a dog I worked with that ended up at Four Paws Shelter in Wintergreen. Little bitty town not quite an hour from here. The shelter serves several small towns in the area. I'm trying to track down the dog's owner. They put a hold on the dog, but I can't get down there before it expires."

"Oh, I know what that means." He cleared his throat. "Sure, that's not too far out of my way, and I have time. You know Meriwether likes well-mannered dogs and my girls will probably want to adopt the pooch. Sylvia and Leslie are missing their Great Dane." He paused. "Do I need anything to claim the dog?"

She breathed with relief. "I'll find out. Probably you'll need to identify it. I need to find the file on the dog and owner for more information. I don't even know its name because they called Lia, only that it had one of my Pets Peeves leashes. Once you have the dog, circle back with me. By then, hopefully we'll figure out how to reunite with its owner. Thanks, Teddy, you're a lifesaver."

"I know." He chuckled. "Hey, it's what I do."

A loud meow replied as if in agreement before he canceled the call. September's smile broadened as she pocketed the phone.

September turned down the street to Nikki's house. A slight figure on a massive motorcycle zoomed past, coming far too close for comfort.

"Crap!" September swerved and nearly took out a mailbox. Shadow yelped and Magic squealed when thrown against the side of the car. "Sorry, boys. Some people shouldn't drive."

She pulled into the Larson's narrow driveway, noting the empty carport. September wasn't sure what cars the family drove. They had at least two, based on what Doc Eugene said. She'd make a quick check, but the place looked deserted.

September climbed out of the car but left it running. She wouldn't be long. "Shadow, wait."

He pawed the door in protest, but the window didn't open any further. "I've got your number, Shadow. I don't need you running after me. I'll only be a minute."

Trotting up to the front door of the modest house, she slowed when she saw the door ajar. The back of her neck prickled. "Nikki? Hey, anybody home?" She put out a cautious hand to push the door open. Something blocked it and she had to push hard to peer through the narrow opening.

Red splotches marred the beige entry tile. A body slumped against the door, the weight keeping it from opening. "Oh my God..." She pushed harder, so the door shifted enough for her to squeeze through. September kneeled beside the figure. Not Nikki, thank goodness, but this blond boy must be her brother, Hank.

She felt for a pulse, and the boy groaned. She breathed again. "Hank, hey there, Hank? Where does it hurt?" He'd bled for a while, but she couldn't see the wound and needed to stem the flow. He struggled to sit up. She stopped him. "No, stay still."

"Nikki, you gotta find Nikki. Please." He gasped and hugged his middle with both hands.

"Don't talk, Hank. Time enough later." September pulled out her phone and dialed 911.

"You don't understand. I'm so damn stupid! Got myself stuck well and good, and now they're after Nikki." He shuddered.

The operator answered. "I've got an emergency and need an ambulance." September rattled off the address. "There's a boy bleeding from his abdomen. Stab wound I think."

Hank's face paled, and he winced and clutched his middle again. "Hurts like a bastard." He struggled to keep his composure, but tears rolled down his cheeks. "Am I gonna die?" His lip quivered. "Please, you gotta save Nikki. I didn't mean to get her in trouble. A favor turned into a stupid-ass mistake…" He pulled out his phone, fumbled to input the code and unlock it, perhaps to call Nikki.

He slumped.

"Hurry!" September yelled into the phone. "I need help here. This kid's gonna die. I just found him. I don't know what happened, please just get here!"

She dropped her phone on the floor beside Hank's and gingerly moved his clammy hands away from his stomach. His shallow breaths slowed. September peeled the blood-soaked tee shirt upward from the boy's slim frame. At least three punctures marred his stomach. Only one bled copiously, but the others could be pooling inside. She pulled his shirt back down over the injuries, bunched it into a wad over the worst stab wound, and applied pressure. She prayed the ambulance arrived in time.

She'd think about Nikki once help for Hank arrived.

Chapter 13 - COMBS

The Buc-ee's travel center swirled with activity. Combs had got the call before he even pulled into the precinct to start his shift. By the time he arrived and met his partner, Detective Winston Gonzales, techs had cordoned off the area around the man's body.

Combs shook his head. "Good luck getting trace. So many people have trampled the scene, we'll never sift through everything."

Gonzales tightened his lips in agreement. "Not to mention collecting accurate statements. Everyone will have an opinion. But any actual witnesses are probably long gone."

The popular pit stop serviced huge numbers of professional travelers, plus the normal daily commuters who zoomed up and down Hwy 75. The main corridor connected Dallas to all-points-north, crossed the Red River into Oklahoma and beyond. With easy access to the highway and 75-mph speed limits, the culprit could be many miles away by now.

The pair crossed the massive lot to the tight knot of onlookers. The police officers keeping looky-loos at bay recognized them, and let them pass. The coroner stood as they reached him.

"No obvious marks on the body, other than a big bump on his head. It's not even bleeding. There's no identification. He has the beginning of a hematoma—that's a bruise—on his throat. Plus petechiae, little red dots from ruptured blood vessels in his eyes."

"Petechiae? Strangulation? Out here in public?" Gonzales sounded incredulous. "How'd they manage that?"

The coroner shrugged. "Don't know, Detective, the how and the why are your job. I just report what I see. I'll do a more thorough exam, of course, when the body is back at the office." He brushed dust from the asphalt off his neat trousers. "My best guess is a punch or kick crushed his larynx. The back of his head cracked against pavement when he fell, he lost consciousness and suffocated." He waved a gloved hand at the body. "Take a look, Detectives, and when you're finished, send the body my way."

Combs watched the man weave through the crowd, then turned to a nearby police officer. "Who arrived first?"

"That'd be me." The man's brow, slick with sweat, belied his calm, professional tone. "A couple of kids called it in. They saw him arguing with another fellow and watched a chase that ended in some kind of skirmish. One of them got it recorded on her phone." He gave a weak smile. "Had notions of posting to social media to get a million views and become famous. But when they found him out cold and couldn't rouse him, they called us."

"Kids recorded something on their phone?" Combs wasn't surprised. Cameras caught everything these days, for good or ill. "Where are they? The kids?" The inaccuracy of eyewitness accounts often frustrated him, but a phone record bore witness without spinning facts.

The patrol officer hooked a thumb toward a distant black-and-white. Gonzales stayed to interview others nearby while Combs followed the police officer.

The officer opened the car door and three flustered college-age girls spilled out, all talking at once. Combs held up his hands, scowled, and waited until they fell silent. His "dad face" worked just as well with his own kids. "One at a time. You first. Name, age, and contact information." If underage, he'd need to contact parents, too. He pulled out his audio recorder for their statements.

All three girls—twenty-one confirmed by driver's licenses— offered similar stories. On the way to south Texas for a spring-break celebration, they stopped for gas and munchies. They pulled into the lot just as a pair of young men ran from the front door directly in front of their car. "One of 'em banged on the hood as he ran by. I thought we'd hit him." The brunette with the nose ring shuddered delicately, and the girl with the blue-streaked ponytail continued. "Yeah, so I followed them in the car across the lot, ya know, to be sure they weren't hurt." She cut her eyes sideways at the third girl.

Combs kept his expression neutral as he listened. From their expressions, he doubted they'd followed the boys for altruistic reasons. "Go on."

The third girl kept her eyes down, hugging herself. "I've heard of people faking injuries for insurance and stuff. My dad sells insurance." She shrugged, arms still crossed protectively over her chest. "So I said we should get them on record with my phone. Get 'em to say that they weren't hurt or nothing. Then we saw them fighting." She finally lifted her head, eyes clouded with worry. "Didn't want to get too close, so I used the zoom on my phone." She uncrossed her arms and held out her cell.

He nodded. "Show me." He took the phone and played the recording. Combs recognized the victim, shouting and brandishing something shiny—a knife?—at another boy. He couldn't make out the garbled audio. He'd have the tech team see if they could clean that up. But the video revealed the pair circling each other, one wearing sunglasses and the other a bright Buc-ee's cap. They barked curses like snarling dogs with hackles raised. Sunglasses flew off the heavyset bearded victim as he slashed the air with his blade. His taller opponent dodged out of reach. They flailed and punched at one another as they ran between rows of parked cars, one seeking escape while the other pursued with relentless anger.

The heavier boy cornered his prey against a large SUV and punched him twice in the gut. The taller boy screamed, clutched his middle and fell backward against the car, and slid down onto the pavement.

Suddenly, a slight figure in dark, form-fitting clothes and bright purple hair—or was it a hat?—rushed into view. Again, the garbled audio sounded, followed by a whirlwind of activity. Combs grunted. The camera jarred at just the wrong moment. The purple-hat figure disappeared from the frame just as the victim fell, and then the video stopped. Combs played back the section again, but still couldn't discern what happened. He turned to the three girls. "Describe what you saw." He'd get a copy of the video, but wanted their statements as well.

"Just what's on the phone. Two guys arguing, one of them chased and knocked down the other. And then that third boy—"

"Boy? No, that was a girl with purple hair rushed in. Protecting the kid on the ground, maybe his girlfriend."

"It was a boy, and he had a purple hat, not hair. Are you blind? But he did something to that man with the sunglasses."

"Are you kidding me? No, the blond kid in the Buc-ee's hat must've shot the guy! He went down like a sack of shi…"

"Enough. One at a time." Combs kept his temper, barely. Typical. Each witness had her own interpretation. "Did you see anyone leave? Either purple-hair or the Buc-ee's hat?"

All three girls shook their heads. Ponytail offered, "After we checked the guy who fell, we called 911." She hesitated. "Can we go now? We're on vacation, and meeting a group tonight."

Combs sighed and looked around the parking lot. So many people, and each one would have a different story. Before he could answer, his own phone chimed, announcing an incoming text. He glanced at it quickly, and his eyebrows shot up. September sent it.

>Heading to the hospital ER. Call ASAP.

Chapter 14 - SEPTEMBER

September pulled into Doc Eugene's parking lot; she had wanted to follow the ambulance to the hospital, but couldn't take Lia's puppy. She glanced at the car caddy beside her where she'd stashed Hank's phone. He hadn't regained consciousness before the ambulance whisked him away.

She collected Magic from the rear kennel. Shadow pawed the back window, so it scrolled open, and hopped out of the vehicle. He grinned with a self-satisfied expression, and September didn't have the heart to stop him. Shadow loved visiting Doc Eugene.

The crowded parking lot testified to the veterinarian's busy schedule, and she looked through the window before going inside. Shadow's training kept him in line, but Magic still had pushy puppy impulses. Thankfully, only two people sat in the waiting room, with a single crated small pet. She pushed inside, keeping the pup on a tight leash.

A young man September hadn't met looked up from the desk as she entered. "Can I help you?"

"Hi, the puppy got a stick caught in his mouth earlier, so just want to check him out. He belongs to Lia Corazon, his name's Magic." At his name, the pup wriggled and turned to slurp Shadow's muzzle. "Lia has a file here, so you can call her with questions and a time for pickup."

The receptionist tried to interrupt, but Doc Eugene exited an exam room and caught sight of September.

"Did you find Nikki?" He smiled and waved at the couple in the waiting room. "I'll be right with you." He turned back to September, one white eyebrow raised.

"Nikki wasn't home." September lowered her voice. "I found her brother, Hank, there, injured, and called an ambulance. I'm on the way to the hospital. Do you have their mom's phone number? Or where she works?"

"Oh dear, that sounds serious. I've already called and left a few messages, to no avail." He took off his glasses, polished them on his sleeve, and resettled them on his long nose. "Nikki said her mom's interviewing for a new job, but I'm not sure where." He cocked his head at Magic. "What have we here? Is that Lia's youngster? Everything fine, I hope?"

September gave him a quick recap as the young man led Magic away. "Sorry to rush off, but I'll circle back with any news about Nikki. I texted Combs, didn't want to call and interrupt his day." She figured he'd call when he could, and had better resources to find the kids' mother.

Shadow did a paws-up on the counter to accept Doc Eugene's chin scratch before following September out the door. He hopped back into the car through the window before she could open the door. "Good dog, Shadow." She'd put the window behavior on command, after he'd figured it out himself. It had come in handy more than once, but September worried at some point he might leap from a moving car into traffic. She wished she didn't have to reset the child lock every time she turned the car on or off.

She had rolled out of the parking lot when her phone rang. "Hey, thanks for getting back so quickly."

"What happened? Are you all right?" Urgent with worry, Combs almost shouted.

Wincing, she pulled the phone away from her ear. "I'm fine. Oh, I'm sorry. You thought it was me hurt and at the ER?" No wonder he sounded upset. "It's not me. You remember Nikki Larson works for Doc Eugene? I stopped to pick her up and found her brother, Hank, hurt and called an ambulance. I'm on my way to the hospital now. His mom hasn't answered her phone. I thought you, or someone on the force, could help to contact the boy's mother to let her know."

"Dammit, September." She could almost see him run his hands through his short hair. "You scared me to death. I'm on scene at what looks like a homicide."

"Sorry, Jeff. I didn't think—"

"Right, you didn't think."

She jerked as if slapped and concentrated to keep the wheel steady. She spoke through gritted teeth. "You'd want to know if something happened to your kids."

He groaned. "Of course I would. I didn't mean that the way it sounded." He blew out a breath. "Look, I've got a dead druggy here at the Buc-ee's, and possibly two more on the run. I love you for wanting to help everybody, September, but let the hospital handle it. Besides, didn't you tell me how busy you are planning the wedding and with Easter rehearsals? Now you drop everything for some kid you don't know?" She heard background noise, a confusion of cars, honking, shouts, and conversation. "I gotta go. See you this afternoon after shift."

September stared at the phone for a moment, lips tight. He hadn't let her explain about Hank's injury, or Nikki. Sure, she had a full schedule today, but a hurt kid trumped plans. Didn't they? She sighed. To be fair, a murder investigation took precedence over the Hank and Nikki drama.

"What do you think, Shadow? Should we go to the hospital or rehearsal? We're already late to the church." At the stop sign, she switched on the blinkers when her phone rang again.

No, not her phone. Hank's phone. A call from Nikki. Before she could answer, the phone stopped ringing.

Chapter 15 - NIKKI

Nikki tried to be quiet underneath the trucker's bed. They'd traveled forever when she finally tried to call Hank. He didn't answer his phone right way, so she quickly disconnected. Nikki hiccupped—she always caught the hiccups when scared—and covered her mouth with both hands, not wanting the driver to hear. Hiding inside the trucker's storage sure ramped up the fear. It stunk like Hank's kicks after he'd run track.

She sat scrunched up with arms wrapped around her knees, head bent forward. A crick in her neck twinged with the rhythm of her heart. Before long, she'd have to move a bit, maybe try to lie on her side. Sometimes Hank got a Charlie-horse in his muscles that hurt so bad he yelled. And if she yelled, and gave away her hiding place, who knows what the trucker might do? He might even call the cops on her.

Nikki worried about Hank. Had the bloody handprint been his blood, or from that other guy? Had that Sebastian person got up from being clobbered? Or had the kung fu guy chased Hank once Sebastian conked out? She hic-hic-hiccupped again, and bit her lip to stop the spasms.

She wanted to know, but didn't want to know, if that made any sense. She couldn't do anything anyway, not by herself. Hank forbid her to call the police. That scared her most of all, because it meant her big brother must be on the wrong side of right.

He'd got in trouble a couple of times, staying out too late with his buddies. One time, Mom yelled at him because he smelled like a brewery, whatever that meant. But nothing like this. Nikki blamed his new girlfriend. He got all woo-woo and starry-eyed talking about her, and would do anything she asked. He had never minded taking Nikki places before, but now he *pitched and moaned*—that's what Mom called it—over anything that kept him away from his latest squeeze.

The big truck shifted gears and for a moment, the grumble-roar stilled. Her next hiccup echoed in the cramped hiding place. Had the driver heard? She stiffened, holding her breath. When the next hiccup came, it hurt inside and she almost squealed.

The truck's grumble changed key when it slowed, lurched to one side, and swapped the hum of pavement for gravel. Blood roared in Nikki's ears, and her heart thumped a counter-rhythm when the engine shut off. If he got out, she could sneak away. Surely, they'd gone far enough that Sebastian couldn't follow.

The driver's seat screed when his weight lifted. Nikki crossed the fingers on both hands, hoping the truck door would open next. It didn't.

Instead, the barrier curtain chink-a-chinked when flung aside. Heavy footsteps. The lid to the bed storage bin creaked open, light spilling into the dark space.

Nikki blinked and squinted up at the man. Her lower lip trembled. What would he do? "Mister, I'm sorry, really sorry, for hiding like this. But I had no choice—"

"Out. Get up out of there, kid. And get out of my rig!" His face turned mottled red, sweaty as watermelon in the sun. "I can't have nobody seeing me with some young girly-girl. You want to get me in trouble? Where'd you come from? How long you been in there?" He huffed, reaching a wiry, blue-inked hand toward her. He grabbed Nikki's collar and lifted her out.

"Ouch, hey stop! That hurts!" He dragged her over the edge of the box; her knapsack hooked on her ankle to follow her out. "I didn't hurt nothing. I'm Nikki, what's your name?" Sometimes asking questions calmed adults. "Didn't you ever need to get away for a minute and hide? I just borrowed your space, that's all..."

"Don't wanna know your name, don't wanna know nothing

about you. Get out, or I'll show you mean, girly-girl! Grab your
crap and get lost." He flung open the rig's passenger door, caught
up Nikki's bag and heaved it out the door. "You want me to chuck
you out, too?" He glared, and the tip of his tongue poked out,
licking his lips repeatedly as his breath quickened. She noticed his
bright blue eyes looked in two different directions. Weird.

"I'm going, I'm going." She stumbled out of the cab. Nikki
hurried to her knapsack and shrugged it on, stretching her sore
neck back and forth.

He stood in the open doorway a long moment, weird eyes
staring at her. Finally, he blinked rapidly, shook his head like a wet
dog coming up for air, and slammed the door. The truck roared
away, kicking up gravel and dust in its wake.

Nikki stared after it then looked around. He'd taken an exit off
the highway and stopped at a dirt turnaround on the access road
miles from nowhere. She blinked hard, but tears spilled down her
face. From the dust, she told herself. She wouldn't cry, she wasn't a
baby. And she'd been in worse spots before, like when the barn
flooded from the tornado and she almost drowned with the rest of
the kids. But being alone made it different. Besides, she hadn't
heard from Kid Kewl in forever. And the other kids had got busy
with their own stuff. Quick hurt stabbed her. Maybe they didn't
want her as part of the secret group anymore.

She squared her shoulders. She'd moved on, too, with a real
part-time job and everything. At the thought, more tears spilled,
and Nikki gulped back a sob. Doc Eugene would never forgive her.
He counted on her, had told her that more than once. Now Hank
wouldn't answer his phone. With cops looking for him, she'd lose
her job, and—oh yeah, she had been dumped along the road like an
unwanted kitten. Just what the hockey-puck had Hank done to get
them in such a mess?

Nikki trudged further into the nearby tree line and sat on a
fallen stump. She shrugged off her knapsack, and again dug inside,
setting the stuffed beaver toy beside her. Pulling out one of the
thermoses, Nikki unscrewed the top. This time, she poured out
some of the ice into the cupped cuff of her shirt. She frowned
when a bunch of Sharpie markers came out of the thermos. She
stuffed them back inside, hesitated, then opened the second

thermos. This time, a bubble-wrapped container followed the ice out of the thermos. She picked apart one edge, just enough to see what it contained. She peeled off tape, and several small glass vials spilled into her hand.

She squeaked in shock. Her hiccups returned with a vengeance. Quickly, she pushed the bubble-wrapped vials—*drugs!* her mind shouted—back into the container and stuffed the ice inside. Nikki screwed the lid back on, and contemplated chucking the whole bag into the trees. Nobody would find it here, and she'd get rid of the evidence against Hank.

How could he? Her big brother had bought, or maybe he stole, the drugs off of that Sebastian guy. Something went *hinky*— she'd heard cops on TV say that—and the *hinky-ness* got Hank in trouble.

Or if she gave the drugs back to Sebastian, maybe he'd leave Hank alone. The last she knew, he got laid out on the parking lot back at the Buc-ee's, miles and miles away. She had no way to get there. But she couldn't just lug around this package full of drugs.

She'd call Hank again and ask what to do. Nobody around to hear, now that the mean old truck driver had left. Nikki would let it ring and ring until Hank answered. And when she finally saw him, she'd give him what-for! After she hugged him.

Nikki felt first one pocket—empty—and then the other. Nothing. She bit her lip, and dumped her tablet and charger, cat-faced purse, the Buc-ee's jerky treats, and the extra sweater next to the Buc-ee's beaver toy on the leaf-strewn ground.

No phone. She must have dropped it in the truck.

Chapter 16 - SEPTEMBER

September drove quickly but still arrived almost a half-hour late to the music rehearsal. She'd tried to call Nikki back on Hank's cell phone, but it went to voice mail. That worried her. At least the girl had access to a phone. Maybe when Hank hadn't answered, Nikki called her mom. There'd be hell to pay once their mother found out what her kids had been up to.

September's lips tightened. Melinda also kept secrets, and acted supremely confident adults couldn't ever understand the importance of, well, anything. At least Willie hadn't yet reached that stage. She shuddered at the thought of two kids giving her the cold shoulder.

In the back seat, Shadow whined his concern. He leaned forward, resting his chin against her neck.

She turned her face to accept his quick kiss across her cheek and felt her pulse slow. "I'm okay, baby-dog. We'll try Nikki again after rehearsal." Combs told her to let go of things she couldn't control. Easy to say, but harder to put into practice. She'd done all she could for Hank, and had to trust the doctors would patch him up and notify the parents. She'd return the boy's phone later.

Before she got out of the car, her phone rang: Arnold Stonebridge. She took a deep breath and answered quickly before she lost her nerve. "Thanks for returning my call. You remember your brother started reworking my garden, before—"

"I remember. He died before he could finish." Arnold paused. "How can I help you?"

She plowed on, eager to get his polite "no thanks" behind her; she'd think about other options later. Quickly, she explained the challenges of the old roses. "So I need professional help. I understand if you're too busy or…"—she hesitated—"or you'd rather not. But if you could recommend someone I'd be grateful."

Arnold didn't hesitate. "I have time this morning. Let's meet so I can see what you have in mind, and we can go from there."

She agreed with happy relief. "If you beat me there, you'll need the code to open the front gate." She gave him the guest code, pocketed her own phone along with Hank's, and swung out of the car. Shadow bounded out when she opened his door then waited patiently for his leash to be attached. He didn't need it, but she leashed him out of respect for others' comfort level. Those who knew Shadow understood his role as her service dog, but for strangers, his black wolfy appearance could raise alarm.

September carefully extricated Harmony from the front seat and slung the cello over her shoulder. She entered through the side door and followed the sound of a sweet alto voice singing a familiar anthem accompanied by lustrous strings. September reached the doorway and paused to enjoy the lovely music. Her sister April stood beside the conductor, singing with a smile on her lips and a new-found spark in her eyes. She'd recovered from her kidney transplant more quickly than anyone could have hoped. This Easter service would be a bittersweet celebration for them, honoring their mother's memory.

After April finished, September opened the door and hurried to take her place as the only cellist in the group. The director said nothing. He didn't have to, his lowered brows and pinched lips shouted his disapproval. The trombone player scooted to one side to give her room to bow, and she quickly set up. At September's hand signal, Shadow settled behind her chair, yawned, and rested his big head on his paws.

They continued to play through the liturgy, interspersed with congregation favorites, including a lovely cello solo arrangement of Morning Has Broken. As she began the second verse, giving herself over to the music, the phone in her pocket jangled with an obnoxious ring-tone. Hank's phone again. Nikki?

"I'm really sorry. I've got to take this." September ignored the conductor's exasperation, and her sister's flush of embarrassment on her behalf. She placed her bow on the stand, settled Harmony onto the floor beside the chair, and hurried out the rear of the fellowship hall, Shadow in her wake.

As she pulled out the phone, September checked the time. Everything about this day felt hurried. Hearing from Nikki, though, would relieve much of her stress. "Nikki? Thank God. Where are you? Oh, this is September. I've got Hank's phone." She rushed the words, eager to get back into the concert hall and mend fences.

"Uhm. That's the kid's name. She dropped her phone, and I found it." The man sounded hesitant and muffled, almost as if he tried to disguise his voice.

"Who is this? Where's Nikki? How'd you get her phone?" September's pulse thrummed.

"Never mind my name. Just doing my good deed, that's all. I didn't hurt her or nothing. Remember that. I found the phone after I kicked her out of my… never mind." His agitation grew. "She snuck a ride and I ain't gonna have nothing to do with runaways, got that?"

September took a deep breath, trying to cobble together the gist of his story. "Why did you call?" She couldn't help the catch in her voice.

"Like I said, I kicked her out. Left her at the first exit just north of McKinney about fifteen minutes south of the Buc-ee's. Took me that long before I heard her, then right away, out she went. It's nice enough weather and all. You can go pick her up. No harm, no foul." He cleared his throat.

"You didn't call the police? She's a kid, and you left her alone out there—"

"I called *you*, didn't I? She was hiding from the cops. And besides, didn't know who-all to call until you started dialing this number. I heard the ring and found her phone. That's it. You should thank me." He huffed, then added, "A little cutie like her, not everyone would be a gentleman like me. If ya get my drift. G'bye." The line went dead.

Shadow pressed hard against September's thigh. She absently

dropped one hand to stroke his sleek brow. September started back into the sanctuary, only to see musicians packing away their instruments. She crossed back into the room and waved for April to join her. "Something's come up. Can you do me a huge favor and take my cello with you?" How long would it take to find Nikki? Leaving the cello in the car for too long asked for trouble. April nodded, and thankfully, didn't ask questions as September quickly slipped Harmony back into the case.

September briefly considered calling Combs again. But he'd already dismissed her concerns and had his own priorities.

"Kennel up, Shadow." He obediently hopped into the back seat, and she slid behind the wheel. She couldn't be sure the man told her the truth. "It's thirty minutes round trip. But we've got to find Nikki. What d'ya say?" He woofed agreement.

She switched on the car, and grimaced when the gas warning light flashed. No time to stop for fuel now, there should be enough to go collect the girl. She prayed Nikki had the smarts to stay put and not wander away. And that no bad actors found Nikki before she did.

Chapter 17 - SHADOW

Shadow stood in the back seat, plumed tail gently waving as he watched the scenery speed by. He pressed his nose to the narrow opening at the top of the window and drank in the smells spilling through. Yawning with excitement, he crossed to the other side of the car to check the sniffs from that window.

Shadow loved car rides. And he especially liked rides with September, without pesky tag-along dogs or kids. It had been a long time since he and September traveled alone together. Recent rides always involved Combs, the kids, or Kinsler. Shadow panted with relief that Kinsler stayed with Lia at the kennel.

He liked Combs well enough. They'd come to an understanding. Shadow knew the big man adored September, and wanted to make her happy and keep her safe, just like Shadow. It was a good-dog's job to protect his person. He didn't like to share, but understood that sometimes people could do things that dogs couldn't. He respected Combs and trusted the man. He didn't have to love him.

At the thought, Shadow whined and moved to rest his chin on September's shoulder. She tipped her head and rested her cheek against his head. "Love you, baby-dog." She stroked his brow and returned her attention to the front window.

Wagging, Shadow resumed his post supervising the view from each window. Soon, the drone of tires on pavement made his eyes droop. He yawned, stretched out on the seat, and dozed.

Dreams made his paws twitch, and whimpers bubbled deep in his throat. Shadow started awake when the car slowed. The tinka-tinka-tinka sound announced a car turn, and he stood again.

Leaving the wide car path, September guided them onto a narrow gravel path that ran alongside the highway. Large trees overshadowed the lane, and Shadow sniffed deeply out the window, noting the fresh smells that spoke of hidden creatures and greenery. His tail swept back and forth on the car seat. Would September stop the car so they could explore? He'd like that.

September broke the silence. "The guy on the phone said he left Nikki somewhere along this road. We've gone seventeen miles. It's the only turnoff I've seen." She glanced in the mirror, catching Shadow's eyes. "You remember Nikki?"

Shadow stood and shook himself. He liked Nikki. She smelled like cats and always fed him extra treats at the vet clinic. He looked out the window again, searching for the small girl.

"Good dog, Shadow." September sighed, slowed the car, and stopped in a small turnaround beneath scrubby trees. "No sign of her. But there are big tire tracks in the mud over there, so maybe that's where the guy dropped her off. Sure hope you can find Nikki. If we at least confirm she was here, I'll have something concrete to tell the police."

Shadow didn't understand all of September's words. He tipped his head one way, then the other and waited patiently. She didn't open his door right away, but hurried to the back storage area to rummage inside one of the canvas bags. He recognized his tracking harness, and slicked back his ears, grinning and wriggling with excitement. He loved games of *seek*. They hadn't played the game in a long time. Shadow particularly enjoyed tracking missing cats. Dogs were okay, but sometimes they got scared and fussy and he had to work extra hard not to scare them. One time he'd found an odd missing creature, something September called a guinea pig. It smelled wonderful and made fun whistle noises.

He hopped out of the car when September opened the door and stood patiently for her to fit on his harness. His paws jittered in the mud left behind from recent rain. Sometimes rain dispersed scent and made it harder to track. But he knew how to find eddies and pools of scent in protected hollows of trees or rocks. Lost cats slunk along in the shadows of barriers like fences or embankments, or climbed trees. Dogs, though, struck off across open fields. He knew how to hunt for each.

September clipped on the tracking line. He waited for her to offer him a scented item that identified his target. But she just stood there for a long moment, looking around. He whined and impatiently pawed her leg.

"You need to think, Shadow. This time, we're not tracking a pet. I don't have a scent cue for you, but you remember Nikki, right?"

He cocked his head and woofed. Yes, he knew Nikki, the girl with treats, who smelled like cat.

"Shadow, *seek! Seek* Nikki!"

His brow wrinkled, and his panting mouth snapped shut. He knew what the command meant. And he remembered the girl, even her scent. Shadow was smart that way. What a fun new game! Instead of tracking pets, he'd find a person.

Without pause, he dropped his nose to the wet earth. Shadow felt September's tension relax. He tugged the tracking line she grasped as he coursed left for several paces, and then right. He knew cat patterns and dog patterns. He'd need to learn people patterns to track better, but Shadow knew how to learn. And when he found Nikki, she'd have a pocket full of treats for him, and rub his ears and call him "you handsome boy."

Shadow moved back and forth, nose several inches above the ground. With no wind, and wet warm ground, any scent laid after the rain still hung in the air and on the dirt and grass. Mud squelched between his toes, cool but not unpleasant. Quickly, he covered the open area of the turnaround, finding no scent-sign of Nikki. So he widened his search pattern. He'd learned to be patient, and methodical; as in the past, his training paid off.

He reached the tree line and alerted near a stump. He lay down. Nikki rested here for a time. He sniffed deeply at the shoe marks on the scuffed earth and wagged with excitement.

"Good boy, Shadow! Good dog. *Seek* Nikki." Her praise meant everything.

He wagged faster in response to September's cheery tone—

he'd tracked a people!—and surged forward. Now he'd found her path, his pace increased. Her scent rode the air dog-nose height, and he towed September faster and faster with the tracking line. The girl had trudged parallel to the car path, underneath the sheltering trees, now and then stopping to rest.

"Nikki? Hey Nikki, are you nearby? It's September, just call back and I'll come to you."

He trotted along the scent cone, pulling hard on the line. September jogged to keep up. His ears pricked forward when he heard the rumble-grumble noise from the highway.

"Nikki? Are you there?" September called again.

Shadow pulled harder, rushing ahead so fast that September lost her grip on the line. He knew he should stop and let her catch up. But something about Nikki's scent and footfalls had changed. No longer plodding along, but running, breaking through slapping tree limbs, and sliding in the mud.

A scream shattered the air. The strange engine roared. Shadow burst into a clearing next to the wide car path and saw Nikki struggling with a stranger. With a roar, he rushed forward, but his trailing lead tangled in a clump of saplings, pulling him up short. He watched, barking and snarling with fury, as the stranger pulled Nikki toward the motorcycle, and roared away.

He yelped. He'd found Nikki, but couldn't stop the stranger. Shadow turned to face September, ears slicked back in sorrow, crying his apology.

Chapter 18 - NIKKI

The motorcycle roared off the road and headed straight at her. Nikki screamed and ran. She didn't recognize the kick-ass girl until a vise-like hand on her arm whipped her around.

"Leave me alone!" Nikki struggled free and backed away. She grabbed up a flimsy stick and switched it back and forth at the other girl. "You kicked that guy at Buc-ee's and knocked him down. He was gonna hurt my brother." The girl had traded the purple do-rag for a motorcycle helmet, and wore a loose-fitting smock over top of form fitting clothes. She'd saved Hank from a beating, or worse. "What do you want? How'd you find me?"

The other girl held up both hands in a placating gesture. "Right, I'm a friend of your brother. He sent me to get you, Nikki. And the package he gave you to hold for him. My name's Quinn."

Nikki stopped waving the stick. "Hank sent you? Is he okay?" Her voice trembled, and she cleared her throat. Package? Quinn meant the drugs! She raised the stick again and jutted her chin. Quinn got Hank involved in drugs.

"Whoa, put down that fly swatter, kid. Listen to me. Hank's in trouble for sure, and he's hurt. He doesn't want you to get hurt, too." She took a step closer and reached for Nikki's backpack. "Just give me the package and everything goes away—"

Spinning, Nikki ran, and put an enormous tree between herself and Quinn. "He gave it to me, to protect. He said to tell nobody, and keep it safe. And don't tell the police." Her brow furrowed with worry. "You don't look like a cop. So if you know about it, you're into illegal drugs, too. You got my brother in trouble! And he's hurt?!"

"You're confused, Nikki." The girl's lips pinched, her brows bunched. "I promise, there's nothing illegal about that package." Her face cleared. "Yes, he's hurt pretty bad. He sent me to get you. And said I should hang on to the package instead, so you can meet up with him. He'll explain everything about the drugs—legal ones, I promise. The pharmaceutical companies charge so much that the people can't afford them. Some people die, Nikki, because of greed. Hank's a hero. He wanted to help get this life-saving legal medication to the people who can't afford it." She stopped and put her hands on narrow hips. "Hank can explain better than me. Can I take you to your brother?" She motioned toward the nearby motorcycle. "You'll have to squeeze up behind me, next to my cat."

"Cat? On a motorcycle?" Her thoughts whirled. Hank a hero. He wouldn't have sent Quinn unless he trusted her. She had no other way to get home. Nikki couldn't help a quick, curious glance behind them toward the bike.

In a heartbeat, Quinn closed the distance between them, grabbed the strap of Nikki's backpack, and yanked hard. The strap scraped against Nikki's shoulders, and she yelped in surprise. "What're you doing?"

Another voice yelled Nikki's name from way back in the trees. Before she could make sense of things, Quinn was pulling her along by the strap. "The cops, they found you. If you ever want to see Hank again, come with me!"

Eyes wide, Nikki stumbled along beside the older girl and clambered aboard the big motorcycle. Sure enough, a cat carrier strapped to the back of the bike had a bewhiskered cat face peering out of a clear bubble viewing port.

Hank trusted Quinn. And Quinn loved cats. Reassured, Nikki wrapped her arms around the girl's slim form, and squeezed her eyes shut, then screamed when her shouted name sounded again, closer. "Hurry, before the police come get me!"

Chapter 19 - Teddy

Teddy nearly drove past Four Paws Shelter. He stopped, backed up, then swung into the parking lot. September hadn't yet gotten back to him with information to reclaim the surrendered dog. He didn't even know the dog's name.

"What do you think, Meriwether? Should I try anyway?" The big cat perched on the dash stretched and yawned before moving to a sunnier spot on the other side of the car. "You're no help. What'll you do with a strange dog in here, kitty-boy?" He smiled at the notion. The Maine Coon cat, close to twenty pounds, had previously proven his ability to put even big dogs in their place.

Teddy carefully exited the vehicle, keeping a watchful eye on the cat. Meriwether liked to explore, just like his namesake, and Teddy wanted to avoid a doorway dash. The dozing cat gave lie to the worries, though, and never moved.

Teddy carried his cane more from habit than need. His leg had mostly healed from the gunshot wound but it still felt achy during damp weather. The appearance of the cane aged him beyond his 68 years, prompting some people to underestimate him. Irksome, but useful in his business cyber-tracking bad guys. Acting the part of the clueless old man might benefit this situation, too.

Adjusting his glasses, Teddy limped from the RV to the front door of the shelter. He glanced around, noting the small cameras

mounted on each side of the building exterior. Barking came from
the rear of the building, and he pictured indoor-outdoor dog runs.
Overall, the place looked and smelled clean, always a good sign.
Still, well-run and reputable shelters raised a lump in Teddy's throat
at the thought of the furry waifs inside. He'd avoided visiting them
for years after he and his wife said goodbye to their last dog. But
after losing his wife, the loneliness took more of a toll than he
expected. Adopting Meriwether had been an unexpected blessing.

Teddy squared his shoulders and pushed inside. The reception
area echoed with meows from resident cats in stacked cages. Teddy
steeled his emotions when one of the felines stuck a paw toward
him from its cage.

The rescue had an adjacent glassed-in room where a couple sat
on the floor interacting with several kittens. A harried young
woman, wearing a smock covered with blue puppies and pink
kittens, bustled out of the room.

"I'll be right with you. We're short staffed today." She
continued through the swinging double door behind the counter
without waiting for his answer. One of the doors stuck open.
Teddy glimpsed a large open room with treatment tables similar to
a veterinary hospital. A woman with a stethoscope carried a scared-
looking dog. When she saw Teddy's curious gaze, she hurried to
close the door.

The first woman returned, the thump-squeal of the doors
prompting more meows from the clowder of watching cats. She
made sure the doors closed before turning to Teddy. "How can I
help ya?"

"I don't know yet." Teddy hooked his cane over one arm,
leaning on the countertop, while he took off and polished his
glasses on the hem of his aloha shirt. He sneaked a look at her
from under grizzled white eyebrows.

Deep lines bisected her brow, and her lips tightened. "Like I
said, I'm pretty busy. So tell me what ya need." She drummed
chipped painted nails on the counter.

That's perfect. "I lost my dog. I'm just passing through and my
dog got out at a rest area a couple days ago." He mentioned one
he'd passed on his way here. "I never got around to a microchip.
But somebody from this shelter called the phone number on my
dog's leash and left a message. Can I get my dog back, please?" He
added a quaver to his voice. "And do you know who turned in my

pet? I'd really like to thank them."

"Aw, sorry you lost your dog. I remember calling when that dog came in. Some lady answered and said the number belonged to a dog trainer. Glad they tracked you down. But I'm afraid I don't know who dropped the dog off, they tied the leash to the outside door handle." She scowled. "The security camera's so old, it got little more than a silhouette as the car drove away. Whoever found your dog probably didn't want to pay the relinquishment fee. At least they didn't leave your doggy out in the traffic."

He kept his expression neutral. The dog hadn't been a stray. The owner dumped it. Teddy had no regard for anyone who would do that. This yahoo didn't deserve to get the dog back!

"We'll need to get positive identification, to be sure it's yours." She put up a hand to stay any objections. "Dogs usually recognize their people, too, and that's a big endorsement. But we don't want wrangling over who owns the pets, ya know. Can't turn over a pet and then have somebody else show up and raise a stink."

"I understand." How would he prove ownership if he and the dog didn't know each other? "What constitutes proof?"

"Oh, medical records, for example. Detailed description of the dog, like three white paws and a pink nose. Photos of you with the pooch. And your picture ID, plus the impound fees and boarding costs to reclaim your dog." She leaned in. "Glad you showed up, though. We only hold them a few days before making them available for adoption. And, well, if they're not adopted…"

He cut her off. He knew what happened to the unwanted pets. "I don't care about the fees, I just want my dog back." Teddy hesitated, glancing at the clock on the wall. "How late will you be here? I don't have the medical records with me. And I need to find a bank to cover the cost." He didn't have to pretend to be flustered. September's favor grew bigger by the minute. "Who carries doggy medical records with them?" He had Meriwether's records, both paper and digital, since they crossed state lines and traveled all the time. But she didn't have to know that.

"Lots of people keep copies. And like I said, the dog should recognize you, right? Watching the reunions ranks up there as one of the best part of the job, Mister… What's your name? Give me your driver's license and we can start the process, and then I can take you to the holding area to confirm identity of your pooch."

Teddy backed away. "Thanks so much! I have pictures in my RV. And how much is the fee?"

She named a figure, and he nodded and hurried out of the building before she could delay him any further. He had the funds on him, but needed the excuse to buy time. And to touch base with September. Without the dog's name and description—hopefully a picture—nothing could be done.

He climbed back into Nellie Nova, grateful Meriwether barely roused. Teddy eyed the shelter's old cameras, guessing the system backed up video for only a day or two before recording back over the old footage. A smile tugged his lips when another car pulled into the lot and someone wearing a similar smock got out and rushed to the front door. The relief person had arrived, meaning he'd have a do-over to convince about reclaiming the dog.

Teddy drove out of the lot, heading for a taco place he'd noticed on the way in. If September could locate the dog's files— he thought she kept pictures of clients and their pets—she might even have some medical information to cinch the deal.

Dialing, he waited impatiently for her to answer. His granddaughters expected him to arrive late tonight. The plan was for them to have a relaxed drive to their home in South Bend.

The call went to voice mail, so he left a quick message to call back. On a whim—breakfast could wait—he circled back to the facility, but parked down the street within view of the building. Meriwether stretched and yawn, then hopped down from the dash to follow Teddy as he made his way to the rear of the RV.

He sat at the desk and opened one of his laptops. The cat pushed into Teddy's arms, and he made room for their usual accommodation: cat belly-up on his lap, while he reached over the top to type on the keyboard. With a few keystrokes, he accessed the software program, searched for the signal he sought, and executed the command.

Teddy smiled. Just as he thought. The shelter's old security cameras might as well be for decoration. Within minutes, he'd accessed the digital recording—a week's worth—and downloaded a copy to peruse later, in case September couldn't find the required info. The poor abandoned dog should not suffer the consequences, and September didn't need to know he'd indulged his curiosity, either. He wanted a look at the scumbag who dumped the pooch.

Anyone who'd dump a dog—or a cat—deserved some payback for doing wrong to one of God's innocents. He stroked Meriwether's tummy, once again grateful he'd inherited the cat after his owner died. If September hadn't stepped in, Meriwether and the other Maine Coons would've had unhappy endings.

His stomach rumbled. "Breakfast burrito time." Briskly but gently, he moved the cat out of his lap, and closed the laptop. Meriwether meowed his objection. "Don't complain, you'll get some sour cream." Grinning, he set off for the restaurant again.

Chapter 20 - SEPTEMBER

S eptember crashed through the brush into the clearing in time to see a figure drag a smaller person to a motorcycle. "Nikki!" She squinted, trying to make out the slight figures perched aboard the bike, but couldn't be sure. On an impulse, she grabbed her phone, and shot video as the smaller figure climbed aboard before it drove out of view.

Shadow yelped and strained against the tangled tracking line, eager to pursue the fleeing vehicle. She hurried to free him. "Come-a-pup, Shadow, good dog." She kneeled in the dirt and opened her arms to him when he eagerly returned to her. He leaned against her shoulder and hid his face against her neck as she struggled to loosen the knots he'd pulled tight. "Was that Nikki on the bike? You saw her, didn't you, baby-dog?"

He whined again and slurped her across the face. "Good dog, Shadow." He'd done as she asked. Or what he thought she wanted, anyway.

Once released from the tangle, she and Shadow hurried back to her car. September debated calling Combs again, then firmly pushed the notion aside. Instead, she got Shadow settled, then dialed 911. *Second time in two hours.*

"911, what is your emergency?"

"I need to report a missing child, a possible abduction." She took steadying breaths, knowing she needed to present the information clearly and without emotion. Combs was right; she couldn't save the world and didn't have the resources or expertise to go further. She'd do as Combs would advise: turn everything over to the authorities.

"Name, age, and gender of the child?"

"Nikki Larson, she's eleven. Slight figure, weighs maybe eighty pounds, with green eyes and shoulder length platinum blond hair."

"Your name? What's your relationship to the child?"

September hesitated and tried not to sound defensive. "I'm September Day. I'm a friend of the family. And I saw her taken." Without prompting, she gave the operator her address and phone number.

The operator didn't miss a beat. "When and from where did the child go missing? Can you describe who she's with? A non-custodial family member, or..."

Shaking her head, September wondered how to explain the situation. "She's been missing for a couple of hours, last seen with her brother, Hank, at their house in Heartland." She rattled off the address. "When I checked on the kids, at Doc Eugene's request—Nikki was late for work—I found Hank hurt and called an ambulance. Before he lost consciousness, he said his attacker went after Nikki. Hank's at the Heartland Municipal Hospital now. I've not been able to locate the kids' mother. That's Ingrid Larson. The father, Rolf, is deployed and can't be reached. I'm told the hospital has resources to find them."

"You waited an hour to report the abduction?" The disapproval dripped from the operator's voice.

"I reported it to the EMTs with the ambulance, but got sidetracked before I could go to the hospital." September couldn't help a defensive tone this time. She would have given a report to Combs if he'd listened. "I didn't know she'd been abducted. Hank just said she'd run away. Then I got a phone call from the man who took her. Well, he said that she hitched a ride with him, and that he dropped her off along the highway." She gave the operator her location. "I'm calling from there now. My dog tracked Nikki—well, I think he did." Shadow hadn't been trained or tested on tracking people. Sharing that with the operator further complicated the already convoluted story. "I saw two people on a motorcycle race away down the highway, going south on 75. The one on the back had light hair. I think it was Nikki."

"When was that?" The operator's tone returned to calm and detached.

"Maybe ten minutes ago."

"Can you describe the motorcycle?"

"I don't know. It was a motorcycle, big handlebars, and two tires. Really noisy. All I could see was the glint of the sun on the rear chrome bumper." She paused. "An impression of blue or maybe purple reflected in the chrome, but I can't say for sure. The bike had one of those canvas saddle bags slung across the rear. Too far away to make out a license or anything. But I did try to get a video." She paused. "Are you going to send someone to look for Nikki?" She started the car and slowly pulled back onto the access road.

"I've alerted the authorities, and they'll coordinate investigators for the last known locations. They'll probably want to talk further with you, Ms. Day—"

September's phone beeped, announcing another incoming call. Maybe Combs? "Listen, I've got to go. You have my contact information. I'll be home in twenty minutes if someone needs more information."

September answered the incoming call without looking. "Jeff? Look, I'm really sorry—"

"No, it's me, Teddy. What'd you do this time, September? I called earlier, but you didn't call back."

She rolled her eyes. "Never mind. Did you get the dog? Oh, and thanks!" She set the phone for hands free and put it in the cup holder.

"The shelter wants me to identify the dog. You know, with pictures, maybe medical records. A name! September, I can't claim the dog if I don't know what it looks like." He paused before adding, "They've got security cameras. I could do a little digital sniffing—"

"No, Teddy." His hacker skills had come in handy in the past, but a lost dog didn't rise to the level of skirting the law.

Of course, they'd need proof. She glanced at the pile of files on the front seat. "I haven't had time to look through the records yet." Her whole day had gone sideways, but she could still meet with the gardener. The hospital would take care of Hank, and the police would find Nikki. She'd done everything she could. But she wouldn't mention any of that to Teddy, or he'd want to dive deeper into the investigation. "I'm on my way home, and will call as soon as I get there."

He cleared his throat. "What if you can't find the file? The girl at the shelter said the dog has a hold, but today's the last day."

"I don't know, Teddy." She hadn't meant to sound so harsh, and softened her tone. "Look, I know you're in the business of poking around the 'net looking for bad guys, but—"

"I know, I know, don't borrow trouble." He chuckled. "You may recall, there's been a time or two that my expertise came in handy."

She laughed. "True. I've dragged you through trouble more than once. And I appreciate all you do, Teddy. As soon as I get home…"

"Hold that thought. I've got an incoming call from my granddaughters. I'll call you back." He disconnected.

September smiled. She knew he'd been looking forward to this trip for months. Teddy claimed hanging out with the teenagers kept him young. He certainly didn't act his age, and often claimed to be "youthening" like Merlin instead of growing older.

She pressed the gas and headed home. September noticed the gas gauge creeping closer to empty, but she didn't have time to stop. Meeting with Arnold would check at least one thing off her massive to-do list.

"Hang on!" Quinn shouted over the roar of the cycle, infusing the command with terse authority. The thin arms circling her midsection tightened. Nikki's white-blond hair surrounded her head like a halo in the wind.

The tracking device Quinn had included in each thermos had led her directly to Nikki. Quinn could have dispatched the kid and the would-be rescuer. But that would bring more cops sniffing around, and neither Quinn nor her employer wanted that. This way, she'd left the would-be rescuer in the dust with no answers. And she could take care of Nikki anytime.

Besides, Nikki reminded Quinn of her younger self: scared but defiant, clueless, yet determined. Nikki had a misguided notion she must safeguard Hank's stash.

Fine. A little of truth mixed into the fiction never hurt, and often proved more convincing than an outright lie. She grinned, recognizing the cat's presence had tipped the decision in Quinn's favor. How about that? Finally, Quinn had a partner in her cat who'd never disappoint.

She'd given herself time to get the answers, and further instructions. Quinn followed orders, which might cut short Nikki's reprieve. To do otherwise painted a target on her own back. You were predator or prey, victor or victim. She couldn't afford empathy.

Nikki broke into her reverie with a scream. "Stop, stop the bike, stop it now!" Her arms tightened, a vice about Quinn's slim waist, then one hand loosened. Nikki leaned sideways.

Quinn gasped and counter-balanced the lurching motion. The girl would cause them to crash on the highway, kill them both! Quinn shouted, reflexively slowing the motorcycle, and glanced behind her.

The cat's carrier had come open. Tigger struggled, dangling from Nikki's hand, which clutched the cat's safety harness. His rear paws skimmed the pavement. Nikki's grip barely kept Tigger from becoming a grease spot on the open highway.

Chapter 21 - COMBS

W hat've you got, Gonzales?" His gaze focused on the dry-erase board. So far, they had one victim, thirty-one-year-old Sebastian Viejo. He had a record—busted for DUI twice. They found his van in the Buc-ee's lot and impounded it.

The person in the purple do-rag appeared to work with the blond-headed man Viejo had targeted. Combs added notes from the girls he'd interviewed at the Buc-ee's, and other witness statements. But no one could identify the blond or Mr. Purple's vehicle. A big rig leaving the area blocked the view on the surveillance cameras. Buc-ee's didn't allow eighteen-wheelers, and happened to evict the driver from the lot at just the wrong moment.

Gonzales figured the killer beat it out of the area during the confusion, and would ditch his or her vehicle ASAP. So he was running down that angle. After the coroner's comments, Combs had run searches on similar bizarre strangulation deaths.

"I found five cars and two trucks abandoned in the past few days." Gonzales cleared his throat and coughed. "Sorry, I'm still fighting allergies. The dang cottonwoods kill me this time of year."

Combs felt his throat itch in sympathy. Spring in North Texas brought boatloads of wildflowers, and pollen filled the air. "The best fits would've been reported in the last hour."

"Yep. Probably couldn't get farther away than the county line in the time they've had to drive. He'd dump it somewhere with easy access to another ride." Gonzales blew his nose. "Based on that, I've narrowed the list to two cars and a truck. Getting the names on the registrations now."

Nodding, Combs made a note on the board. "That'll help. Unless the abandoned ride got boosted, too." The location of the vehicle could point to connections and motive behind the killing.

The video helped only a little. The recording clearly showed Viejo chasing down Blondie, a tall guy, and accosting him, maybe with a knife. That could explain the blood. But with so many people and cars milling around, it barely caught the flash of movement—did the guy *kick* Sebastian in the neck?—before the slight figure disappeared. "We've got a damn ninja drop-kicking people," he muttered. That took skill.

He'd turned the college girls' video over to the tech guys, hoping they could augment pictures to better identify the pair. They'd found blood on the pavement and taken samples. Combs guessed it came from the blond, since Sebastian's only injury appeared to be the throat punch. The amount of blood on the ground made him worry they'd have another dead body before they found and questioned either Blondie or Purple.

Gonzales came back on the line. "Just got it narrowed further. A fifty-three-year-old Joey Davenport owns the truck. Bald, over 300 pounds."

Combs made a face. "Not our ninja or Blondie. Anything else?"

"Still waiting on one of the cars. But a lime-green VW comes back belonging to Tanner Rudolph, twenty-seven. According to his family, he's on vacation in South Texas, but they've not heard from him in a few days. He's not answering his phone. What do ya think?"

He wrote the name on the whiteboard. "Hey hold on a minute, I got a call coming in from the Buc-ee's manager. Maybe better info." He accepted the other call. "Yeah? This is Detective Combs."

"Uhm, right? I wondered, did you find out who did it? I mean, my staff, they's really worried. Oh, this is the manager over at —"

"I know who you are." He prepared to disconnect the line. "I can't share details of the investigation. Thank you for your help, but I need to keep this line open."

"Wait, I know. But I maybe have something that'll help. News, that is."

He could almost picture her wringing her hands. "That's fine. What do you have to share?"

"Ya know, we don't allow nobody to spend the night here. Folks try. We got to run off truckers now and again, and RVs and such. So we keep track of who parks in the lot and for how long. Ya know?"

Impatient, he prompted her. "No, I don't know. Why don't you cut to the chase? Please."

"Okay. See, there's this old car. It's been sitting here since you left. On the cameras, it's time stamped arriving not too long before all that awful stuff happened." She hesitated. "Once the po-lice talked to everyone, most folks beat it outta the Buc-ee's lot. I never seen it so empty. That's why I noticed. I sent out my assistant manager to check, you know, for a registration to see about calling the owner."

Combs ran a hand through his hair. "Stop him, don't let him go through the car. I'll send someone."

"That's okay." She sounded pleased with herself. "He was real careful-like, didn't touch nothing important. I watch those FBI TV shows, so I know what to do. Anyhoo, we got the name of the owner of the car. You want it? I mean, we don't want to warn some criminal by asking about the car, right? So that's why I'm calling—"

"The name?" She'd already potentially had her employee contaminate the car. "You said you got the name of the owner?"

"Uh-huh. Registered to Henry Rolf Larson."

"Thanks. Sit tight, I'll send someone out to you. Stay out of the car! And keep others away from it." He reconnected to Gonzales and brought him up to speed.

Gonzales whistled. "Henry? Even money he goes by Hank. Wasn't that the kid September called you about? Trouble sure follows her around."

Combs sucked in his breath. Gonzales nailed it. "You go check out his car back at Buc-ee's. And I'll head to the hospital. If

Blondie and Hank are the same kid, somebody had to give him a ride back to his house."

"Yeah, maybe the ninja. We need to get a line on them."

Combs could imagine his partner smoothing his mustache. "Somebody had to see something. Then we'll compare notes, and if need be, follow up on the VW's owner."

He'd need to question September, too. When her phone went to voice mail, he disconnected without leaving a message, and hurried to his car.

Chapter 22 - QUINN

Q uinn pulled off the road, heart pounding louder than the motorcycle's engine. She leaped off the bike, then gently grasped Tigger beneath his forelegs, as Nikki scrambled off and unhooked the safety leash.

"What the hell happened? Did you open his carrier?" Quinn cradled the big cat in her arms, while he buried his face against her neck, mewing and shivering. His rear legs dangled, quivering, the top of one paw completely raw, like ground meat, where it had dragged against the pavement.

"Of course not! I wouldn't risk him getting out while going about a hundred miles an hour. Duh!" Nikki peered at the cat's legs and whistled. "He needs a veterinarian." She hugged herself. "I watched my boss treat a dog with that kind of wound before. It could get infected real easy."

Rocking back and forth, cradling Tigger like a baby, Quinn shook her head. Her employer would never allow that. Leaving the cat with someone for treatment required records, answering questions, leaving a trail.

Nikki gently stroked the back of the cat's neck. "He's a beauty. Cats are my favorite. Doc Eugene can fix him up, I know he can. I can show you how to get to his clinic, and—"

"You work for a veterinarian?" Quinn stared at the girl over the cat's head. "You're just a kid. You know how to treat Tigger?" She eyeballed the broken catch on the cat carrier. If it was intact and the girl lied about opening it, Quinn would kill her. But the kid didn't know that, and had no reason to lie about how to treat Tigger's wounds. They looked excruciating. One leg looked worse than the other, but fur and skin had scraped off the knuckles of one paw and the other hock.

"I've worked for Doc Eugene nearly a year. I saw how he did it." Her age and expertise challenged, Nikki's tone sounded defensive rather than boastful. "It's better for a vet to do it, and give Tigger medicine and stuff for pain."

"But you can do it? I told you why we can't go to the cops. And an animal doc probably would have to report us, right? But I need to get Tigger help. He's my buddy. He's got me through some tough times, ya know?" She cleared her throat, hating the catch that betrayed the emotion Quinn strove to banish from her life.

"I've got a cat like that. Her name's Hope." Nikki again stroked the odd striped fur, and pursed her lips, tipping her head to take in the extent of the injuries. "We need to clean his legs good first. And I need supplies. Probably we could get what I need at a pharmacy." She smiled shyly. "Lucky I caught him."

Quinn raised her eyebrows. "Yeah, just born under a lucky star." The kid better come through. First aid would suffice until after she recovered the rest of the stolen product from the other kids.

With a grimace, Quinn gingerly placed Tigger back into the carrier, crooning to him. "Sorry, I know it hurts. Be a brave boy for a little longer." Surprisingly, the cat didn't object. She clipped the safety leash back on to his harness, and flipped the clear cover back in place, before helping Nikki back on the bike. "The latch broke, so you need to keep a hand on it so Tigger won't get out again."

Nikki nodded. "We need bandages. A couple of different kinds, like gauze pads. Betadine solution. Tape, oh, and an elastic ACE bandage with Velcro would work. That's better than Saran wrap, that wouldn't breathe right." She listed the items on her fingers, talking to herself. "I'll give you a list."

Nodding, Quinn mounted the motorcycle, and they continued She kept checking behind her, to be sure Nikki kept one arm on the carrier, while the other was clamped around Quinn's waist.

Within twenty minutes, Quinn saw a sign advertising the

downtown area of the next small town. She turned off to look for a store. These days, cameras tracked every move, but nobody paid much attention. Pharmacies had more stringent, up-to-date security, so Quinn couldn't risk shopping there. She didn't trust the girl to go alone—hell, Nikki's parents had probably already lodged an Amber Alert.

Quinn caught sight of a mom-and-pop grocery on the corner. Surely they'd carry the first aid supplies needed. And if they had security cameras, they'd probably be old or not even work. She'd learned property owners either forgot or neglected to keep on top of such details. Quinn leaned into the turn and pulled into a parking spot in the building's shade. She took off her helmet, but left on dark glasses, and tucked stray bits of hair back under her purple hair-covering.

"You wait here. Tell me your list again."

Nikki wrinkled her nose. "I don't know if this place'll have—"

"So give me some alternatives, if they don't have the exact brand of Band-Aid." She typed the list into a note on her phone, raising her eyebrows at a couple of Nikki's suggestions, but didn't take the time to question. "Oh, and if I come back out here and find you gone, I will track you down and turn you into the cops. And your brother Hank."

Hands akimbo on her hips, Nikki tossed her hair. "Just where would I go? Somebody's got to watch your cat, and take care of him." She tapped the clear bubble cover on the carrier. "Just get the supplies and then find us someplace to bandage up the poor thing."

Swearing under her breath, Quinn strode into the store, grabbed a small basket, and hurried to the home health shelves. They stocked plenty of things for scrapes and stings, but only limited bandage supplies, as Nikki feared. She dumped two boxes of the largest Telfa pads into the basket, added a couple of elastic ACE bandages, a roll of bandage tape, scissors, and a large bottle of contact lens saline solution. Then, shaking her head at the odd request, she prowled the aisles until she located the last two items: two pairs of plain cotton socks and a bag of granulated sugar. She took everything to the register, grabbed a gimme cap from the nearby stand, and declined the cashier's cheery attempt at small talk. She paid cash.

Quinn stuck the bag of supplies into the saddlebag, donned her helmet, and got them rolling again. It hadn't taken long, but every minute counted. She needed to track down the last two on her list, couple of girls not much older than Nikki, but they should be a piece of cake.

She pulled into a newly renovated rest area. She feared it might be too public, but saw only a few cars parked. Quinn parked, took off her helmet, rummaged in the saddlebag for her purchases, and pulled on the gimme hat to hide her hair. "Moment of truth, Nikki. Let's see what you can do." She thrust the bag of supplies into the kid's arms. Then she disengaged the carrier from the bike, slung it over one shoulder, and led the way into the building. "Keep your head down, don't talk to anyone. We go straight into the ladies. Hey, don't forget your backpack."

"Got it." Nikki sounded excited and had already slung her backpack across her shoulders. She skipped to keep up with Quinn's long strides.

Once inside, the building's AC blew chilly air that gave Quinn goosebumps. She quickly scanned the area and spotted the bathroom. Tigger mewed softly, then more loudly, and Quinn whispered comforting words. "Gonna fix you up, hang in there, buddy. I got you, trust me." She hoped nobody questioned the presence of the cat. These days, people took pets everywhere.

The lady in the lavatory washing her hands raised her eyebrows, but thankfully minded her own business. Quinn waited until she'd left then locked the door after her.

"Okay, we need to work quick. Hey you don't think Tigger's gone into shock or something, do you?" She wasn't sure exactly what that was, but knew it couldn't be good. "Should we give him some sugar right away? I thought honey was good for that. Oh, I got some Tylenol, too, for Tigger's pain."

Nikki had dumped all the supplies onto the countertop, and quickly tore open one package after another, preparing the workspace. She picked up the small package of pills and tossed it back to Quinn with an expression of distaste. "That's poison to cats. Don't ever give Tylenol to Tigger, you could kill him."

Quinn fumbled with the pill bottle, aghast at what she might have done. "What about his pain?"

"I said he needs a veterinarian. They've got special medicine that's safe for cats." Nikki softened her scolding tone. "But I don't think Tigger's in much pain, or he'd act different." As she spoke, Nikki washed her hands thoroughly with hot water and soap, then dried them with a paper towel. "One time, Doc Eugene treated a cat that got burned. And he said at least the kitty didn't feel it, cuz it destroyed some of the nerves. Maybe that's what happened with the road rash on Tigger's legs." She drew herself up to look as tall and imposing as possible. "I can put on the first bandages. But Tigger needs a professional. Doc Eugene says first aid is only that—the *first* aid, until you can get medical help."

Quinn nodded. She didn't like being lectured by a kid. But Nikki made sense. Soon as she could—once she completed her assignment—she'd get Tigger the best care in the world. She set the carrier on the counter next to Nikki's preparations. "What now? Should I take him out?"

"Almost ready. I'll need your help, too. He trusts you. You'll need to hold him."

Nikki tore a dozen strips of bandage tape and stuck one end of each along the edge of the counter. Then she opened the first pair of cotton socks, and scissored each one from cuff to toe, spreading them open on the counter. Finally, she opened the package of Telfa pads, and stacked them two deep the length of each sock. Finally, she cut open the bag of sugar and poured a generous amount on top of the pads.

"What the hell?" Quinn's eyes narrowed. "You're putting sugar in the bandage?"

"Yes." She ignored Quinn's incredulous question. "Now get Tigger out. We need to rinse off the injuries first." She opened the bottle of contact lens solution. "Hold Tigger with his legs over the sink."

Quinn dutifully followed the direction. She'd expected Nikki to run the water over the injuries, but the kid ran a steady stream of saline solution all over the raw areas on Tigger's legs. "Doc Eugene says saline works best because it's more like the body's natural fluid." She didn't touch the injuries at all, but peered at the two raw spots closely. "I don't see anything stuck in there. But that doesn't mean anything. There could be sand or dirt, or other bad stuff pushed into the sores. That's where the sugar comes in. Doc

Eugene said it's an old-fashioned remedy that prevents bacteria from growing. See, the dragging rubbed off Tigger's skin and fur, and maybe some of the muscle. But a sugar bandage helps the skin and tissue grow back." She nodded wisely. "He said the ancient Egyptians used honey. But that's a lot messier to use. We just need to get Tigger patched up until you can get him professional help."

Following Nikki's direction, Quinn positioned the first, more badly injured, leg on top of the mound of sugar and held him steady. Nikki poured more sugar on top of the injury, until the granules hid the raw tissue. She gently pulled both sides of the split sock up around the sugar-covered leg and grabbed one piece of tape after another to stick around the leg and hold it together. They repeated the process with the second leg. Then Nikki opened the second pair of socks and gently rolled one over the top of each sugar bandage. She used the Ace bandages and tape to secure the cuff of each sock to the furry britches on the cat's upper thighs.

Tigger mewed and only struggled as they completed the operation. Quinn wondered if he'd fit back in the carrier with the two enormous snowman-size leg bandages.

Pounding on the locked bathroom door startled them all. Tigger mewed again and struggled.

"Hey, you in there. Unlock the door. What's going on?"

Pounding again

"Open up right now, or I'll call the police."

Chapter 23 - KALI

Kali picked up a cigar, clipped the end with gold-plated scissors, then lit it with a matching lighter. Both had belonged to her husband. She puffed slowly, enjoying the sweet smoke that wreathed her face. It calmed her, especially the secret ingredient designed for her exacting specifications. Her eyelids blinked lizard slow, and she nearly purred with pleasure.

At any moment, she'd receive an update on her special project. Although these things required time—rushing things could spoil everything—her patience only lasted so long.

Quinn had begun well enough. She knew the girl had quickly tracked down the first thief. He hadn't been able to resist taking a taste of the product, which she'd made sure would be his last. Kali smiled again, drew deeply on the cigar, holding her breath a long, long time before letting it out in a rush of fragrant smoke.

She'd wanted the mutt to lure September Day out of her protective nest. Kali made sure September learned of the animal. She'd banked on the woman's soft spot for such creatures, a flaw she herself never understood.

But September refused to answer the call. She sent others to do her bidding. Kali smiled again. The eventual meeting between the old man and Quinn would serve as an appetizer, the others along the way as side dishes. September she'd save for dessert. She wished she could taste that deliciousness personally. But Mr. Fright would share all the details. Kali could hardly wait.

One of a dozen cellphones on the desk beside Kali lit up, announcing the expected call. Her staff had routed it through several other switches, hiding her location. She had many agents throughout the world, to see and hear for her, and on her command, reach out as her fist. Most of her operation ran well without daily oversight, but this most intriguing and entertaining project held her focus. "Tell me." Her voice would be distorted by the software, untraceable and unrecognizable. She'd learned well from her husband—the bastard.

"Our agent has the girl with her."

Very good. Quinn had done well. September felt a strong kinship with Nikki. "And the target?"

A pause, as if the voice at the other end anticipated her displeasure. "She took the bait, but then let go of the hook. She's headed home."

Kali crushed the cigar into the ashtray and stood, feeling the heat creep up her neck. "Home?" *September let Quinn take the girl?*

"She called 911 but had little information to share with the dispatch. Another call from the old guy came through, the one surveilling the dog. He's calling her back at home later."

Kali paced from one end of the opulent room to the other, before dropping once more into the massive leather chair that swallowed her tiny form. "Escalate."

A pause. "Repeat to confirm, please?"

She smiled, the possibilities chasing circles in her imagination. This project became more intricate and entertaining. The woman didn't know anything yet, but after all that had gone before, soon she'd seek answers. The longer she remained alive, the potential for her to derail Kaliko Wong's entire Organization grew. She needed September Day to revert to type and allow emotion to fuel her decisions. And leave home, away from her protectors, to where target practice got a clear shot.

"I said escalate. Message our agent the deadline has shortened."

She chose a fresh cigar and snipped off the end. Kali imagined doing the same to each of September's fingers.

Chapter 24 - TEDDY

Hold on, girls. Give me two minutes." Teddy hurried from the fast-food restaurant back to Nellie Nova, juggling the bag of spicy burritos in one hand and his phone in the other. He'd called September while waiting for his ordered food and now wanted to relax while he caught up with his granddaughters.

Meriwether meowed loudly when he climbed into the RV, and Teddy quickly shut the door. He switched the phone to speaker before setting it on the table. "Okay, how're my favorite granddaughters?" He pulled out the extra container of sour cream and fingered a dollop into the cat's bowl to keep him busy.

"We're your *only* grandkids." Leslie giggled, and Sylvia added dryly, "You always say that."

"And you always say that back." He grinned, enjoying the banter. The girls, barely a year apart in age, had finally prevailed upon their parents to join senior classmates for the traditional spring trip. The pair shared a strong family resemblance, but their personalities offered stark contrast. Leslie's outgoing nature and quirky sense of humor kept everyone laughing. Sylvia's serious character and tendency to self-isolate worried Teddy.

"We've had such adventures, Grandpa! And they're not over yet," said Leslie. "Took three years to get here. Thank you thank you thank you for saying yes."

"Adventures, really?" Not the description he expected. "What about you, Sylvia? Having fun?"

"I guess."

That had been part of the deal. Leslie campaigned each year to attend the annual trip, but Sylvia never seemed interested. This year, the girls worked together to convince Grandpa Teddy to campaign on their behalf. So he talked with his son and daughter-in-law. They felt Sylvia would keep her impulsive sister in check, while also reaping the benefits of socializing with her more outgoing sister.

"It's fun. But I'm ready to go home. I worry about Kismet." Sylvia sniffled a bit.

Their old Great Dane had been part of the family for seven years, a long life for the giant breed. Teddy had a soft spot for Kismet. The dog protected him from an attack during a visit over the holidays. "Oh, I'm sure he misses you, too. I won't be long. I'm working on... It's a surprise."

Heck, he'd just surprised himself at the brain burp, but it just might work out, depending on what happened with the shelter dog. "Hopefully, it won't take long, and I'll still be there by supper. I'll keep you posted. We can take our time driving back. Your folks don't expect you until Monday night." For once, the girls' school hadn't used all their snow days, and opted to add vacation time rather than shorten the school year.

"That's why we're calling, Grandpa. There's been a teensy-weensy change of plans." Leslie couldn't hide the glee in her voice.

"I told her not to do it." Sylvia's sullen tone. "I'm oldest, she's supposed to listen to me. That's the only reason I agreed to come. But no, she's gotta go all Don Quixote—"

"You're tilting at windmills?" As far as he knew, most of the wind turbines were in the northwestern part of the state. Or across the border in Oklahoma.

"Don't be such a toilet fish, Syl." Leslie countered with her own excited chatter. "It's not windmills, it's part of the adventure I mentioned." She added, if a bit grudgingly, "Guess it's sorta like a quest, only it's not make believe. It's real, and truly important, helping the less fortunate. Dad said you always do stuff like that." Her wheedling tone showed Teddy she knew exactly what buttons to push. His son's comment referred to Teddy's penchant for helping the underdog, but hadn't been meant as a compliment.

When the pair began talking over each other, he interrupted. "One at a time. You said change of plans? What's this crusade you mentioned?"

"Crusade, for sure." Sylvia harrumphed.

"Like I said, just a minor change." Leslie interrupted. "We'll tell you all about the adventure when we see you. It'll make more sense in person." It sounded like she covered the phone with one hand to talk with her sister and then returned full voice to the conversation. "Me and Syl met up with these really nice kids, and—"

"What?" Teddy added another dollop of sour cream to Meriwether's bowl when he tried to stick his big head inside the paper bag with the rest of the meal. "I thought we'd already confirmed our plans."

"I know, I know, Grandpa. But we just couldn't pass up this invitation. And it'll save you driving time, too. We caught a ride early this morning from Corpus Christi with one of the guys heading back north. Casper said there's some awesome painted churches we just gotta see."

Teddy pushed his wire-rim glasses back up his nose. "A church tour?" Had the girls got caught up with some religious group? He supposed most were harmless. Teddy had nothing against religion, figured it comforted lots of folks. But he'd lost any shred of belief he'd ever had when his wife died. "Leslie, let me talk to your sister." He didn't have to add "the level-headed kid."

Leslie made her own harrumph sound, but handed off the phone.

"Okay, kiddo, tell me straight. You girls converting or something? Anything I need to know about your sister's hedging?"

"We're not converting, Grandpa. Duh." Sylvia hesitated, and then blurted out in a rush. "Leslie says she wants to see the artwork. You know how she's into all that artsy-craftsy stuff, wants to be an architect or something. And I looked them up on the internet. It's not some scam or anything, they're truly historical. They do look pretty amazing. For churches, anyway." She took a breath, and added, "And it's a way to finish the adventure stuff." In the background, he heard Leslie raise her voice, so Sylvia had to talk over her. "I promised I wouldn't say anything more. But, well, I think Leslie's crushing on Casper."

"Am not! Give back the phone!"

Sylvia continued, "I had nothing to do with it, so it's only fair my sister gets to tell the story."

He cocked his head. He'd never known Sylvia to lie, and she wasn't good at it. He scooped up Meriwether and gently placed him back on the floor, away from the bag of burritos. He lowered his voice. "Are you girls in trouble? I won't get mad, I promise."

Leslie grabbed back the phone. "I'll text you the new address. You'll get to see the painted churches for yourself, Grandpa. And then I can tell you about our—I mean, *my* amazing adventure. Oh, and you're the best grandpa ever. Love ya bunches." She disconnected.

Teddy couldn't help his disquiet. Over the years, he'd learned to pay attention to the odd prickly feeling on the back of his neck. "They're good girls," he said, trying to convince himself.

Meriwether meowed back and hooked his claws on Teddy's pant leg.

Grinning, Teddy dumped the contents of the bag out on the small table. "You can have a bit of cheese, but only a little. Gives you gas."

Opening the laptop, he ran a quick search for painted churches. "What do you know?" He stared at the picture of a small, unassuming church, and scrolled down for interior pictures of spectacular bright colors, gilt designs, vaulted ceilings, iconography, and more. The article listed more than a dozen places of worship, most available for touring. Teddy shrugged. At least the girls had been straight with him. It seemed legit. And, as Leslie said, that meant he wouldn't have to drive all the way to south Texas to pick them up.

He'd have time to work on his surprise. Teddy scrolled to the downloaded video from the animal shelter. If September didn't get back to him soon, he wanted to be ready to act. So he reviewed it as he munched on his breakfast burritos and drank Dr. Pepper.

Chapter 25 - SEPTEMBER

When September pulled off Rabbit Run Road, and through the newly installed gates, she found the Stonebridge Landscape truck already in her circle drive. A big man appeared from around the side of the house, scrutinizing a tablet. He raised a hand in greeting and waited for her to park in the rebuilt carriage-house garage. The car's gas gauge flashed a red warning light as she turned off. She blew out her breath with exasperation. Nothing to do about it now.

The contractors' restoration of her historic home had taken longer than expected, but the upgrades were worth it. They'd matched the original brick as closely as they could, or added contrasting materials as accents. Anyone new to the home would believe it was planned that way. The automatic garage door beat the old swinging wooden barn doors all to heck.

September climbed out of the car, then let Shadow out of the back. He sat, waiting for her to grab the stack of file folders, but his front paws jittered, eager to meet and greet the man by the truck. "Shadow, okay. Say hello." She gave the big dog the permission he wanted, and with a soft woof he raced out of the garage.

"Hey, Arnold." She keyed the garage door closed while she strode to meet him. Shadow stopped three dog-lengths away from the man, high-held tail moving slowly as he sniffed from a distance.

"Thanks again for meeting on short notice. Sorry I'm running late." She showed the dog her closed fist, and he yawned and sat beside her, satisfied she accepted the man as safe.

Arnold held out his hand to shake and smiled. She caught her breath at the family resemblance to his brother. Broad shoulders, over six feet, his work kept him fit.

"No worries, September. I had to pick up a package out this way." He shrugged. "Got a steel oven stone, supposed to make the best homemade pizza. I eat a ton of pizza. And work it off." Arnold took off his hat and then put it back on. He whistled through his teeth, looking around the house and shuffling his feet. He acted as nervous as she felt. "While I waited for you, I looked at the back garden and made some notes. I hope that's okay? I've not been out here since…" He cleared his throat and looked away. He'd insisted on helping decontaminate the garden of the tainted bone meal that killed his brother, Aaron, and so many others.

"That's fine. I wouldn't want anyone else touching Aaron's design." Mark still mourned his husband's death. She hoped her brother would find happiness again, but knew all too well that everyone grieved in their own time. "Let's go inside, where we can talk."

She led the way to the front door, then put up a hand to stop Arnold as it swung open. "Shadow, *check-it-out.*" They waited on the brick steps as Shadow raced inside. The security system bee-bee-beeped a warning.

He waited patiently. "I understand. Can't be too careful."

They heard claws scrabbling on the hardwood entry, and the thumping gallop of paws up and down the stairs. In less than a minute, Shadow returned with a happy grin and waving tail, his okay that the house remained empty of scary intruders.

She entered ahead of the big man, waited for him to step inside, then latched and locked the door before tapping in the security code. The beeping stopped. September pointed him to her office then joined Arnold at the big desk, dropping the files to one side. Within minutes, Macy paced into the room, rubbed the full length of his body against September's ankle, then leaped onto the desk. The Maine Coon settled himself on top of the stacked files.

Absently stroking Macy's neck, September explained the garden challenges. "A lot of old roses got ripped apart during the tornado. I planted a few new ones, but Willie's dog loves to dig.

Hopefully, some survived."

"Some roses live for decades, especially the old-fashioned *found* roses. Those aren't really appropriate for cut flowers, though."

September nodded, thinking of the tangle of prickly vines threading over and around the back fence. She had stitch-looking scars from those. "We probably need new plants after all these years. I know it takes time to rebuild a garden, but we'd really like to have our wedding reception here. I'm thinking lots of different colors around the perimeter. And open spaces so we don't have to navigate a jungle to mow. Oh, and are there any roses that don't take a lot of maintenance?" She caught herself and shrugged. "I mean, we'd call you to help with all of that. Would that be every month, or once a year, or... Combs works long hours, and my schedule varies. And kid labor only works so well." She could just imagine Melinda's rolled eyes when asked to help deadhead bushes.

Arnold laughed. "Lots of questions. Luckily, I've got answers. Yes, you'll need new plants. We might save a few of the old ones. Antique roses survive nearly everything, and pruning them prompts new healthier growth." He reached out and offered his rough hand to Macy. After a preliminary sniff, the big cat pushed his head into the man's palm.

September smiled. "Macy loves the garden, too. I want to cat-proof it later so we can spend time out there. I love that roses are pet-safe, even edible." She hesitated. "Except, I've pulled off some of those weird-looking growths on some plants. That's not dangerous, is it?"

He grimaced. "That's witches' broom. Technically, it's called rosette disease. I noticed several infected bushes. Unfortunately, we can't save those—need to dig out any infected plants and burn them. We can put new roses in those spots after we wait a few days for the infectious mite to die." He stroked Macy's neck. "I don't know about witches' broom being safe for the pets."

September bit her lip. Maybe roses wouldn't be part of her wedding, after all. She'd wanted to bring back the house's historic glory, but perhaps she'd have to give up that dream.

At the look on her face, Arnold said, "We can plant fewer roses farther apart, so they don't touch. That helps prevent new infections and also reduces maintenance."

"Tell me about the maintenance. Be honest. Can I manage by myself? How much time will it take? Your brother and I hadn't talked much about that." She had done little with the garden for months. A simple yard to mow was looking more and more appealing.

He grinned again. "Aaron enjoyed making things beautiful. I'm more practical, and can set things up so you wouldn't need more than a once or twice weekly to-do list." Arnold glanced at his tablet, avoiding her eyes. "No pressure, but if that's too much for your schedule, I'd be happy to stay on retainer and take care of the garden for you. That'd be pruning in December or January, adding new mulch as needed, and checking for other things during the growing season. We can prevent black spot and spider mites and weeds. I'll set up a drip irrigation system for the new roses, so you'd just turn it on and off on a schedule." He looked up, expectantly. "This old Victorian lady deserves to get her rose petticoats back. And"—he cleared his throat—"I want to bring Aaron's design to life."

She met his eyes. "I'd like that, too. He'd already dug lines for the irrigation. I think he wanted that set up before putting in new plants."

"Exactly!" Arnold turned the tablet so she could see. "We have hundreds of color choices and sizes, with or without thorns, climbing or—I take it you prefer shrub roses?"

She nodded, intrigued by the simple but elegant design on his tablet. He'd incorporated the ornate fence surround in the schematic, with a spiral pattern path interspersed with stained glass paving stones. Lots of open space, but little mowing required, and a place she could hold cat or dog behavior consults when needed. She wouldn't need to rely on Lia's training facilities.

"That's lovely! Mark's paving stones, right?" He nodded. "But Arnold, it takes years for some roses to mature, to look like this. With the wedding only a few months away, is the plan realistic?"

"Let me worry about that." He smiled gently. "Now's the perfect time to order and get them in the ground. With proper care, and the right weather, they should bloom within six weeks, if not sooner. And, if we need more mature plants, I can find a few locally that fit the bill."

September loved the design. She could almost smell the perfume. She hesitated. *Better to be disappointed now than later.* "Could we do this in stages? Maybe just the fence area first, then finish the rest later?" The insurance money to rebuild the house didn't cover the garden. She couldn't justify spending too much at once, but wanted to turn the old house back into a showcase.

"I know what you're thinking, September. I'll give you a cost for the roses, and you can decide how many. Yes, we can add more later. But consider my work a wedding present." When she would have protested, he held up his hand. "Mark and I already discussed this. Let me put up a sign—tasteful, I promise—dedicating the garden to Aaron Stonebridge. You'll have a garden worthy of this property and bless my family into the bargain. Please?" He held out a hand to her. "Maybe each spring you could open up the garden for tours to showcase what Stonebridge Landscape can do?"

Her mouth dropped open.

"You're gonna catch flies." He laughed. "Sorry, my dad always said that. C'mon, September, let me do this for you. And for our brothers, Mark and Aaron."

Tears flooded her eyes. Shadow whined and leaned against her leg. "I thought maybe you blamed me for, you know, losing Aaron that awful way." She sniffed. "I don't know what to say." Her hand dropped to touch the dog's brow.

"Say yes. Unless you don't want Aaron's name—"

"No! I mean, yes! Of course, I want him honored. What a truly wonderful, thoughtful gift. For sure, we could open up the garden for you and potential clients. So next steps?"

"We pick out roses. Colors, sizes, how you want them situated. We could do masses of one color, or mix it up with a rainbow."

"Simple decision then, Arnold. Rainbow colors, all the way."

The landline in the kitchen rang, startling them both.

"Let me get this, and then we can put together a wish list." September skipped from the room. The news had turned the horrible day around. She reached for the old-fashioned wall phone. One of the few survivors from the storm, she'd kept it as a reminder. Most business came to her cell phone, and only a handful of close friends had the number. "This is September Day. How may I help you?"

"Did you leave your phone on silent again? I've called four times."

"Combs?" September groaned. She pulled out the cell and saw the missed calls. "Sorry, it's been a crazy day. What's up?" She hesitated. "I'm sorry about earlier."

"Never mind that. I'm at the hospital, waiting to see Henry Larson."

"Hank? Is he going to be okay? Did you find Nikki?" She unconsciously crossed her fingers, eager for good news.

"We need to talk. Will you be home for a while?"

She glanced at the office where Arnold sat at the desk, just in time to see Macy paw-pat-pat and dump the files onto the floor. "Yes, I'll be here."

Chapter 26 - QUINN

Just a minute." Quinn called to whoever pounded on the other side of the locked restroom door. "Give us one minute. Please." Quinn waved frantically at Nikki, and together they cleaned up the counter. They dropped handfuls of paper towels on top of debris in the trash can, and bundled leftover bandage material into Nikki's backpack.

"I don't think he'll fit in the carrier with the bandages on." Nikki stroked the cat's throat, soothing him. She had a real touch with Tigger. He rarely wanted strangers messing with him.

"The carrier expands. Check that zipper around the base." Quinn tamped down her emotions. It wouldn't do to get upset, and really, Tigger had no choice. None of them did. He had to squeeze into the carrier. She wouldn't leave him behind.

The banging on the door increased.

Nikki smoothed her white-blond hair behind each ear. "I know kitties aren't allowed in the rest area, but they got to understand. He got hurt. We had to get him help." She cooed to Tigger.

It didn't matter what the girl thought. Bad enough someone else would see her with the cat's carrier. Quinn needed anonymity to do her job. The detail of a pet cat could get her killed. "Make him fit. It's important."

With a sigh, Nikki unzipped the carrier. She reached into her pocket and brought out a cellophane-wrapped package. At Quinn's raised eyebrows, she said, "Jerky from Buc-ee's."

What? Before Quinn could snatch it away, she realized what the girl planned.

"I know it hurts, Tigger. I'm super sorry, boy, but you need to get back in your bed. You like jerky?" She held out a piece and the cat sniffed, tentatively tasted, then chewed enthusiastically. "Good boy! How 'bout more yummies? You deserve treats for being so brave." Nikki offered a bit more, and coaxed the cat into the carrier, dropping the rest of the package inside one of the carrier pockets. With his padded rear paws, Tigger fit, but barely.

Quinn taped the broken opening on the carrier closed, slung it over her shoulder, and motioned for Nikki to unlock the door.

The woman from the information desk stood with arms tightly crossed, one foot tap-tapping. A family of vacationers pushed past, barely waiting for Nikki to open the door. "You can fasten the stalls. No need to lock the door. What were you doing, anyway?" As if to punctuate the question, one vacationer slammed her stall door.

"My little sister's puppy had an accident, we had to clean it up." Quinn didn't hesitate to lie. A pair of sisters traveling with a puppy threw shade over the reality. She glared at Nikki, willing the girl to stay silent.

"You better not have left a mess." The woman sniffed and looked around the area, making a face at the waste can.

"Let's go, Sis." Quinn grabbed Nikki by the arm and pulled her out the door.

"Ouch! Let go." The girl pulled away.

She should have eliminated the kid right away. Too late now, unless she wanted to take out a half-dozen strangers. Her employer prized discretion above all. Tanner Rudolph had taken care of himself, and she'd taken care of Sebastian. Her employer didn't need to know she'd only meant to disable, not kill.

Quinn stiffened her jaw. She'd do better the next time. Nikki's brother, Hank, had probably bled out by now. Collateral damage. Stupid to get mixed up with someone like Sebastian, and drag his little sister into the mix. But Nikki the firecracker, more nuisance than help, had saved Tigger's life. She owed her a reprieve. At least for now. "Come on. We've got a long trip ahead."

"You're taking me to see Hank now, right? You said so. You promised."

"Shut up!" Quinn hissed, very aware of the attendant's sharp ears and side eye. "Sure, kid, I keep my promises." *If it serves my purposes.*

Nikki beamed. You'd think she'd won the lottery.

Quinn tamped down the sudden twinge of guilt. Guilt got you nothing but trouble. No, she had to recover the last of the stolen product from the last two thieves, and eliminate them. If Nikki cooperated, maybe she'd let her live. If she didn't cooperate... Sometimes life sucked.

She fixed the cat carrier securely on the back of the bike. As she waited for Nikki to climb aboard, Quinn's phone announced another incoming text. She stiffened and then looked.

>Targets moving, collect ASAP. Hold at church for next instructions.

Chapter 27 - NIKKI

Nikki double-checked the tape closing Tigger's carrier before she climbed back onto Quinn's bike. She hitched her shoulders, trying to get the now-stuffed knapsack more comfortable.

She felt proud of putting the sugar dressing on Tigger's huge paws. He looked way bigger than her own Hope-kitty. That made her sigh. Hope hadn't acted well for several weeks now. Doc Eugene said probably the kitty's rough start in life exposed her to bad stuff that made her sick. She seemed sad, too. Nikki wondered if another cat friend would help. Hope's fur, though, looked nice and shiny, not like Tigger's fur.

Most cat fur lay smooth and silky against the body. But Tigger's uneven short tabby coat, though clean, seemed jagged and uneven. Maybe he'd had a skin condition. Nikki had helped treat dogs at the clinic, shaving and bathing them with strong-smelling stuff to get rid of skin mites. She made a face at the thought of creepy-crawlies inside a poor dog's skin. It made her itch.

Maybe Quinn shaved off Tigger's fur to keep him cool. Some kitties got a lion cut in the summer that left a fluffy mane but clipped the rest of the fur close to the skin.

But none of that explained why gray and black color ran off his paws when she washed his injuries—as if he walked through paint that turned his white paws to tiger stripes. Weird. She'd never seen cat fur where only the ends looked dark, with white fuzz next to the skin. Maybe Tigger was some rare cat breed? She'd ask Quinn once they stopped again, when they got to Hank.

Hugging the older girl's slim waist, Nikki squinted her eyes to keep the wind from making tears run. She'd already cried enough worrying about Hank. She used to cry all the time, like a baby. But now she'd gotten more grownup. She'd seen some pretty scary things, and lived through dangerous times with September and the other kids. Nikki figured kids matured quicker when they lived through danger than if they just read about scary things in books.

She'd make Hank proud she'd kept the medicine safe and hadn't let that Sebastian guy take it from her. Nikki couldn't wait to see Hank, so he could explain everything. Sometimes brothers could be stoopid-heads, but mostly she liked him. He didn't tease her too much anymore. And even when he did, she knew he did it cuz he liked her. Her lip trembled again, hoping he hadn't got hurt too bad. She dared a peek through slitted eyes to see their progress.

The scenery whipped by. Nikki's hair became a silken cloud around her head. Quinn sure liked to go fast! At this rate, they'd be back to Heartland in no time. How lucky that Hank had a friend like Quinn. And how amazing Quinn found Nikki just before the cops arrested her for hiding Hank's drugs—no, Quinn called it medicine. She knew Doc Eugene kept some of the medicine at the veterinary clinic in a locked cabinet because he said bad people might want to steal it and use it *illicitly*. She smiled. He'd taught her big words she'd otherwise never have learned.

That made Nikki think about missing work. She'd never done that before. Doc Eugene really counted on her to keep her promises. Now she'd broken her word, he'd be disappointed in her. That hurt more than anything. Heck, he might find somebody else, someone older who could drive and not have to rely on a stoopid-head brother for rides.

Tears welled again, and Nikki pressed her face hard against Quinn's back, sniffling and hiccupping. She just wanted this day to end, to see Hank and have him be okay—not a thief or nothing, or hurt too bad. And she wanted Mom to say *everything's okay*, and hug her, and hold her on her lap like when she was a crybaby little girl. Even if she was too old for that baby stuff. She sniffled, yawned, and listened to the sound of wind and tires on the road.

As they traveled farther and farther, soon to see Hank and where everything would become right again, Nikki dozed...

She roused when the motorcycle rolled to a stop. Nikki looked up and wrinkled her nose. She stared right and then left, remaining on the pillion seat when Quinn dismounted. "Where are we? You said we'd go see Hank." An old church stood prim and proper with an old tree leaning beside it. A chain across the narrow road blocked access to the distant parking lot, empty except for a single dark vehicle.

Quinn drove off the road, following the other car's tracks down into the ditch, and up the other side to bypass the barrier. She drove right up to the church and parked under the ginormous tree. She unfastened the cat carrier and the saddle bag, slinging each over a shoulder. "This way. Follow me."

"He's here? In a church?" Nikki's lower lip trembled. "Is he okay? You said he got hurt. What's he doing here?" *He should be in Heartland hospital.*

And this wasn't Heartland. They'd ridden for a long time. Why hadn't she paid attention to the road signs? Nikki climbed off the bike, stretching stiff legs, and hiking her knapsack to a more comfortable position. The weight left her muscles sore after wearing the straps for so long.

Quinn just tightened her lips and walked away. Nikki hurried to catch up as the older girl strode toward the double doors of the old church. One of the unlocked doors hung open and Quinn pushed it wider to enter.

When she stepped inside, Nikki gasped. The plain exterior hid an interior that gleamed with a bright sky-blue ceiling flecked with golden stars. The walls held painted religious figures surrounded by fancy decorations like on a pastry chef's wedding cake. Colored light streamed in through massive stained glass windows on each side of the sanctuary's old dusty wooden pews.

A line of gothic arches supported the vaulted ceiling and drew the eyes upward toward multiple carved figures—statues with halos, old melted candles at their feet. At the front of the sanctuary, a beautiful altar on blood-red plush carpeting held shiny brass candlesticks and tall metal stands holding crosses. "Why are we here?" Nikki whispered. Something about churches always made her shy to speak out loud.

"Meeting people." Quinn had stopped only briefly at the sight of the painted interior. She turned to face Nikki, and put a hand on her shoulder, squeezing to emphasize her words. "I work for someone and have a very important job to do. I don't always like my job." She cocked her head. "Do you like everything about your job at the veterinarian's office?"

Nikki scrunched her nose. "Cleaning the poopy kennels sucks. And I hate it when one of the pets hurt, or ends up dying." Her voice caught. Could you say *poopy* in a church? "But all the good stuff outweighs the bad. That's what Doc Eugene says. And it's true, mostly." She didn't like that question, though. Nikki had a bad feeling. She tightened her grip on the backpack straps.

"My job's like that. I get to help people that have nowhere else to turn." Quinn's earnest expression matched her tone. "Your brother Hank wanted to help people, too. That's why he took the medicine from Sebastian. Sebastian wasn't a good guy." She squeezed Nikki's shoulder again. "I think bad people should get what they deserve, don't you? That's part of my job, too." She let go of Nikki and looked around the church. "I'm supposed to meet a couple of people like your brother. They picked up three thermos canisters just like the ones he gave you, to help get that medicine to the people who need it but can't afford it. You need to help me." It wasn't a question, but a demand.

"Where's my brother?" Tears spilled, and Nikki impatiently scrubbed them away. "Is he even a-a-alive?"

"I told you, Nikki. He was hurt but alive." Her impatience sounded in her raised voice. The sound echoed in the big open space. "Now listen to me. People we're meeting might not be as nice as me. They might scare you. I need you to trust me. I don't want... and Hank, he wouldn't want you to get hurt, either." Her jaw tightened. "You helped save Tigger, so I know you're a good person, Nikki. But I can't do my job and make sure innocent people stay safe if you get in my way. Can I count on you to do exactly what I say?"

Tigger meowed, but before Nikki could answer, they heard footsteps approaching from behind one of the doors beside the altar at the front of the church. A loud man's voice carried easily. Voices echoed here, like singing in the bathroom. The man sounded like a tour guide, expounding on the various architectural and artistic aspects of the building. Two girls followed in his wake, one with a knapsack slung over her shoulder.

"Hi! Are you taking the painted church tour, too?" The taller thin girl pushed by the short muscled man. "I'm Leslie Williams, that's my grumpy sister Sylvia." Leslie gestured to a pudgy brunette. Both girls looked older than Nikki, maybe in high school or even college. Nikki glanced at Quinn, eyebrows raised.

Quinn frowned and gave a slight head shake, so Nikki looked down, saying nothing. She wondered why the girls didn't recognize Quinn. That didn't seem to discourage Leslie, who chattered on. "This is the third one, and the best church so far. Right, Syl?"

The other girl shrugged and crossed her arms.

"How many more to go, Mr. Fright? I want to see all of them before me and Syl gotta leave. Grandpa's gonna pick us up when I text him the last address."

Mr. Fright's short bushy hair haloed his head, and a tight tee shirt and stretchy athletic pants outlined his muscles. "Oh, I think we've seen the best of them. What's your name?" He stared pointedly from Nikki to Quinn.

"You know my name, *Mr. Fright.*" Quinn's posture stiffened. "What're you doing here?"

"Oh, our employer sent me to help. You got the message, right? Here's a hint: never disappoint our employer."

Nikki stared at the long cylindrical shaped bag he had over his shoulder. His lips parted, revealing glistening white teeth with one gold tooth in front. "Special camera. To document important details of the *tour.*" He nodded at Quinn, and her nostrils flared like she smelled something bad. "Speaking of cameras, what do you say we commemorate this moment?" He pulled out his cell phone, motioned to the girls to pose—Quinn declined—and took a picture of the trio. Leslie quickly took her own selfie before Nikki pulled away.

"I don't need your help." Quinn slowly and deliberately settled the cat carrier on one of the wooden pews. Her eyes never left the man. It reminded Nikki of the way Hope-kitty stared at something threatening and gathered herself to fight or run. She wasn't sure which Quinn had in mind.

Quinn licked her lips, took a big breath, and spoke to the sisters, still with eyes staring at Mr. Fright. "Girls, this is my friend Nikki. Why don't you show Nikki the rest of the church? Mr. Fright and I need a private talk." She glanced briefly at Nikki and nodded at the two girls.

The man cocked his head when Nikki joined the sisters.

"Make it snappy before grandpa gets here. Bet it'll be a delightful surprise for Teddy Williams."

Nikki stiffened. She knew that name. At the soft breath of shock, Nikki twisted to stare at Quinn. But despite the other girl's ashen face, her expression gave nothing away.

Chapter 28 - SEPTEMBER

M acy!" The big cat met September's eyes from across
the room, then paw-patted two more files onto the
floor. "Just stop. It's not treat time, not for another
hour."

At her tone, Shadow stood and sniffed the cat's tail, and then
nose-poked the big feline in his soft tummy. Macy swacked at the
dog, but with claws retracted, then hopped off the desk. September
hung up the kitchen phone and hurried back into the office, just as
Arnold caught and rescued the rest of the stack before it also slid to
the floor.

"That cat's a piece of work." Arnold grinned broadly, and bent
to rescue files from the floor, straightening them into a tidy pile on
the corner of the desk. "Reminds me of my mom's cat,
Stormageddon, or Storm for short. She's a brown-on-brown tabby
with a big bullseye spot on her side."

"Classic tabby. Must've arrived during a storm?"

He nodded. "She never sits still. Bounces from sofa to cat tree
to laps. And she can get into the attic to the central air louver
located right over mom's bed. Hey, do you know why Storm wants
to suck on ear lobes? Last time I spent the night, I woke with a
purring, kneading cat attached to my ear lobe."

September laughed. "Cats weaned too early sometimes do that.
What does your wife think?"

Arnold shrugged. "Not married. I work all the time or I'd have a whole clowder of them. I recently lost my dog, Kami, and not ready yet for another."

Macy darted into the kitchen, leaped onto the counter, and meowed plaintively. "Whenever he feels ignored, Macy finds a way to get attention." She couldn't help but smile at the cat's antics.

"Is that why cats knock stuff over, or push it off tables?" He nodded at Shadow. "My dog used to just stare, paw my leg, and expect me to read his mind."

"I'm sorry you lost your dog friend." She'd felt that pain. "Cats enjoy gravity experiments. In Macy's case, he's trained me well." When Macy called again, September relented, pulled a treat out of her pocket and tossed it to the top of the refrigerator. The Maine Coon trilled happily, leaped to the tall perch, and began munching.

As she returned to the office, September noticed Shadow watching Arnold with interest, and smiled. Shadow knew when her stress grew. Scheduling tasks always helped keep her on track, but much of today's plan had skidded sideways. Shadow's behavior—on alert much of the day—reflected her own frazzled nerves.

So her own shoulders unclenched watching the big dog relax. He stretched his neck to get a close-up sniff of the big man's boots. His black tail wagged. They must smell of fresh dirt, greenery, and maybe squirrels, one of his favorite things. She grinned again, remembering his new tree-climbing skill, then returned her attention to the laptop computer, open to a display of antique roses.

Shadow moved closer to Arnold and sniffed the man's pant leg. "Shadow, don't bother him."

Arnold chuckled. "That's okay. I miss my old dog, Kami"

"When can you start? What's next?"

He nodded. "I can start anytime. Do you want to choose or leave it to me?" Arnold cocked his head. "Me, I'm very particular about colors. There are dozens of pink roses, each a different shade, with some that bloom only once a year and others repeat blooming all summer long. Same for yellow roses, or white ones. So you want ruby red, or orange-red, or... and do you want roses with a subtle or more strong perfume?"

"Yikes, Arnold." She rubbed her eyes. "I guess I like roses that repeat bloom. And perfume, that'd be nice. But you're the expert. So bright vibrant colors, no two of the same color side by side. And at the price listed"—she calculated in her head—"no more than fifty plants. Will that be enough?"

He whistled. "More than enough, maybe too many. We don't want them crowded."

"Okay, I leave it to you." She let Arnold out of the back kitchen door to take the needed garden measurements.

Shadow raced to the kitchen's stained glass window to watch his progress. "He doesn't need your help, baby-dog. You worried he'll find one of your Frisbees, or shoo away the squirrels?"

He barked twice at one or both of the words, and paw-danced in excitement. "Settle, Shadow." September returned to her desk, glancing at the stack of file folders. She sighed. Shelters sometimes held back pet descriptions and relied on identification to confirm ownership and avoid potential conflicts. She gave away leashes in two sizes: thin red ones for smaller dogs, and wider blue slip leashes for big ones. Teddy's visit to the Four Paws Shelter hadn't yielded any helpful information. Without more details, she had to guess based on timeline and narrow it down to big dogs.

She pushed the stack aside, impatient for Combs to get home. "What's he want to talk about, do you know, Shadow?" He'd been investigating a homicide. She hoped Nikki's brother had nothing to do with it, but why else had he gone to the hospital? "Maybe he has news about Nikki."

Shadow woofed and wagged when he recognized the girl's name.

On a whim, she opened a new browser page and searched for local news. "Nothing about Nikki." Shadow whined at her tone while she continued to type on the keyboard. "Oh wow. Somebody got attacked at the Buc-ee's." But it didn't seem to have any connection to Nikki's disappearance or Hank's injuries.

When a car door slammed, Shadow raced to the front door. A frisson ran icy fingers down her spine. Shadow didn't bark, though, and she relaxed when keys grated in the lock and the door squealed open.

"September?"

"I'm in the office." She stood as Combs strode into the room. Deep lines trenched his forehead, the expression appeared every time he worried over difficult or upsetting cases.

He crossed quickly to her, and without preamble, pulled her

into his arms. At first surprised, she reflexively returned his hug, and kissed him back, hard.

"I'm sorry, Jeff—"

"Sorry, babe." Their words spilled over each other, and they both laughed. Shadow jumped all around the pair, doing his best to separate the snug embrace. "Splitting?" Combs asked.

"Yep." He'd learned a lot about dog and cat behavior over the past few years. She pulled away. "Shadow, settle. Good dog." And she'd learned a lot about police business. "Tell me. Is it Hank? He's involved in something bad, isn't he? And Nikki..."

He motioned for her to take a seat and sat beside her. "Is that Arnold's truck in the drive? Can we afford garden costs right now, with the wedding?"

"I'll tell you about that later. Don't worry, I promise it won't be a financial problem." When he would have argued, she added, "Trust me."

He closed his mouth and grimaced. "I do. Trust you, that is. And I should've listened to you earlier. Yes, Hank's involved. I just need to figure out how." He set a digital recorder on the table and switched it on. His tone changed, and he became the police detective, questioning a witness. "How'd you come to find Henry Larson? Take me through everything, September."

She'd done this before, more than once. September straightened, and Shadow laid his head on her lap. She stroked his forehead, smoothing his silky ears, fingering the bullet notch in one ear tip. "I got a call from Doc Eugene asking me to run by the Larson home. Nikki, that's Hank's younger sister, works for him at the vet clinic, but didn't show up. He couldn't reach her mom. Doc thought maybe Nikki needed a ride." She swallowed hard. "She's only eleven, and doesn't drive."

The furrows in his brow deepened. "Nikki abducted? Wait, strike that. Go back to the Larson's house. What'd you see when you got there?"

She took a breath and closed her eyes briefly to help remember. "The door, unlatched. Blood on the door and the entryway."

Shadow licked his lips, and she soothed him with a gentle stroke.

"So you went inside?"

She nodded and shuddered. "Hank was on the floor. He sat against the door. I had to push hard to get inside. He was bleeding from his stomach." She caught her breath. "You saw him at the hospital? Is he going to be okay?"

"Don't know, he's in surgery. He sustained serious stab wounds. The hospital hadn't yet located his mother." He hesitated. "It didn't look good."

"I called 911, tried to slow the bleeding while we waited for the ambulance. Jeff, Hank said whoever hurt him went after Nikki." She impatiently dashed away tears. "Who would go after them, Jeff? They're good kids. Does this have anything to do with the attack at Buc-ee's?"

He started. "How'd you know about that?"

She gestured to the laptop. "Local news. You mentioned a homicide investigation, so I wondered."

Combs rubbed his eyes. "We don't know how Larson's connected, but we have description and video that sure looks like him; and his car is still there."

September laced her fingers together and squeezed hard. "They've already been through so much. Their dad's deployed, mom's working two jobs and looking for something better, Nikki's working to help. I think Hank works somewhere after school, too." She gasped with sudden realization. "Nikki must have been at the Buc-ee's, too."

He tapped the desk in front of the recorder, bringing her attention back to the interview. "Tell me about Nikki. She wasn't with Hank at their house? Where'd you see her?"

"That was weird." She wrung her hands. "I'd picked up Hank's phone, and didn't realize it. After I talked to you." She looked away. "Instead of heading to the hospital, I went to the church rehearsal."

He grimaced, but didn't interrupt.

"Nikki called Hank's phone."

He raised his eyebrows. "Lucky break."

"You'd think so, right? It wasn't her. Some trucker—at least I think it was a trucker—had her phone. He said she'd sneaked a ride in his cab, and told me to come get her. He'd dropped her off on the side of the highway."

"Kicked out a little girl? Along the highway? She's how old?"

He rubbed his chin.

"I know! I would've reamed him a new one, except I wanted to know how to find her. You were busy, and I didn't know enough specifics to call anyone else."

He frowned again. "I said I'm sorry."

She touched his arm. "I'm not belaboring it. Just wanted to explain why I went off on my own again." She quirked a grin. "I know you hate when I do that. I called 911 for Nikki, too."

He nodded. "Go on."

"Shadow and I headed down the highway, and got off at the mile marker the trucker indicated. Shadow found Nikki's trail. He's never tracked people before, but he did it! He really loves Nikki—she gives him treats—knew her name, or it probably wouldn't have worked." Shadow pawed her leg at the sound of his name. "Yes, you're a good dog, Shadow." She gritted her teeth. "We nearly caught up to her when some crazy woman on a motorcycle zoomed in and took off with her."

"Motorcycle?" His eyes widened. "That would explain some things. We couldn't figure how Hank got away from Buc-ee's without being seen. On the video, a big-ass eighteen-wheeler blocks the view. That'd be long enough for a motorcycle to spirit the kid away."

"I didn't think truckers were allowed." September unclenched her hands. The puzzle intrigued her. "Hank sometimes drives his dad's old car."

"The big rigs aren't allowed. The manager gave me an earful about it. Wait." He smiled grimly. "You said Nikki hid out in a trucker's rig?"

"Yeah. And you think Hank made his get-away on a motorcycle?"

"That would explain Hank's car still at Buc-ee's."

Something niggled the back of her memory, and September struggled to dredge it up. "When I drove to the Larson's, someone on a motorcycle nearly side-swiped me. Oh, and I got a video of the bike that took off with Nikki. It's not very good, but could be enhanced."

He stood, unable to hide his excitement.

September's cell rang, and with an apologetic look, she picked up. "Sorry I've not got back to you. I'm still tied up."

She whispered to Combs, "It's Teddy."

The old-man voice grated with excitement. "That's okay. I know you didn't want me to go all extra-curricular, September. But my timetable unexpectedly moved up and I can't hang around much any longer. Gotta pick up the pooch, and go meet my girls."

She explained to Combs about Teddy's rendezvous with his grandkids. "He's doing me a favor. I'll be done in just a minute. Hey, maybe he could enhance the video of Nikki on the motorcycle."

He shook his head. September knew he disapproved of civilians' involvement in investigations, although they had benefited from some of Teddy's methods. "Say hi for me." Combs reached to turn off the recorder.

September put the phone on speaker and set it on the desk. She pulled the stack of files closer. "Combs says hey. You're on speaker. If you've got the owner's name, I can find a match in my files to the dog's home."

Teddy growled his answer. "This owner doesn't deserve the dog. He dumped him at the shelter. I got video of a green VW pulling up, tying a white three-legged dog to the front door handle, then speeding away. What kind of jerk does that?"

Combs switched the recorder back on. "Did you say green VW?"

"Yep, lime green, Detective. Don't suppose you know this yahoo? Took some finagling from the video, but I got the license plate number. I traced the tags, and it's registered to a feller named Tanner—"

"Tanner Rudolph." Combs finished the name.

"I don't believe it." September stared at him, eyes wide. "That's got to be Lefty, a three-legged Great Pyrenees. I don't believe it, Tanner would never abandon his dog. Let me grab that file. I'll send you the details, Teddy, so you can claim him."

"Where are you, Teddy? We need to talk." Combs looked at September. "Can you send me that video? Oh, and September has another one for you to review."

Chapter 29 - TEDDY

Teddy was looking forward to seeing this town in his rear-view mirror. As requested, he'd sent Combs the video of Tanner Rudolph abandoning his dog. It broke his heart. Clearly, Lefty hadn't wanted to be left, crying piteously, and tugging against the leash looped around his neck. The dog got not even a farewell pat, or backward look from his owner. He looked scared, ears pressed flat, and fluffy white tail tucked, yet cried and yipped when the piece-of-crap Tanner Rudolph strode away. Whatever September thought, he knew what he'd seen.

"How can anyone do that? Dump a pet they've lived with and cared for. Dog doesn't understand what he did wrong to deserve getting kicked to the curb. And the answer is nothing. Nothing at all!"

Meriwether meowed his agreement, or disdain—with cats you could never tell—as Teddy pulled into the shelter parking lot. He'd stopped by a store to purchase a proper leash and collar for Lefty. He'd added a custom tag that documented the dog's name with Teddy's own address on the back. He smiled, figured the added detail wouldn't hurt. Clearly, the former owner hadn't cared enough to even leave a collar on his onetime friend. He'd made a collar tag for Meriwether, too, but had to hyphenate the name to fit.

Teddy also got a small bag of food, not knowing exactly how

long they'd be travel buddies. Armed with the dog's name and a more detailed description from September's file, Teddy felt confident he'd soon spring the pooch from incarceration. "You're in for a better life. I promise."

Teddy wanted to hurry so he could rendezvous with his granddaughters, even if he didn't have to drive all the way to the Gulf. He promised Combs to stop by Heartland on the way back for questions about the dumped dog and the video. Combs had said cops had found Tanner Rudolph's car abandoned. Huh. Dumped his dog, then dumped his car. Interesting, and made Teddy wonder what he had to hide.

But the detective rarely shared much. Teddy didn't mind. He had ways to find out the details. Maybe Rudolph's sins went beyond dumping dogs. When he got a spare second, he'd do more digging.

The girls wouldn't like interrupting their trip. But he could sell them on the excitement of being part of a police investigation. He smiled. Girls their age liked the idea of adventure. And they'd like the rescue dog.

He scooped up the big Maine Coon and carried Meriwether to the rear of the RV. "Hate to do this, but you need to wait in your bed until I get the new guy situated." He grabbed a plastic container of the cat's favorite crunchies, shook out two or three and tossed them into the carrier, then set the longhaired feline near the opening. The cat looked from Teddy to the open carrier, and back again, sniffing delicately. Then with a resigned air, Meriwether paced into the roomy soft-sided cat house, and picked up each morsel, taking his time to crunch each thoroughly. Teddy gently pushed the extra-long tail inside and zipped up the opening.

"Thanks, buddy. Shouldn't be for long, I just want you safe."

September had noted Tanner Rudolph wanted Lefty trained as a service dog. That meant the pooch knew to act respectfully around other people and animals, plus whatever special skills he'd learned. "Dumping a service dog? That's evil." And unbelievable. Specially trained canines rarely left their partners. If need be, they'd find new placements—like Shadow had been trained for September's autistic nephew, Steven, but once the boy had no need of the dog's help, Shadow found his life-partner in September. Teddy had never seen a human and canine so connected.

Teddy steeled himself. He'd once again have to turn a blind

eye to other worthy animals in the shelter. Picking up Lefty would only be temporary. But he knew how to make better arrangements for the pooch, so Lefty could live out the rest of his life in a forever home that truly appreciated him. Teddy smiled at the thought, took a big breath, gathered up the leash and collar, and left the RV.

Teddy noticed the camera again. He'd looked at that video twice more since talking to Combs. The dog's owner had worked hard to keep out of the picture, and he'd worn a hat.

The door squealed as he entered, and the muffled sounds of barks and meows rose from several cages. This time, a short, balding man with kind eyes manned the front counter. "Hey there, sir, I lost my dog. And I got a call that he's here. I'm here to get him back."

"Okay, that's a lucky break if you know he's here. Somebody called?" He did something on a keyboard, and printed out a form. "Please fill this out. Then I'll need your identification, and you'll need to pay any fees." He handed Teddy several pages on a clipboard with a pen and motioned for him to take a seat. "I've got staff cleaning and feeding our guests. I'll be right back." He disappeared through the door.

Guests? I kinda like that guy. Teddy took a seat and quickly filled out the required information. Since he and his wife had adopted their dog, years ago, the questions had become more intrusive and all-encompassing: Name, address, employer, rent/own/lease your home, fenced yard or not, kids ages, previous pet adoptions, and even "have you ever given up an animal before, if so, why?" Many of the questions didn't apply in his situation since, rather than adoption, he was reclaiming an already owned animal. He'd heard complaints from people who'd had pet adoptions turned down for what they considered unreasonable concerns. He could see how the organization wanted to ensure the animals they placed stayed in the home. *Two sides to every situation. Glad I don't have to make those decisions.*

The balding man returned, and Teddy gave him the form back, along with his driver's license. "Which dog? Do you have a description?" He made a copy of the driver's license and stapled it to the form.

Teddy showed him the picture on his phone. "That's Lefty. He's my traveling buddy, we're on the road in my RV, and he got away at the rest stop." He repeated the story told earlier to the woman. He held up the collar and leash. "He slipped out of his collar." He made sure the attendant saw the name tag. "Can I get him now? I sure miss that fellow."

The man leaned forward to peer at the picture on Teddy's phone. "Always best to get them micro-chipped. Lucky you got a call at all. Yep, the pup looks familiar. Follow me." He opened the half door in the counter and motioned Teddy inside.

Teddy breathed easier, and clumped after the other man. He knew this would be tough and stiffened his jaw. At the far corner of the room, another set of double doors opened onto two long corridors, each lined by wire encased, cement-floored runs. Most held a single animal, but some runs held pairs of dog friends. Some dogs stood barking for attention, while others curled into furry balls of despair. Teddy swallowed hard.

"Lefty? Lefty, where are you, boy? Ready to go home? Let's go." Teddy called out, having to do something to relieve his stress.

A sharp yelp followed by a deep bark answered his cry. Midway down the left side, he saw a Great Pyrenees missing his right front leg. The dog levitated into a single paws-up posture, balancing his one front paw against the wire door. "Lefty, there you are!" The dog matched the description September had sent. Smaller than most of his breed, the white dog at about eighty pounds still looked solid and imposing. The picture on Teddy's phone, though clearly not recent, still caught the dog's winning personality.

As he came abreast, the dog hopped back down and backed away, whining. His tail, at first a whirl of excitement, slowed and stopped. Lefty whined and licked his lips, straining to look beyond Teddy. He clearly expected Tanner to appear and rescue him.

Teddy's throat tightened. He grabbed the wire with one hand and leaned down, whispering fiercely. "Lefty, I know you don't understand. But I'm a friend, I promise. Let's get out of here, and we'll figure things out." He straightened and turned back to the attendant. "That's my dog, that's Lefty."

The young man checked the file clipped to the front of the kennel door. "Okay, looks like there's just an impound fee and..." He looked from the dog to Teddy, checked the picture on Teddy's phone one last time. "Lefty? What a great name. How'd he lose his leg, if you don't mind me asking?"

"As a puppy. An infection that wouldn't heal." Teddy rattled off the detail that September had supplied, glad he'd asked. "He's never missed a beat since."

The attendant grinned. "Never mind the boarding fee. I'm just glad you found each other. He looks all fierce, but he's a sweetheart. That made my day." He took the collar and leash from Teddy, opened the wire door, and placed both on Lefty. He handed the end of the leash to Teddy.

Lefty stood with ears slicked down, tail tucked, turning his head away. "C'mon Lefty, let's go." Teddy wheedled. He tried to keep his face cheerful, but inside, he panicked.

"Don't worry, Mr. Williams." The attendant patted him on the shoulder. "Shelters can stress them out. The sensitive ones take a while to bounce back. Betcha once he's back in familiar surroundings, Lefty will be back to his old self."

"Hope so," Teddy muttered, and gently guided the dog out of the kennel. At the front desk, he signed the forms, and left quickly. As they crossed the lot to the RV, Teddy noted the dog's missing limb didn't hamper him. Lefty walked on a loose leash with a kind of bunny-hop motion that made his ears flop with each stride. When Teddy stopped to thumb the key and open the door, Lefty sat. The dog looked around, sniffing the breeze, and finally fixed his gaze on Teddy.

"Good dog, Lefty. I think we'll get along. It's just temporary. Up you go." Rather than unlocking the driver's or passenger's door, Teddy opened the side entrance that offered more open space. He took a step up into the Nova, beckoned, and Lefty obediently jumped up, carefully sniffing the steps. He paid particular attention to the passenger seat. "Yep, that's Meriwether, the cat. Heck, you already know that, right? Oh, and just so's we're clear. He's the boss of you." *Of me, too.* Teddy grinned.

Teddy closed the door and let go of the leash. Lefty wagged tentatively and let Teddy scratch the side of his neck. Then he put down his nose, moved toward the back, sniffing with increasing enjoyment. "We've got a bit of a ride to get where we're going." He heard Lefty find the bowl of kibble he'd set out. He seemed like a fine dog. Tanner Rudolph's loss.

Teddy took his place in the driver's seat, started the RV and pulled out of the lot. He hoped to reach the girls and pick them up from the painted church tour before nightfall. He knew the general area and wanted a head start before they sent him the specific church address. Then they'd find a nice hotel to stay overnight, and head back to Heartland in the morning. With luck, answering the police questions wouldn't take long.

That reminded him: he needed to look at the video September sent. He remembered Nikki, a nice kid. He wondered what kind of trouble she'd found this time.

Chapter 30 - SEPTEMBER

"W hy do you have a file on Rudolph?" Combs asked as she disconnected from Teddy.

"He came to me for dog training." She reviewed the intake questionnaire. Most of her clients came by referral, after Doc Eugene or another veterinarian ruled out health causes for a behavior problem. "It was right after I moved in with Lia after the tornado, during the repairs on this house."

Combs grimaced. That had not been a happy time for either of them. "Any insight into the man?"

"Here's a picture of him, with his dog." It looked like a desktop printout from the computer and didn't offer the best likeness.

"What'd he want you to do for him and his pooch? Wave a wand to fix something after a year of putting up with the behavior?" He rubbed his eyes, and she knew he itched to grab the file from her and read it himself. She appreciated his restraint.

"Actually, he looks like a pro-active dog lover." She complained too often about the ones who wanted her to "fix" everything in an hour's session. "He called Lia for the training. He said the dog had been nose-boinking him really hard, for no apparent reason. But it coincided with him being diagnosed—"

Both of their phones and the computer chimed in concert,

announcing an incoming email from Teddy. "He sent the video. Playing it on my desktop might bring out more details."

Despite the poor quality of the shelter video, they could see what mattered. The green car pulled into the frame and parked. The position obscured the license plate by accident or design. A slight figure climbed out, head covered by a snug hat and wearing form-fitting athletic clothing with a large pale shirt tenting over the top. Keeping his face averted, the driver crossed around to the rear hatchback, opened it, and grabbed up the blue slip leash to tug out the reluctant dog.

September's throat grew tight at sight of the dog's tucked tail, and odd lurching form. According to the notes in his chart, the eight-week-old pup had been left at a shelter with a broken and infected leg. Tanner adopted Lefty after amputation saved the dog's life. Great Pyrenees typically stood tall, barked loud, and devoted themselves to pleasing those they loved. But in the video, Lefty was clearly terrified. She recognized the leash as one she and Lia gave away as an advertisement for services. Tugged along by the neck, the dog moved as low to the ground as his missing leg allowed, casting furtive eyes away from the driver. Lefty continually lip-licked, a behavior designed to calm and defuse any perceived threat.

"That can't be Rudolph?" Combs leaned forward, squinting at the screen as if to bring it into better focus.

September ran a hand through her dark hair. "Everything's in shadow or blurry, but he doesn't seem as big as in the photo in the file or my vague memory of him. And look at the dog. Lefty wouldn't act like that with a trusted partner."

Combs backed up the video, and they watched again, pausing as the figure looped one end of the leash around the shelter's front door then returned to the car. "According to Tanner's DMV license, he's six-four, 240 pounds, with brown hair, brown eyes."

She froze the video and backed it up to the best image, offering a silhouette profile as the driver slid back into the driver's seat. "Hair's covered with that hat. No way to see eye color. But,"—she nodded—"that driver's 100 pounds, maybe 115 at most. Moves like a dancer. Way shorter, too. Look at the height compared to the car."

Combs snorted. "Tanner would need a shoehorn to get behind the wheel. His folks said they had a running joke with him about that VW but he loves the car. He'd set up the hatchback area to accommodate his big white dog."

She looked at him. "You talked to his folks? What'd they say?"

He shrugged. "Not much. He traveled to south Texas for spring break, and they haven't heard from him since he left Corpus Christi. Gonzalez called and scared 'em half brainless, asking about him. They hadn't known he was missing. Oh, and they swore up and down he'd never dump his dog anywhere. He and the pooch were tight."

September's throat ached, and Shadow pressed hard against her side. You don't throw away chosen family, and most especially not a service dog trained to keep you healthy. "So they don't know where he is?"

"No clue. But the shelter camera gives us a timeline. The driver must've been with Rudolph, took the dog to the shelter and ditched the car shortly afterward." He started the video again and grinned. "There it is. Wondered how Teddy got the license number." He stopped the video again and pointed.

The driver's efforts to hide the license failed when the shelter window caught the reflection. "The geriatric hacker strikes again."

He laughed. "Gotta hand it to Teddy. Without him, we wouldn't know the connection." He stared at her and cocked his head. "He picked up that dog for you? How'd you know—"

"Got a call from Lia." She explained what had happened.

He cracked his knuckles. "I'll buy one coincidence. But we've got a whole rash of 'em, and they're spreading like poison ivy. Makes me itch, September."

She shrugged, but agreed with him. "I don't know what to tell you. It's either coincidence or some nefarious outside force orchestrating everything. That makes even less sense. Why would someone steal a dog to drop it at a shelter anonymously but leave a leash that traces back to me?"

"And what," he picked up the thread, "does the dog—okay, let's make that Tanner Rudolph—have to do with Sebastian Viejo, my vic at Buc-ee's? Why did he and Hank fight... over what, exactly?"

"Yeah. That fight scared Nikki into running. But how did the mystery bike rider find Nikki out the back of beyond?"

She looked at Combs expectantly.

"A biker who resembles the one who stole Rudolph's car and dog. A biker that looks kind of like the purple-head suspect we think killed Sebastian." He showed September the brief video the witness had shot. "The witnesses couldn't agree on whether it was a man or woman, purple hair or a hat."

"Could be a young man, or a woman, now that you mention it." A unique hair color wouldn't be easy to hide. "Took out someone twice his—or her—size? Sheesh." September shivered, remembering the stalker, now dead, who had made her life a living hell for so long. "Feels like I'm connected somehow, in the middle of everything."

He hugged her. "You have nothing to do with this, September. At best, you're a tangential connection, whatayacallit, six degrees of separation. You helped train a dog once upon a time, that's all."

She hugged him back, and relished the warmth of his arms, but thought his assessment wishful thinking. "We just need to figure out the identity of the biker. That'll answer a lot of our questions…"

He pulled away. "What's this *we* and *our questions*? Yes, finding the biker will help. But that's *my job* with Gonzales. Your job"—he waved in the garden's direction—"is to finish planning our wedding. That's what you told me this morning, right?" He leaned in and kissed her to soften the words. "I appreciate the brainstorming and Teddy's help. But please don't let Teddy tempt you into poking another hornet's nest."

"I… well, of course not." She crossed her arms and jutted her chin. "Just as long as the swarm doesn't come after me."

He laughed. "Fair enough. We'll talk more later, and I may have more questions along the way." His phone rang, and he glanced at the display. "It's Gonzales." He listened a moment, and his lips tightened into a grim smile. "That's the break we needed. I'll catch you up on the way there."

She watched him, trying not to scowl, and walked with him to the front door. "Did Gonzales find the biker?"

Combs shook his head. "Not yet. But they found Tanner Rudolph's body at a fleabag motel down in Wintergreen."

Shadow stayed close to September's side until Combs climbed into his car and drove away. As much as she liked Combs, he didn't like it when the detective made her heart thump too fast.

The busy day had kept him alert. He knew September didn't fear the stranger working in the back garden. And the man smelled of green things, and other creatures. That made his tail wag high, concerned but interested. Would Arnold bring another dog here, too? Shadow already shared the garden with Kinsler. And he had to share September with Combs. Too much change made his fur bristle and itch.

He followed her back to the office and watched as September retrieved the papers from before. She read aloud; he didn't understand all the words, but didn't care. He just liked to listen to September's voice.

"Nose-boinking behavior. How about that, Shadow. You only cold-nose my armpits if I sleep too late. But you nose-boink Macy-cat, and he doesn't appreciate it at all."

He woofed and wagged, happy to hear his name. She smiled and turned back to the pages. At her soft intake of breath, he pushed his head against her thigh, and she dropped a hand to his cheek. "Now I remember this case. After his diagnosis, the nose-boinking made sense. And that's why we trained Lefty to call 911 by nose poking Tanner's phone."

Shadow tipped his head to one side and closed his mouth. So many words. He knew what "boink" meant. To prove it, he poked her in the thigh with his nose as she closed the file. "Yes, okay, thanks for the boink. Just don't do it too hard, baby-dog, not like Lefty. We needed to teach Lefty to soft-boink. He self-trained to alert."

He nosed her thigh again and grinned.

"I've heard of spontaneous training before. It only happens with an incredibly strong bond. Like what we've got." She smoothed the tender notched place where a bullet had stolen a piece from a good-dog's ear.

"Thank goodness Tanner recognized the dog acted intentionally, not out of spite or inappropriate behavior. He just wanted it confirmed and wanted to learn how to reinforce the behavior. How to have a positive relationship with his service dog and reduce the bruise quotient on those boinks." She smiled sadly. "Now he's dead, and Lefty got dumped at the shelter. Poor dog must be terrified."

Chapter 31 - TEDDY

Teddy pulled into a rest stop. Lefty roused from his doze in the passenger seat, sat up, and yawned loudly. The dog crashed as soon as they pulled out, finally able to relax once out of the kennel. "You gonna stay awake now? Ya know, that's the cat's place, doncha?" It had impressed him that Lefty had only given a cursory sniff in the cat's direction, and that the kitty hadn't thrown a fit. "Time for a potty stop for both of us." He'd give Meriwether a chance to use the facilities, too. He couldn't risk having both animals loose in the RV while he drove, not before he figured out how well they tolerated each other. Or not.

He drove Nellie Nova down the RV ramp and parked at the far end of the lot near the dog walking station. "Okay, ready to go?" Teddy picked up the end of the leash. He'd left it attached to Lefty's collar, not wanting to chance having to chase the dog around. His computers and other equipment cost a tidy sum and he'd only recently reconciled himself to the cat using it for perches.

After he unlatched Meriwether's carrier door, Teddy hurried the dog out of the RV. He glanced inside and smiled when Meriwether padded after him. Yep, the explorer cat let nothing phase him, and hopped up on the dashboard for a fine view as Teddy led the dog down the sidewalk.

Lefty followed closely on the leash in his rocking-horse gait, ears flopping in rhythm. Teddy wondered what sort of service the pooch provided. He still couldn't wrap his brain around the man dumping his dog.

At the garbage bin, a prominent sign reminded pet owners to pick up after their dogs, and even provided baggies. Teddy wrinkled his nose. He hadn't thought of that when he stopped at the pet product store. He grabbed half a dozen, stuffed all but one in his pocket, and continued down the path. September used some kind of command that told Shadow to go to the bathroom. If she'd trained this dog, would Lefty also understand the potty word?

"What was it, anyway? *Hurry up.*" No, the dog continued to sniff whatever wonderful story he'd found to read on the sidewalk. Teddy urged Lefty to leave the sidewalk, and led him into the taller grass, the baggy over his free hand at the ready. "*Go potty.*" Lefty ignored Teddy's efforts. "Good dog, Lefty. We both needed the break."

That was it! September said some clients might use stronger language in private. But they didn't want to use rude words in public dog parks. "*Take-a-break,* Lefty. Good dog." The dog looked up, grinning, and took a few steps before squatting and finishing his toilet.

As Teddy gingerly retrieved the dog's deposit using the disposable poo-bags, it reminded him of the stinker on the bike who drove off with Nikki. September had tried to text it, but even the fifteen-second clip took too long. He'd told her to upload to a cloud link he'd sent. From what she described, he'd need time to enhance the visuals to get anything usable for the police.

"Might as well take a quick look, Lefty." The dog barked as if in agreement and wagged. The pooch seemed to feel better out of the shelter, even if he missed his owner. It amazed Teddy how dogs forgave even the worst offenses. He knew if Tanner Rudolph showed up, Lefty probably would ecstatically run to him, despite having been abandoned.

Teddy opened the RV door carefully, first checking to see the cat's location. The big Maine Coon still claimed his spot on the dashboard. Tightening his grip on the dog's leash, Teddy urged Lefty up the steps and to the back of the vehicle. He knew September would give him more detailed introduction tips, but he figured Meriwether could put up with the inconvenience for a day or two. So far, Lefty hadn't been too intrusive. "You stay with me, pooch." He looped the dog's leash around the leg of the built-in table and settled behind the laptop.

As he downloaded September's video Teddy felt something against his leg and looked down. He smiled when Lefty settled his chin on his shoe. He adjusted his glasses and brought up the video.

Teddy grimaced. The quality suffered from September's unsteady hand, shooting in the shadows, and the fast-moving target. "Piece of cake. Bet I can get a clear shot of the license in twenty minutes."

Meriwether meowed at his words. Teddy watched with concern when the cat jumped from the dash and moved to take his normal place in his lap. But the dog didn't move his head, only thumped his tail and sighed. "Hope you get along with other dogs as good as Meriwether." If his plan worked, Lefty would have a new home that appreciated him.

"We'll brighten the first part. And sharpen the contrast." He had a filter that worked wonders. "Then on the back end, damp down the brights. We'll go frame by frame and find a good shot of the license and fudge with the resolution." Rubbing his hands together in anticipation, Teddy called up his video enhancing software, plugged in the clip, and worked his magic.

It only took fourteen minutes. "Well, I'll be…" Teddy had isolated the license plate, made a screen-shot and sent it to Combs. He could guess the rider's identity. Before Nikki climbed on the back of the motorcycle—maybe willingly—he'd sharpened enough frames of the video. The driver wore the same clothes as the dirt-bag who dumped Lefty.

"What the heck has Tanner Rudolph got to do with Nikki?" After he dumped his dog, he abandoned his green car, then carried off some random kid on a motorcycle? Teddy watched the short video again, this time paying particular attention to Rudolph's mannerisms.

He couldn't see much. The figure's silhouette faded against the bright sun. Still, something about the turn of the head looked familiar. The face remained hidden, but when the figure half-turned in the bike saddle, it reminded Teddy of — something? Someone?

Teddy switched programs and logged in to another database

using an ID and password created specifically to keep him anonymous. With a few keystrokes, he input the license from the motorcycle and clicked the process button. In less than a minute, the answer came back. "Too easy," he muttered. As he suspected, Rudolph didn't use his own name on the bike. "Quinn Donovan. Wonder just who you really are? Let's find out, Mr. Dump-Yer-Dog Donovan!"

Forty minutes later, he was no closer to discovering any details. Enough of that rabbit hole; he could spend hours chasing phantoms. Best to report to Combs and September, and be on his way.

He uploaded the finessed video, along with the enhanced screen-shot of the license to his cloud storage. He pasted the download link into a text that he sent to both Combs and September. He started to share his thoughts in a text, but called instead.

"Hi Teddy. Just got the link with the cleaned up video. Thanks for the fast turnaround." September paused, then added, "I put you on speaker for Combs."

"Combs will come to his own conclusions after comparing the two videos." Teddy took off his glasses and rubbed his eyes. "I cleaned it up the best I could. To me, it's the same person. Same size, and similar clothes, anyway.

"Same person?" September's confusion made her voice raise. "You know who took Nikki?"

Teddy grimaced. "Sorry, I wasn't clear. The video of the guy dropping off Lefty—by the way, I got him, and he's fine—and your motorcycle driver." At his name, Lefty looked up and wagged, before settling his head once more on Teddy's shoe.

"Can't be Tanner. Combs says he's over six feet and 240 pounds."

"Like I said, hard to tell for sure, but the clothes look the same. I got a better picture of the license on the bike, too, and ran it. Figured I'd save the cops some time. "If it's any consolation, it looks like Nikki willingly climbed on the bike. I couldn't get anything from the sound, too much wind noise, yelling from you and Shadow barking."

"Combs said that Rudolph's family hadn't seen him in a while, not since he left for vacation with his dog. And they said he'd never willingly give up Lefty. Are you sure about the rider?"

He adjusted his glasses. "No, not sure at all. Quinn Donovan licensed the bike. I didn't go too deep, but my quick search showed very little about Ms. Donovan. No history prior to about six months ago."

"So the rider is a woman?" September's confusion carried easily over the phone line.

"September, I don't know. That's the license holder's name. But the bike or the tag could be stolen, too. The name's a nym for somebody hiding their business."

"Nym? Oh, pseudonym. Right." She paused. "I guess the rider with Nikki could be a woman. They took off so fast."

Teddy nodded. That's what he'd figured, too.

His phone pinged, announcing an incoming text. He grinned. Probably one of the girls.

"Hey, I'm happy to help with anything else. But I need to hit the road again. Hold on, just got a text." *At last, the pick up address for the girls.*

He switched to the text and smiled at the selfie. "What the hell…" The faces of three smiling girls filled the screen: Leslie, Sylvia, and a younger, worried-looking girl with white-blond hair. "That's Nikki! What's she doing with them?" Then Teddy read the caption. His breath caught. His right hand clutched his chest as if to keep his heart from leaping from his breast.

<Tell cops & all die. 3-for-1 swap. Bring September Day if you want them back alive. Further instructions TK

Chapter 32 - SHADOW

September spent lots of time staring at the computer or her phone. Shadow liked phones more than computers. He could hear people talking out of the phones, even though he couldn't see them.

People knew things good-dogs didn't, but that was okay. September couldn't hear or smell important things that Shadow could. Together, they made a good team.

Shadow heard her phone made that funny music sound that told her somebody wanted to talk.

When Teddy's voice came out of the phone, Shadow stood up and woofed, and wagged. He remembered the old-man smell: dust, spicy cologne, and burritos. Sometimes Teddy shared the burrito. Shadow licked his lips and sniffed. But he couldn't detect Teddy-smell or burrito. Phones puzzled him. His tail fell silent.

He didn't understand most of the conversation, only a word here and there. Teddy mentioned Combs, and his brow wrinkled. Would the man come back? And his ears came forward when September talked about Nikki. He whined because he knew September worried about the girl. He'd tracked her but found Nikki too late, and she left on the motorcycle. He'd failed September. He pushed his head into her lap and sighed when September smoothed his brow.

"I'm okay, baby-dog. I'm waiting for Teddy to finish a call from his grandkids." She leaned down and looked into his eyes.

"You won't tell Combs I discussed the case with Teddy, will you?" Shadow whined. "Of course you won't. That's why I love you, Shadow. You wouldn't tell on me even if you could." She sighed and leaned down to press her forehead to his. "I wish Combs understood how I feel. I get he doesn't want me playing hero, but how do I stop caring? And everything does seem connected to me."

He slurped her face, and she laughed. He liked the sound of September's laugh.

She sat up and looked at the phone that sat on the desk next to the computer screen she kept watching. "If I can help, I have to try. Don't I?" She picked up the phone. "Teddy? Teddy, are you still there?" September tapped her fingers. "Maybe we got disconnected. I need to call Combs and update him—"

"No! No, September, are you there?" Teddy nearly screamed into the phone, and Shadow yelped and jumped away. "Don't call Combs, September. Or the cops. You'll get them all killed!"

Chapter 33 - QUINN

Quinn paced back and forth in front of the altar, keeping her voice low. "Let me do my job. My way. I have everything under control." She glared at Casper Fright, sure he'd chosen a name to mock her. As an employee of the same Organization, she figured he didn't exist any more than Quinn Donovan.

Mr. Fright smiled, and shed the canvas carrier from his shoulder. "I'm here to make sure you honor your obligation. Failure always brings consequences, correct?" He tapped the long container.

Knowing the bag contained a specialized weapon, Quinn nodded stiffly and stopped pacing. She crossed her arms, then attempted to drop both hands to her sides. No room for mistakes with her employer. And this man smelled her defensiveness as readily as a jackal stalking prey. "Look, I've recovered all the stolen product." She ticked off each accomplishment on a finger. "To do that I tracked down Tanner Rudolph and his stash. Made him tell me where—"

"Messy. I'd dealt with him anyway after he reneged on his agreement. But you drew the attention of the authorities. You know our employer values privacy. Discretion above all, Quinn. That's what you call yourself now—Quinn?" His lips tightened in a bloodless smile.

She ignored the jibe. "Unavoidable. And I covered my tracks.

Even dumped Rudolph's dog at the shelter, just like I was told." Quinn had hated the thought of killing the pooch, so the instructions to leave him at the shelter relieved her. "I made sure nobody has anything on me."

Pattering footfalls on the second floor drew their eyes. Quinn gestured to the sound. "The little girl has Sebastian's product in her bag. And the two sisters with you have the last package of three thermoses. All tidy. And none of the girls have a clue what's going on. I made sure of that. So I don't need your help. Unless you'd care to deliver the recovered product to our contact?" She couldn't help the jab, turning him into an errand boy.

He ignored the comment. "Consequences, Quinn. Never, ever use amateurs. Too many things go wrong that draw unwarranted attention." He reached for the case and unpacked the gun. "Don't you understand, girl? You failed the test."

Her throat tightened. She clenched her fists. Eyeballing the possible exits, she knew he could cut her down long before she gained safety. But he wouldn't expect her to attack...

Mr. Fright paused and stared hard at Quinn. "Our employer has a soft spot for you. Don't know why, don't care. But you get a do-over. Fail again, and I won't waste breath on conversation." He aimed a finger at her, with his thumb cocked like a gun.

Quinn closed her eyes and let out her breath. She spoke stiffly, careful with her words. "I appreciate the opportunity to redeem myself." She licked dry lips, silently berating herself for overconfidence. Of course they'd test her. And they had set her up to fail.

The footsteps overhead grew louder, girl chatter interspersed with laughter. "Hey, Mr. Fright, can we go see the bell tower?" one of the sisters called from the top of the stairs.

Fright didn't take his eyes off Quinn as he answered. "I'll be right there, ladies. You stay where you are. Just finishing up our private convo." He dropped his voice to a whisper. "Forget about collecting the drugs. They never mattered anyway. Consider them a MacGuffin."

She wrinkled her forehead. She'd spent weeks planning the Mexico buys, pitched the plan to her new employer via appropriate channels, recruited the amateurs, even killed one man and probably let another die. She tamped down her anger. She'd expected to eliminate the sisters, and would regret doing Nikki. *All part of the test.* But to earn the trust of her employer—and spare her own life—she couldn't argue or question.

He continued to unwrap and set up the specialized gun. She'd trained with a dozen different firearms, but had only seen one like it. The AR15 had a pistol grip with a short-barrel rifle, less than 16 inches, so legally categorized as a pistol. The Mutant chambered 762x39 caliber ammo, with the same easy-to-find magazine designed for the AK47. Easy to transport, handle, and fire, with a sling, scope, and light attachments. It was the perfect assassin's weapon. "The kids'll freak when they see that."

"You keep them calm and clueless and they won't see it. That's your new job, girl." He snapped the last piece into place. "They're bait. But expendable. Just don't want to lose the leverage too soon."

Bait for the grandfather, Teddy Williams.

Quinn hadn't wanted to include the two sisters. Sebastian insisted. *He'd have been taken out in any case.…* A plant! Hired to involve Teddy's grandkids?

The part she'd played became clear. Who else had been targeted and lured into her scheme just to hook the old man? Sebastian recruited Tanner Rudolph, too, arguing his medical condition would convince others. And it did.

She'd been set up to target Teddy Williams. Why? She'd only known the old man for a few days. He'd helped her when she needed a friend. But she had no choice. *Can't fail again.*

She couldn't let the old man stand in the way of the rest of her life. Quinn steeled her resolve. "That's for Teddy Williams?" She gestured toward the custom gun, her voice steady.

"Eventually." He picked it up, cradling it in one arm like an extension of himself. "The grandkids lure him here. But he's bigger bait for bigger fish."

"Who?"

Fright put a finger to his lips, eyes twinkling. "You'll see." He draped a soft cloth over top of the gun. "Now let's get this special *camera* situated upstairs, before our visitors arrive. And remember, you've got one job left to do. Keep those kids quiet and under control until I say different. Otherwise, I've got more than enough ammo to go around."

Chapter 34 - COMBS

Combs parked outside the police cordon; local PD had secured the area. As he got out of the car, he saw Gonzales raise his hand and wave from outside one of the shabby rooms at the far end of the motel. Other guests stood in doorways of the ranging building, staring and pointing cell phones to see more detail. He flashed his badge to an officer and hurried to join Gonzales.

"What've we got?"

"Tanner Rudolph." Gonzales tilted his head toward the open doorway.

He peered inside, but so many techs crowded the room, Combs couldn't see enough to matter. "You already checked it out?"

"Yep. Nobody went inside before me. Office manager says the do-not-disturb door-hanger's been there for days. He called it in." Smoothing his neat mustache, Gonzales pulled out his phone, and replayed the video he'd taken of the scene, while narrating. "I got stills, too. It's definitely the guy in the DMV photo. But no ID on the body, or anywhere in the room, other than the name he gave the front desk to register. No luggage, no toiletries, no nothing, which fits. They found those in his car. Also, no sign of trauma. No obvious COD. Somebody took his identification."

Combs cracked his knuckles. Waiting for autopsy and lab results always delayed things. "Huh. Somebody killed him, then cleaned the room, probably put up the door-hanger. The killer didn't want him identified, at least not at first. Maybe they got sloppy, figured he registered under an alias, rather than his real name?" *Either an amateur, or nothing to hide.* "Pretty clean kill, though. You thinking drugs?"

Gonzales nodded. "Drug score gone bad. Rudolph OD'd and his dealer cleaned up to cover his tracks and skipped out. Already had the techs bag the door-hanger to check for prints. Killer knew it'd only delay the inevitable."

Combs directed his attention to the walk-through video, noting the position of the body. Rudolph sat slumped in a chair like a deflated rubber doll. The lighting—or the decomp—turned his skin into a marbled green tone. "The office manager find him?"

Gonzales jerked his head in assent. "Haven't taken his statement yet. I already talked to his neighbors. They didn't hear or see anything, but they just arrived and he's definitely not fresh." He smoothed his mustache again. "Motel guests rarely stay more than one night. Some only a few hours."

Combs knew what that meant. And those "guests" wouldn't be eager to talk to the cops. "Maybe we'll have better luck with the office manager."

As they turned to leave a technician called out. "Found something." Combs and Gonzales waited for her to bring the object to them. On the palm of her gloved hand rested a flat plastic orange circle, perhaps an inch across.

"What is it?" Combs poked it with the end of a pen.

"Found it under his shirt. Must've fallen there when he shot up." She raised an eyebrow. "Need tests to see what, but looks like a vial cap off some kind of injectable. I'm guessing pain meds."

Combs grunted. Whoever cleaned up took any syringes. "Makes sense. The black market traffics in all kinds of stuff." He remembered Doc Eugene mentioning a rash of break-ins at area veterinary hospitals. "There's a market for everything from morphine to Metacam and fentanyl. Are the vial caps specific to a particular drug?"

She shrugged. "They're pretty generic, but we'll check for trace and narrow it down as much as possible." She ducked back into the room to bag and tag the cap.

Gonzales blew out a breath. "Autopsy should pinpoint whatever he injected." He pointed to the motel office. "Let's see what this guy has to share."

Combs followed the smaller man down the long, broken sidewalk to the front of the decrepit building. Gonzales pulled open the door, motioned him to go first, then joined Combs at the abandoned front desk. "Hey? Where are you?" He slapped the counter three times. "Told you we need to talk." Gonzales scowled and peered past the high counter.

A hidden inner door squealed open and the squirrel-faced skinny manager scurried out. He had a wad of something beneath his lip; Combs glanced around, looking for a spit can. Right on cue, the guy produced an empty plastic Ozarka water bottle, and deposited a disgusting expectorant into the receptacle.

Combs pulled out his recorder and set it on the counter. "You called it in? What's your name?"

"The body? Yeah, I already told the cops. Who're you?" He pulled a rickety padded stool up to the counter and perched his bony butt. For someone so thin, he had an enormous gut that pushed into the edge of the counter each time he swiveled back and forth. Combs scowled, but both he and Gonzales presented their badges.

"I'm Sammy Bangs."

Gonzales leaned forward. "Mr. Bangs, why'd you wait so long to call? The ME says he's been dead for days."

"Man paid for privacy. Said his name was..." He chawed and spat, pulled out a registry and jabbed a dirty finger at one line. "Tanner Rudolph. Some little girlfriend of his showed up, after he'd registered, and paid for two more weeks." He sat back on the stool, scratching his stained shirt, and leered. "Usually, it's one night. But hell, she was worth two weeks, if ya know what I mean. Besides, feller hafta be dim to turn down two weeks plus the doggy deposit—" He clamped his mouth shut. His eyes shifted down and to the left.

"Dog? He had a dog?" Gonzales raised his eyebrows.

Combs said nothing. He'd share the dog details with Gonzales later. Right now, he wanted to hear what Sammy Bangs had to say.

"So you left him alone for a week. No maid service, no fresh towels, no nothing?" Gonzales continued the questioning.

The man shrugged his bony shoulders. "Man had a dog. I didn't wanna get bit. And he put one of them 'private' signs on his door handle."

"So what made you check on him? Party too loud? Complaints about the dog?" Gonzales leaned in, despite the man's powerful aroma. "Did you get the girl's name?"

"See, that gave me a puzzlement. Any dog I ever had barked its fool head off with the slightest noise. And most nights here, 'specially weekends, we get a fair amount of party noise. Know what I mean?" He winked. "But nary a sound from the pooch. Or the room. And I only seen the girl that once."

"You have security cameras. We'll need the video." Combs couldn't help the hope in his voice, but expected the disappointment that arrived with the man's next words.

"Yeah, the camera's digital. It over-writes every so often, but you can have it. But like I said, it's been a week." He spat, wiped his mouth again, and his brow puckered. "Come to think on it, I don't recall seeing the dog either, only that once on the day Rudolph checked in." He made a face. "The owner ain't gonna like having dog pee and turds all over that room." He sniffed.

"Not to mention a dead body," Combs said dryly.

"The owner's got a policy, no pets allowed. He's gonna take it out of my pay." He spit in the bottle again and wiped his glistening mouth with the back of one hand. "You gotta talk to him. Wouldja? I couldn't go against the law, that'd be worse."

Combs sighed with exasperation. "What made you check on Rudolph today?"

Gonzales added, "Why'd you let him bring a dog? Just how much was that doggy deposit?" He grinned at Combs. "Bet it didn't go on the books."

Bangs crossed his arms. "I follow the law. Have to let service dogs stay. Besides, what goes on inside them rooms, that's private between consenting adults. People pay, they get their privacy." He raised his arm to mop a suddenly damp forehead on one sleeve.

"You called today. After just a week when you got a two-week payment. And no noise complaints. Why?" Combs sharpened his tone.

"It'd been too long for housekeeping to ignore anymore. I got complaints about the smell. So, ya know, I figured the dog did his business inside." He hesitated, then added grudgingly. "Glad I got the extra deposit money to get the room cleaned up. I knocked on the door and yelled out. But there wasn't no answer, not even a whimper. Opened it up, and man-oh-man, the smell, like something died—" He spit again. The bottle made a hollow *thunk* sound when the wet hit. "Guess it did. Died, that is. So I called the cops, I didn't even go inside, just shut and locked the door again and waited for y'all to show up."

"What'd the girl look like? Height, weight, eyes and hair color?" He'd said she looked worth a two-week rather than one-night stand. "She come with Rudolph or arrive later?" Combs pulled the recorder out of the line of spit-fire.

"Let's see. Little thing, thin but strong. Had muscles but wiry like a cat, ya know? Maybe a hundred pounds, give or take, came up to my shoulders."

"So about five feet four or five." Gonzales nodded encouragement.

"Yeah, and she wore that athletic gear for working out. And a purple hat of some kind." He spit. "So I dunno about hair color. Cain't 'member the eyes, neither."

Combs started. "Purple cap?"

Gonzales caught the mention, too, and met Combs's eyes with sudden understanding. "That's helpful. Oh, about the dog…"

Bangs rolled his eyes. "I done told ya. The feller said it's the law, that service dogs get exempted from rules and suchlike." He pointed to a laminated card stuck to the computer terminal. "The owner don't want no trouble. I followed the rules, like he said. You cain't turn 'em away and only get to ask what service the dog provides." He snorted. "Even if they make up some crazy-ass story, you gotta take their word."

Curious, Combs pressed the man. "Why'd you think he made something up?"

"I heard about seeing-eye dogs. And some fellers served in the war got blowed up and caught that post trauma stress stuff. Some of them got dogs to chase away the nightmares. But I never heard-tell of some dog what can tell a body when to take a shot."

"A shot? You mean, the dog alerts to giving medication?" Gonzales smoothed his mustache to hide his smile.

Smirking, Bangs smacked one hand on the countertop. "Crazy, right? But that's what Rudolph said. His dog told him when to shoot up for his diabetes." He spit.

Chapter 35 - SEPTEMBER

"Teddy, what's wrong?" September's chair tipped over when she leaped to her feet, staring at the cell phone on the desk. Shadow barked, and jumped around.

"Shadow, settle! Down." He dropped to the carpet, tail "I don't know what's going on." His voice shook with emotion. She'd never heard him so upset. "I got a text from my granddaughters."

"Oh my God, are they okay? Oh Teddy, how can I help?" Teenagers were accidents waiting to happen. That made September think of Combs's kids.

"They sent a selfie. Well, somebody sent a picture, anyway." She heard him swallow hard. "Nikki was with them."

"Nikki?" Her brow wrinkled. That made no sense. "How— why? Where are they?" At least Nikki was safe. It would relieve Doc Eugene to hear they had found her.

"You don't understand. Leslie and Sylvia called earlier and changed plans, said they'd meet me partway. They want to take a church tour." His voice grew more and more agitated.

"Calm down, Teddy. A church tour? It could be a lot worse." She had yet to convince Melinda and Willie to attend church with her. Combs went reluctantly, but only to please her.

"What the hell? September, they aren't religious. I figured some handsome boy convinced them—mentioned someone named

Casper. Anyway, they promised to send me the address to meet. Instead, I get this threat."

September blinked. "How's a selfie a threat?"

"Will you shut up and listen to me?" He yelled so loud, she backed away from the phone, and Shadow growled.

"Okay, fine." She waited. "Teddy? Are you there? I'm listening."

A sob.

September pulled out the chair and sank into it. "They texted you a picture? The three girls together? Are they hurt?" Her breath quickened.

"Not yet." He sniffed, then honked his nose before continuing. "The picture's fine. The girls look happy. Maybe they don't know what's going on." He sniffled again. "They threatened to hurt them if I tell the cops. I'm supposed to wait for instructions for a-a-a—" He gulped. "They want a trade."

"But we have to call the police." She couldn't lie to Combs.

"No! Please, no September. Don't call the police. Help me get them back. You're the only one who can help. Combs can't follow up on Quinn Donovan. I think she's the one who has them."

She shook her head, then realized he couldn't see her. "I can't help you, Teddy. That's a job for profes—"

"They want to trade." His voice was raw. "The text said a three-for-one swap, but they die if the police get involved." He hiccupped. "Thank God you didn't tell Combs yet. And don't you dare clue him in now! I helped you before. More than once. And I know it's asking a lot. But I don't know what else to do." The words ended in a strangled wail.

"Swapping all three girls for one. One person." A sudden chill shook her to the core. "They want me, don't they?"

"I think so. I'm sorry, I'm sorry, oh God, September, I'm so sorry, I would never ever ask but it's my granddaughters, dear God they're so young I don't know what to do..."

It all fell into place. The dog she'd trained, dumped at the shelter. Nikki taken. And now Teddy's grandkids. "Stop crying, Teddy. Deep breaths. Where are you now?"

He struggled to control himself. "I couldn't lie or try to trick you. I won't blame you for saying no. I'll figure something out." He cleared his throat. "Please don't hate me, September."

"Hate you? Never, Teddy. You're my chosen family, never

doubt that." Combs would try to stop her, but she was the only one who could meet their demands.

Time to stop making excuses. Some promises should never be made.

She took a big breath, squared her shoulders, and placed one hand on Shadow's shoulders. "Of course I'll help."

Chapter 36 - NIKKI

Nikki backed away from the narrow church stairwell when she heard footsteps on the lowest step. Her tongue wanted to stick to the roof of her mouth when she swallowed. She wondered if the other girls could hear her heartbeat.

No way. The sisters bobbed their heads in time to whatever tune flowed through the earbuds they shared. One chatted nonstop to the other more serious girl as they wandered down first one side and then the other of the odd open balcony that overhung three-quarters of the perimeter of the ornate sanctuary.

Small painted panels of religious figures framed in pointed arches lined the walls of the narrow walkway. Between the stain glass windows, ornate tapestries covered the wall spaces. The sisters paused in front of each to read the brass plate description and took selfies in front of their favorites.

The acoustics transported even whispers, but only Nikki heard Quinn and Mr. Fright's conversation. Quinn had lied to her. Nikki suspected the man lied to Quinn, too. She shrugged her knapsack higher on her back, very aware Hank's contraband had brought her here. From what she'd overheard, the sisters also bought into Quinn's fiction about the drugs, just like Hank.

The man called the drugs a MacGuffin, maybe some kind of off-label drug like what they'd recovered during the tornado last year. Nikki crossed her arms, hug herself hard. Kid Kewl promised the bad guys got caught, and nobody would hurt the kids ever again… but he hadn't answered messages in weeks. She'd comforted herself he had important stuff to do, not that he ignored her.

Mr. Fright appeared at the top of the stairs holding a long object covered with a blanket and mounted to a tripod. She'd seen no camera shaped like that. Nikki looked away, not wanting to meet his eyes. Mom always knew when Nikki did something wrong, and this man looked like he'd do more than scold her for eavesdropping.

"Enjoy looking around, girls. I need to situate things for a special guest arriving later." He smiled, showing his gold tooth, then jogged up the curvy second flight of stairs.

Nikki gulped. He meant Teddy Williams, that nice old man. She'd bet anything Mr. Williams wouldn't like the *special plans*, whatever they were. She'd heard Mr. Fright say *ammo*, and that meant ammunition for a gun. She'd seen enough exciting scary TV shows and movies where all the bad guys, and sometimes the heroes, carried long guns. *I may be a kid, but I'm not stoopid.*

"What's up there?" Leslie scurried over to Nikki. "We've seen everything on this floor."

"Bet it's the steeple." Sylvia readied her camera phone. "I saw the bell when we arrived. I want a picture from up top."

"No." He turned, sharp tone giving the girls pause. "No photos allowed, didn't I tell you that? You got your selfies, that's enough. Let me hold on to them for now. No arguments." He held out his hand.

Nikki flinched. They shouldn't challenge him. But then, the sisters didn't know Casper Fright was just pretending to be a tour guide. Who named their kids something like that? She bet it was fake. And she wondered what he'd done with the real guide. Nikki shivered at the thought.

Leslie lowered her phone. "It's about out of juice anyway. I'll just shut it off." When he kept his hand out, she reluctantly gave him her phone. "You'll give it back when we leave."

"Of course." The man softened his words, adding an excuse that somehow rang false. "Not enough space up there for everyone. Nothing interesting to see. Just dust and tarnished hardware. Not like all the windows on the second floor, or the painted arched ceilings on the first floor." He turned to nail Nikki with his gaze. "Are you enjoying the tour too, little girl?" His smile didn't reach his eyes. Snake eyes. Creepy.

Nikki shrugged and looked away, both hands fisted hard in the straps of her knapsack. She needed to warn Mr. Williams. September would know how to reach him. What would happen to them, though, if Mr. Williams never came? And where was this church, anyway? She hadn't paid attention when Quinn zoomed into the church parking lot.

She waited until Fright disappeared around the curve of the stairs and gestured the two girls close. Nikki remembered how easily she heard the conversation downstairs. She chose her words carefully, not wanting to alert Mr. Fright or Quinn.

"Hey, pretty neat church, right?" Her knuckles whitened. She shrugged off the bag, and dropped it on the floor, pulling out the bloodstained beaver toy to retrieve her tablet. Following the other girls' example, Nikki took pictures of the glorious artwork, betting on them not to give her away. None of it said anything about the name of the church, though, and she didn't want to ask and have Quinn or the dangerous man hear.

She turned to lean over the balcony, and took pictures of the sanctuary below, paying particular attention to distinguishing characteristics like the cluster columns and high-pitched roof. The first-floor walls included repeated patterns of crosses, glorious windows depicting religious symbols and stories, and brightly painted statues. Surely Mr. Williams could identify the place based on that. Before she lost her nerve, Nikki opened up an email, attached the pictures, and sent a terse note to September. She closed her tablet and stuffed it back into the knapsack, putting the stuffie back on top. She'd contact Kid Kewl and beg for help, but needed more information before she did.

Nikki reached out to tap Sylvia on the arm. "Can I ask you something?" She hated how her voice trembled and coughed to cover up the sound.

"What?" The girl pulled out her earbuds with a frown. "You're Nikki, right? How'd you meet Quinn? Did she go to Mexico, too?"

Putting a finger to her lips, Nikki shook her head, then said loudly, "I just met her but she's helping me out of a jam." Mexico? Had Hank's drugs come from there? She leaned forward and whispered, "Did you pick up drugs for Quinn, too? It's okay, so did my brother."

"Drugs?" Leslie joined them, not bothering to keep her voice quiet. "Oh, you mean the insulin? Yeah, what an adventure!" She elbowed Sylvia with a smirk. "Grandpa's going to have a cow when he hears about that."

Nikki blinked, eyes wide. "Insulin? You mean, for diabetes?" Some pets at Doc Eugene's got insulin, but she'd never helped with that. "That's not illegal." Nikki's mind raced. Maybe Hank's latest girlfriend had diabetes. She was way older than him, and Mom didn't like them dating. And now she'd got Hank into trouble. Surely she had a prescription, though, so why would Hank have to meet up at the Buc-ee's to get it?

Leslie rolled her eyes. "Didn't Quinn tell you? See, the drug companies make it too expensive for people. Nobody should have to risk their life if they can't afford something that keeps them alive. When that dreamy guy, Sebastian, told us about it and how you can get it for cheap right across the border, we had to help. So we made a day trip into Mexico. Pretty exciting! Right, Syl?"

Sylvia huffed. "*You* had to help. And I couldn't let you go alone, could I?" She turned to Nikki. "We met Sebastian at a party."

"Sebastian, he's so dreamy…" Leslie grinned. "I would have helped, anyway."

Nikki couldn't believe what they said. "So a bunch of kids went to Mexico to bring back drugs?"

"No, it's not like that. We bought it at a pharmacy, all legal and everything. At a huge discount." Leslie fairly bounced up and down with excitement. "Sebastian handed out the cash before we got there. We took turns buying the medicine. They didn't ask for proof or a prescription or anything." She shrugged.

"Is that legal, though? Bringing insulin here from Mexico? What if it's not the same and doesn't work?" Nikki wondered how they knew it was safe.

Sylvia frowned. "I worried about that, but Leslie wouldn't listen." She shrugged. "I looked it up on the internet. And it's not legal, not really." Leslie objected, and her sister talked over her. "They look at you funny at customs if you bring back too much.

But in smaller amounts, like what we each got, the authorities don't care. Quinn asked everybody to do a solid for the people who can't afford it any other way."

"But why? Are you diabetic?" If not, would they sell it? That might be fine in Mexico, but Nikki felt sure nobody had blind eyes about such things in the states.

"No, we don't have diabetes. One of the others, Tanner, had a service dog and everything." Sylvia opened up her oversize bag and pulled out a set of three thermoses identical to Nikki's. "It's got insulin pens and vials inside. Tanner said his parents' insurance dropped him when he got too old. So he'd been rationing his doses, cutting down the amount he really needed."

"Risking his life!" Leslie reached for the canister, but Sylvia stuck it back in her bag. "We had to help. Sebastian said we'd meet up with his distributor, hand off the insulin to him, and they'd get it to the people who need it." She leaned forward, pointing a finger to the ceiling, and said half voice, "But Mr. Fright offered to take 'em on to the distributor for us, after the church tour. Wasn't that nice?"

Quinn appeared at the top of the stairs. "I told you everything's legal." She carried the cat carrier. "Tigger started meowing a lot. I think he's in pain. Isn't there anything you can do for him?"

"Ooh, a kitty!" Leslie hurried to see. "What's wrong with him? Poor thing. And all stuck tight in that carrier. I bet he just wants out."

Quinn opened the cat carrier, and Tigger slowly came out. The cat head-butted Quinn's hands, and she murmured softly to him, gently checking the bandages.

"Why does anyone have to sneak around for insulin?" Nikki pulled out Hank's identical package and shook it at Quinn. "My brother got hurt over this." She glanced pointedly up toward the bell tower where Casper Fright waited for Mr. Williams with his *special camera*, probably to hurt him.

For a moment, Nikki's anger and fear overcame good sense, and she nearly shouted, "And what's a *MacGuffin*?"

Chapter 37 - SEPTEMBER

T eddy, where are you?" September dropped her phone into her shirt pocket to keep her hands free. "And where are your grandkids?" She caught up her windbreaker and shrugged it back on. Shadow knew that meant going somewhere, and whined with anticipation.

His gravelly voice steadied now she'd agreed to help. "I'm at a rest stop. The girls said they'd send me an address, so I could meet them. But I have no idea how this… this fiasco might have changed things." He blew out his breath, and September could imagine him taking off his glasses to polish them, but only making the smears worse.

She'd heard of the painted churches, but never visited. "Okay, Teddy. I'll come and meet you there." She ran one hand through her hair, tucking the wavy strands behind both ears. "There can't be that many painted churches." *No guarantees the girls will stay in the church anyway.* "We can get all the addresses and check each one."

"I already looked, September. Some references say fifteen and others say twenty, located from east of San Antonio to an hour north-east of Houston." His voice rose. "Dubina, High Hill, Praha, Ammannsville… Schulenburg has four. Those are the ones on the historical record and included in the tours. Who knows if they'll stick to those? I don't want to wait and give them the power, but there's no way to visit them all. We'd waste time."

She did a quick calculation in her head. "You're about three hours away from me if I drive like a maniac. The most distant church, though, is over four hours away. They know that. So they won't expect us for at least a couple of hours after you get the address. We've got time to plan." She paced, running one hand through her hair over and over.

"Plan what? How to sacrifice you to these criminals? Why?" He breathed hard, and muttered, "Calm down, calm down, Williams. Think. Think!"

September wondered what they'd need to rescue the girls. She'd take her gun, of course. And Shadow's ready-bag. Grabbing up a pen, she scribbled a list on a yellow pad.

"They'll expect us to react emotionally, without logic." Teddy continued to think out loud. "They want me to trade you for the three girls. How do they think I'll convince you to go?"

She wrinkled her nose. "Ask?"

He barked a humorless laugh. "Hell, no. Nobody sane would agree. Bad guys believe people think and act the way they would. They'll expect me to lie and say or do anything to save my grandkids... Why the hell do they want you?"

Her heart thumped hard. "If they want me, why not come here? Why take kids to force a meeting hours away?"

Teddy didn't speak for a long moment. "My God in heaven, Combs didn't tell you? You don't know?"

Her packing stopped so suddenly, Shadow bumped into her legs and woofed in surprise. "Know? Didn't tell me what?" Her mouth turned to dust.

He groaned. "Now's not the time. Don't blame him. Combs worries about you, September, especially after our South Bend adventure. He didn't want to argue with you over protection."

"Protection?" She strode to the front of the house and peered out the front windows. "He's having me watched? Followed?" September's throat tightened with the familiar terror she'd thought banished with the death of her stalker. "How could he?!"

"Combs loves you." Teddy raised his voice. "He asked if I had some connections that could provide discreet security. To keep you safe." He whimpered. "And it'll kill my girls."

Her face grew hot. She grabbed the chair to steady herself and tamp down the emotional turmoil. Combs had installed new cameras around the house. And they changed their security codes regularly. But she'd noticed no one following her. Hell, she hadn't looked for it, either. "So if I leave, Combs knows. He can follow or send police. Teddy, there's no way to keep the authorities out of this." She didn't doubt his love, but she felt betrayed by Combs—violated by this secret.

Shadow leaped up against her side. She opened her arms, and he settled his paws around her waist, chin on her shoulder. For a long moment, she stood stiff, eyes squeezed shut, fighting the urge to collapse into a fetal position. She felt Shadow's warm, wet tongue wash away the tears leaking from her eyes. Her stomach clenched. She gritted her teeth against bitter bile that burned her throat. With a final powerful hug, she released Shadow, and he dropped back to the floor, still pressing his comforting shoulder against her knee.

No wonder Teddy sounded wracked with guilt. He'd made it all but impossible for her to help him without alerting the police. "We can't think about anything right now except getting the girls safe." She stoked anger to replace more debilitating emotions. "I don't want to die, Teddy. I've got a new life, a wedding to plan, and want to live long enough to ream Combs out." Her breath quickened. "I'm sick to death of surprises screwing everything up, just when things go right." She walked into the kitchen, and strained to see Arnold's imposing figure striding around the garden. "We can't let them call the shots. We need to get there before they expect us. That gives us more control. But Combs will know."

He spoke with hesitant hope. "I could disrupt the cameras."

She shook her head, even though Teddy couldn't see. "That'd make him more suspicious. Let me worry about that."

"We don't know where they are."

"Then we go with what we know so far. Quinn Donovan. Find out everything about her. Her connections to Tanner Rudolph, and to that Sebastian character. And the dog. Does she know you? Was she caught up in one of your investigations? There has to be a reason she targeted you by taking your grandkids."

"To get to you." His voice trembled. "I don't think this is about me. I'm so very sorry."

She didn't want to believe that, but couldn't deny the

possibility. September shivered. She prayed that picking apart just one of the puzzling threads would unravel the whole tapestry of deceit. Teddy's expertise in computer forensics had to find something.

"What about tracking the girls' phones?" In the past, he'd been able to follow the ping from towers to narrow a search.

He groaned. "Don't you think I tried? Whoever they are, they know about my skills. The girls' phones are off. Maybe destroyed. While we've talked, I've finagled every way I can think to narrow the search. And I come up empty." His frustration grew with each word.

September paced back into the office and jotted down a few more notes on the yellow pad. Macy hopped onto the desk. The cat grabbed at her pen and gnawed the end. A sudden tightening in her throat prompted her to embrace the big Maine Coon. He'd need his heart medicine later today. And she wouldn't be here to give it. She made another note on the pad.

"We can't wait, Teddy. You're not that far from some of the churches, but I need to hit the road right away. When you call me with the location, I want to be closer than four hours away." She tore off the paper from the yellow pad. "I'll call you when I'm on the road." She disconnected and grabbed up her phone charger as the back door opened.

Arnold stared down at his feet and sighed. "Tracking in dirt. Do you have a broom and dustpan? I'll clean up."

"No worries. Shadow and Kinsler bring in mud every time they go out." Dirty floors were the least of her worries. Eager to be on her way, she wanted Arnold gone as quickly as possible. "Did you get the measurements you need?"

He shifted from foot to foot, still reluctant to track further into the pristine kitchen. "Better than that. I called my supplier, and they've got exactly the mature specimens we need. Just a few will make a huge statement and set the tone for the rest of the garden." He grinned, clearly pleased with his accomplishment.

"Fantastic, Arnold. I can't thank you enough." She grabbed her car keys and small purse, then urged him out the door. "I've got to run, so I'll walk you out. Shadow, let's go."

The big dog bounded ahead of them, waiting briefly once outside for September to set the alarm and lock the deadbolt on the kitchen door. Together, they walked to the garage, and she waved at Arnold as he proceeded to the front drive to his truck.

September opened the back door. "Shadow, kennel up." He hopped inside, always ready for a ride. She checked Shadow's go-bag with all of his tracking and other gear. Would she need it? Who could tell? She had to hope Teddy would have a clearer idea of what they needed the next time they spoke.

She climbed behind the wheel and checked the glove box for her gun. A box of ammunition sat behind the umbrella, gloves, and other paraphernalia. Once she caught up to Teddy, she'd load up and ready herself for... whatever. *I'll think about that later.* She needed answers for Combs first, for why she headed south. He'd stop her, or have his security follow her... did her car have a tracker? She shuddered. *Shades of her stalker...*

Shadow woofed as if he read her thoughts. And maybe he did.

When she turned the key, the car started, then sputtered and died. The red gas warning light taunted her. "No!" September beat her fist against the steering wheel. Now what?

September scrambled out of the car and ran to catch Arnold. His big truck was heading down the drive to the big gates. "Hey! Hey Arnold, wait up!"

He stopped and rolled down his window. "What's up?"

"Out of gas. I don't suppose you have any to spare?" She knew he had gas cans in the truck bed.

Arnold shook his head. "Only stuff mixed with oil for the equipment. It's not what you'd want in your car. I could drop you in town." He shrugged his big shoulders. "You'd need to catch a ride back, though. I'm heading to Brenham to pick up your roses."

"Wait. You're going now? To Brenham?" She smiled. "Would you like some company? I've always wanted to see that garden center."

His eyebrows rose. "Sure, I've got room. I'll have to move the pizza stone to the back." He patted the heavy metal pan—still in the shipping box—sitting in the passenger seat. "But I thought you were in a hurry going somewhere."

Her smile broadened. "It just so happens somewhere is on the way to Brenham."

Chapter 38 - COMBS

Gonzales wrote bullet points on the whiteboard, recapping what they knew. Beneath the blurry picture of the purple-hatted girl he had **Name/Alias** with a question mark. Combs replayed the three videos of the girl, each one augmenting understanding.

The spring-break girls only glimpsed her, but she'd clearly been at the Buc-ee's and dropped Sebastian Viejo. Combs cracked his knuckles. "Manager at the motel got the best look at her, said she moved like a cat. So, based on Sebastian's injuries, I'd bet my pension that she kicked him in the throat. Quick, silent, efficient."

Gonzales nodded and wrote **martial arts?** on the whiteboard beneath **5' 4" and athletic.** "They won't have the COD on Rudolph for a while. But the ME reported no obvious injury. His prelim said hyperglycemia. Kid needed insulin, went into diabetic coma and died. Waiting for confirmation."

Combs shrugged. "Still, she was there. Everyone who comes in contact with this girl ends up dead." He swiveled back and forth, the chair squeak adding a nails-on-the-blackboard sound. "After she laid out Viejo, she must've taken Hank Larson back to his house. September says a motorcycle rider nearly side-swiped her as she arrived."

"That's a big maybe, though." Gonzales added it, but with two question marks. "If Hank regains consciousness, we can ask him."

"God willing, yeah." Combs couldn't imagine how the boy's

mother must feel, especially if Hank died. Sebastian Viejo's record showed a history of assault with knives. The punches on the Buc-ee's video recorded the stabbings.

They'd finally located the mother, and got her to Hank's bedside. She'd been in interviews all day, and beat herself up since she'd been out of touch. Combs could offer no news about the little girl. What the hell had the ninja wanted with Nikki? "The hospital promised to call if there's a change."

Combs once again watched the video September shot of Nikki riding off on the back of the motorcycle. The distance and sun glare distorted too much, and the driver wore a helmet that hid any head covering—purple or otherwise. Nikki's unique white-blond hair made it easy to identify her.

Smoothing his mustache, Gonzales wrote the note on the board: **_Picked up Hank's sister??_** "That ties our ninja-girl to Hank. Maybe she didn't stab Hank, but she left him for dead. If September hadn't shown up, he'd be toast." He thumb-erased one of the question marks on the girl taking Hank home.

"Teddy Williams sent me a link to another video." At Gonzales's blank look, he added, "You remember. Calls himself the _geriatric white collar hacker?_" He laughed. "Don't ask me how he and September got pulled into this."

Frowning, Gonzales lowered his voice. "You still have eyes on September? Did you ever tell her?"

"No. I haven't figured out how." Combs pulled out a stick of gum, peeled it and stuck it in his cheek. "She's been kind of prickly lately."

"It's been months since you set all that up. And if she finds out before you explain, woo-wee! Sure wouldn't want to think what my Mercedes would do to me if—"

Combs's glare shut Gonzales up. "It's for her own good. She'll understand. I've been busy with work, and she's been busy with her stuff, the house, the wedding, and anyway, why are we talking about this?" He cleared his throat. "September asked Teddy Williams to collect a shelter dog, which happened to have belonged to Tanner Rudolph. And guess who dumped the dog?"

"I don't know, the dog fairy? Santa Paws? I'm not in the mood, Combs." His mustache twitched, and he returned to gnaw the bone. "She's gonna kill you when she finds out, Combs. And you've sold your house, so don't beg for a place on my sofa. Mercedes would kill me."

Combs softened his tone. Gonzales meant well. "I know. I'll tell her tonight." They'd discussed and agreed on the new cameras. He just hadn't told her all the details about the monitoring system, or that he'd hired a discreet guy to watch out for her when he couldn't. He'd thought they'd be on their honeymoon though, and had given the fellow this week off. So probably a good time to come clean with September.

He straightened and walked to the whiteboard to pick up the thread. "Our favorite ninja dumped the dog after she left Tanner Rudolph at the no-tell motel." He added a note.

"I don't get it. How'd September know about Rudolph's dog?"

"The shelter tracked September down. She trained the dog. Remember the motel manager said Tanner's dog alerted him when to take medicine? It's a diabetes-alert service dog."

Gonzales stared, eyes wide. "Don't you think that's just a little too much of a coincidence? Owner of the dog she trained dies, and she gets called to travel who-knows-where to pick it up?"

Tucking his chin, Combs sighed and nodded. He'd had good reason to hire the surveillance. He didn't know why, but she'd become a magnet for danger, another reason he insisted she leave sleuthing to the pros. At that thought, he went back to the cloud link that Williams had sent, and downloaded the image file named enhanced license. "How about that? I'm surprised Williams didn't gloat about this. The old man must be slipping."

"What?" Gonzales left the board to lean over Combs's shoulder and stare at the screen.

"He cleaned up the motorcycle license plate picture." Combs grinned. "Let's run this asap and get a BOLO out." His phone rang, and he stopped the scree-scree swivel to take the call. "Got it. Will be there shortly." He stood. "The hospital says the kid's out of surgery. And he'll wake up soon. They'll give me a few minutes to talk to Hank, if I get there asap."

"Go, fill in the blanks. I'll run the bike license. And we'll reconnect after and compare notes." Gonzales smiled.

Combs checked in at the nurses' station and got directions to the Larson kid's room. He cracked open the door, then knocked when he saw Hank's mom look up from her chair by the bed.

"I'm Detective Jeff Combs, ma'am. We met—"

"I remember." She nodded at the resting boy. "He fades in and out, but the doctors say he'll be okay. Eventually." Her lip trembled. "Have you found Nikki?"

"Working on it." He entered, and let the door fall closed. "If he's up to it, I need to ask Henry some questions."

The boy stirred. "My dad's Henry, call me Hank." His skin matched the hospital bed sheet and only a shade or two darker than the white-blond hair. "Did you catch Sebastian? He's the one stabbed me."

Combs pulled a chair to the other side of the bed. "Don't worry about him. He won't hurt anyone else." He leaned forward and placed his recorder on the nearby tray. "I need to record our conversation, okay?"

Hank nodded, and Combs glanced at his mother.

"Should he have a lawyer?" She twisted a tattered tissue between her fingers.

"Mom, I didn't do nothing wrong. I promise." Hank shifted in the bed, and hissed in pain.

"Take it easy, son. I just need you to tell me what happened. You're not in any trouble." *Not at the moment, anyway.* "But if your mom wants to call a lawyer, that's your right."

Hank shook his head, and his long blond hair fell over his eyes. His mother smoothed it out of his face, and he turned away. "I want to tell you. It could help you find Nikki." His shoulders hunched. "I never meant for her to get caught up in this."

Combs switched on the recorder. "Take your time. Let's start with why you went to Buc-ee's, and how and why you connected with Sebastian Viejo."

Hank licked his lips and looked away. His mother took his hand and squeezed. "I'm here, honey. Whatever happened, it's okay. I'm here for you."

He looked down at their joined hands and squeezed back. "You warned me, Mom, but I didn't listen." He met Combs's eyes. "My girlfriend—she hooked me up with Sebastian. Gave me the money and asked me to pick up her medicine." He looked back at his mother. "I swear, Mom, she said it was legal. She needs insulin for her diabetes. I wouldn't have done it otherwise. For sure, I wouldn't have taken Nikki along." His eyes welled. "Nikki just wanted a ride to her stupid job. And then everything went south." His lip trembled. "I paid Sebastian, but he said it wasn't enough, so I grabbed the bag and he stuck me. Then I ran, and stuffed Clarabelle's medicine in Nikki's backpack and told her to run, but Sebastian went after her, and…" His face crumpled, and deep furrows crept across his forehead, before he drifted back into unconsciousness.

"Can you finish this later? He needs to rest." Mrs. Larson stood and motioned for Combs to leave.

He nodded and grabbed his recorder before he stood and walked with her to the door. "Just one thing. Do you know her name? His girlfriend?"

She made a face. "She's not his girlfriend. That's a wish without a hope. She's too old for him. And she's just playing games, got all the high school boys hot after her. I know the type. Wants the attention, uses her looks to get whatever she wants." She sniffed, a momma bear in defense mode.

"Her name's Clarabelle?" *An unusual enough name.* "Do you know a last name? Or where she lives?"

"Clarabelle Freedom. Probably a stage name. I think she lives over in the trailer park, but I've heard she moves around a lot." She raised her eyebrows, implying more. "She's at least twenty-five, maybe older. She sings at Hog Heaven BBQ, that local cowboy bar. You know it's got quite the reputation." Her voice dripped with disapproval. "The girls who work there bat their eyes at all the men, sashaying up to them to get extra tips. Or more." Mrs. Larson spoke through clenched teeth. "Please go arrest her, Detective. I know how young boys get wound up over girls, and get talked into all kinds of trouble. But she had no right to get him involved in this drug business. Or my daughter." She dabbed her eyes. "Go find my Nikki, Detective Combs. Now if you'll excuse me, I need to figure out a way to tell their dad."

Combs thanked her and pocketed his recorder. On the way back to his car, he called Gonzales. "Just leaving the hospital. Any news on the owner of the motorcycle?"

"Yes. And no." Clearly frustrated, Gonzales spoke quickly.

"The plates come back registered to Quinn Donovan. Female. Twenty-four years old, five feet four, brown hair, brown eyes. No outstanding warrants, no record of any kind."

"Well, that's a start." He unlocked his car and climbed behind the wheel.

"You don't understand. When I say no record, I mean nothing, nada, zilch. Quinn Donovan miraculously materialized about six months ago. All the records look good on the surface: DOB, and school records match. Parents, both deceased, moved around a lot, but if you dig deeper—it's smoke and mirrors. The parents listed are dead, but died before the girl's DOB. The schools are fabricated, no such places exist. Somebody went to a lot of trouble to create a cipher."

Combs started the car. "They want her invisible. I'm surprised she uses a motorcycle. That's a tell, and more easily tracked than anonymous cars."

"She's young." Gonzales chuckled, adding, "If that's her actual age. She'll get better at staying invisible, or she'll get caught. Or maybe whoever's behind this wants her caught, so she takes the fall. Combs, this smacks of a bigger deal than some regional black market insulin scam."

Combs agreed with Gonzales. He flexed his shoulders. It had already been a long day, and he looked forward to relaxing later with September. Thank God she'd agreed to stay out of the investigation. While he loved September's soft heart and instinct to champion the underdog—literally and figuratively—he couldn't focus on his job when she put herself in danger. For as long as he'd known September, she'd been unlucky, targeted by everyone from a relentless stalker to a medical conspiracy. And while she'd grown stronger emotionally, he knew she remained fragile—only one step away from a meltdown. He'd tell her about the surveillance, and make her understand he had to protect her, and keep her safe, no matter what. That's what you did for people you love.

But right now, he had a job to do. "Could you run a name for me? The Larson boy gave me his girlfriend's name. Clarabelle Freedom, maybe lives in the trailer park. She apparently put him up to buying insulin from Sebastian Viejo. I want to talk to her, find out how she knew Viejo, maybe connect him to Quinn Donovan."

"Sure. Hold on."

Combs drummed his hands on the steering wheel, then turned the car toward the cowboy bar. If Clarabelle worked there regularly, he'd quiz the owner and staff. She might already be there.

Gonzales came back on the phone. "You won't like this, Combs."

He sighed. "Hit me." This whole day had been a study in frustration. "She another ghost like Donovan?"

"Yeah, in a manner of speaking. She's dead."

Chapter 39 - QUINN

Quinn stared at Nikki. The kid was too smart by half, and clearly had overheard her conversation with Fright. Even though they hadn't yet sent the address, she knew Teddy Williams could arrive at any time. The old man had skills that Mr. Fright didn't understand. Williams knew what awaited him.

No time to mess around with Nikki's questions and alert the other two girls. Better to deflect. She motioned to the sisters. "Can you help me with Tigger?" The cat had finally stopped crying when she let him out of the carrier. Although he moved slowly, he walked well and barely favored his bandaged rear legs. The injury at least spared the paw pads.

As Sylvia and Leslie drew closer to the cat, Quinn grasped Nikki by her arm and pulled her to the edge of the balcony space. She whispered urgently. "You need to be careful. Do what I say, if you want to live."

Nikki whispered back. "Answer me, Quinn. I heard you and him. I heard what he said about ammo." Nikki shivered and pulled her arm free. "How can I trust you? Why should I? What did Mr. Williams ever do to deserve to get shot?"

"Shot? What did you say?" Sylvia whirled.

Nikki smiled with a sour expression. "This church has great acoustics, Quinn."

Leslie stood up, too, and clutched her sister's arm. "Who got shot?"

"Nikki said Grandpa's going to get shot!" Sylvia pointed a finger at them. "Is this about the insulin? It is, isn't it?" She wailed. "I knew we shouldn't have gone to Mexico!"

"Shut up!" *They'd get them all killed.* Quinn frantically hushed the trio. She hadn't signed up for killing innocents. Maybe old-man-Williams had it coming—he claimed to be a hacker, and that business got you sideways of all kinds of bad actors. But these three girls got dragged into the mess through no fault of their own.

Sebastian had enlisted the sisters to hook their grandfather. But Hank—and Nikki herself—never went to Mexico. They were collateral damage. Unless the boss had many more balls in the air than Quinn could imagine.

My fault. All because Quinn got full of herself and figured she could be bad-ass and a do-gooder at the same time. She'd naively believed what they told her, what she wanted to believe. They played her. This test, as Mr. Fright characterized it, forced her to prove her loyalty by betraying what she'd always believed about herself.

Her employer had allowed her to destroy the man who'd wanted to destroy her. She'd sought redemption for having her innocence, her family, her name stolen from her.

What she'd lose here today meant no way back. But she had no choice. It didn't matter why, it only mattered that she did the job without question. Even if it meant further blackening her already tarnished soul. Keep the clueless kids quiet, so Mr. Fright could finish his job.

"Come with me. Do exactly what I say." She grabbed Nikki's arm and guided her down the narrow balcony.

Nikki waved her free hand at her knapsack. "My bag, let me have it."

Leslie scooped up one strap as she and Sylvia followed with her own bag.

Quinn steered the girls to the end of the balcony and jerked open a small door. It wasn't much, but better than nothing. The tiny office offered no safety, but would distract the girls and keep them out of the way. It had a desk with a computer, landline phone; small shelves and files; and an ancient air conditioner smushed into a tiny window. "Stay in here and close the door." She held out her hand. "Give me your phones.

"Mr. Fright already has mine." Leslie whimpered.

"You can't call the police. That will get Teddy—get your grandpa killed."

Leslie folded up into a ball on the floor. Sylvia relinquished her phone with a snarl and put her arms around her sister. "Told you we shouldn't go to Mexico," she muttered.

"Shut up. None of that matters now." Nikki's tone vacillated between fear and outrage. "Are you going to let him kill Mr. Williams?"

Crossing to the tiny desk, Quinn yanked the cables from the computer and phone. She figured they'd call for help, no matter her warnings. She had to convince them to trust her one last time. "Don't try anything stupid, Nikki. The acoustics are great, like you said, so you'll hear a lot of talking and yelling. Just know that anything I say or do, no matter how outrageous, is to protect you. To save innocent lives." She crossed back to the door. "Shut this behind me, lock it or block the door if you can. And stay quiet, so nobody knows you're here. Don't let anyone in." She hesitated, then added, "Not even me."

Quinn squared her shoulders, left the room, and latched the door behind her. She strode down the wrap-around balcony to the stairs, and bent over the cat carrier. Unzipping the storage compartment, she pulled out a pair of knives and sheathed one on the outside of her thigh, the other behind her back. She dug deeper, pulled out her 9mm SIG Sauer, checked the magazine, and holstered it under her loose blouse.

Something felt off. The hair rose on the back of her neck; she looked around, then stood quickly.

Tigger had disappeared.

Chapter 40 - TIGGER

Tigger ignored the jabber of the humans. He wanted to stretch his legs and get rid of the awful material clinging to his rear paws. If he could shed the wrappings, the hurts would go away. Then he'd find a place, a private and safe place, to defecate. The vibration of the bike always made him need a potty place as soon as they stopped.

Usually, he enjoyed riding with Quinn on the noisy, rumbly motorcycle. He slept most of the time while in the carrier and loved to explore all the new places they visited once they stopped. So this place intrigued him, not at all like the carpeted small rooms that smelled of old cigarettes and strange animal pee. This place smelled dusty and old. But in a good way. Cobwebs meant spiders, and shadows rustled with munchable critters.

As Quinn led the strangers away from him, Tigger cheek-rubbed the carrier. He wrinkled his nose at the smell of the item that lived inside one zippered pocket. The powerful odor scared him. He remembered that scent from the-time-before, when he lived with many other cats and a soft-lapped old woman. The old woman died amid fear and blood, and the gun-odor lived on in Tigger's memory. Not too long after that, though, his new person found him and he learned to be happy again.

One pocket contained a soft bag filled with his new favorite treats. His purr rumbled with anticipation, and he sat down—grimacing at the sting in his back legs—and pawed at the zipper with a forepaw. He switched to sharp teeth and quickly got it to move. His purr increased. Usually when they stopped, once Quinn let him out, she locked the carrier behind a door that not even his paws could breach. So he worked quickly before she returned and opened the zipper just enough to paw-fish the bag out.

His mouth watered. He blew bubbles at the idea of the entire bag of treats at once. Tigger grabbed the bag in his teeth, lifted it high, and looked around for a place to make his meal. He wanted to leap up high to the ledge, but his rear legs had stiffened. Instead, he turned in the direction where air stirred his sensitive whiskers, and padded toward the stairs.

The stairs fell away in one direction and climbed high in tight circles in the other. Tigger loved finding the highest place he could. From a tall perch, Tigger could watch for approaching trouble, and stay out of sight and reach of danger. Even with his sore, throbbing legs, Tigger could manage to climb one stair step at a time.

He began to climb.

Chapter 41 - COMBS

So much for his shift ending on time. Combs arrived at the trailer park, squeezed his car into a tiny spot, and hurried to the swirl of activity. Before he showed his badge, the uniform officer waved him through. "Hope you haven't eaten. It's messy." The officer's face shined with sweat, and the odor of vomit was unmistakable.

Grimacing, Combs hoped the cop had spewed far away from the scene. "Just got the call. This may relate to an ongoing investigation." He hesitated. "Who called it in?"

The officer pointed toward a heavyset good-ol-boy in overalls leaning against a pickup with the Hog Heaven BBQ logo on the side. "Keep him here, I want to talk to him."

Combs hurried to the small trailer with the door propped open. He slipped on shoe coverings before climbing the steps, then poked his head inside, and stopped. Blood painted the walls and clotted the furniture. For a moment, Combs's head spun. *Deja vu.* The copper smell and image took him back to his mother's death scene. He blinked, swallowed several times, and the room came back into focus. "What've we got?"

"Strangled, then throat slashed. Or vice versa. Somebody wanted to make sure." The ME stood, revealing the rest of the young woman's body. "You want to look more, Detective? Or can I transport?"

"Give me a minute." Combs pulled on gloves and stepped gingerly around the body.

She'd been a beauty. A poster-sized picture mounted on the wall showed Clarabelle posed in sequined cowgirl fare: pearl snap-buttons on a low-cut blouse with a fringed miniskirt and silver-studded boots. He could see why Hank and his friends crushed on the woman. He'd heard the restaurant hosted a band on weekends. But Combs hadn't been back since they'd busted the previous owner. "Would you check her for diabetes while you're at it?"

The ME shrugged. "Sure." He hooked a thumb at the refrigerator. "But easy enough to find out. She'd have insulin in there. It's got to be refrigerated." He pointed to the small kitchen table holding a box of chocolate-covered cream-filled doughnuts. "If she was diabetic, those aren't hers."

Nodding, Combs carefully stepped around the woman's remains. He opened the refrigerator. "What am I looking for? Vials? Syringes?"

"Or insulin pens. Yep." The ME joined him, stooped to peer inside, and shrugged. "Nothing there. So I guess the doughnuts are hers."

Combs left the trailer, after giving the okay to transport Clarabelle's body, and crossed to the restaurant owner and introduced himself. "You're the new owner of Hog Heaven? I'm Detective Jeff Combs." He turned on the recorder, showing it first to the man.

"I wanted to change the name, but Hog Heaven's already famous. I'm not dumb enough to throw publicity like that away. No such thing as bad publicity. I mean..." He turned up both his palms in apology. "That didn't come out right. I'm Cliff Delong." He leaned forward to speak into the recorder, then crossed his arms. "That poor little thing. Who coulda done such a thing?"

"You found her? Why'd you come out?"

"She missed Thursday rehearsal, didn't show last night, and I got a full house tonight, the Saturday crowds expect her. It's the last night of spring break for the locals. I hadn't seen her since last weekend, and she usually hangs out even when not gigging. It's good for business. All the young fellows like her. I figured she'd lost track of time." He rubbed his face. "Not to speak ill of the dead, but she partied. A lot. And probably got a little sum-sum on the side, ya know?" He offered the palms-up gesture again. "I run a clean business, but I can't control what they do on their own time."

He'd heard that before, but Combs didn't press it. "So you don't know any reason someone would want to hurt her?"

Delong shook his head, and his jowls jiggled. "Everybody loved her. I mean, she was gorgeous. Fun to be around. Great for business, too. The men came to drink and dream; the boys just dreamed. Clarabelle weren't a great singer, but with those looks, nobody cared."

"So she had lots of men friends. Anyone special? Anyone new?"

"Maybe. Until recently, she made it clear she didn't want to be exclusive." He half smiled. "Then suddenly she flashed extra cash and started brushing off some regulars. I had to talk to her about it. I mean"—he blinked owlishly—"you don't piss off my customers. You make nice with them, keep them buying drinks, that's part of the job. And we got muscle on staff to keep her and any of the girls safe from too much... unwelcome pestering." He cleared his throat. "Like I said, I keep things honest at Hog Heaven."

"Extra cash from somebody new. Did you meet him?" *Or her?* Combs leaned forward, half expecting a description of the purple-hatted ninja. Had Quinn Donovan paid Clarabelle to convince Hank Larson she needed insulin?

"Never so lucky. But Clara called him *steamy-hot.*" He batted his eyes. "That's what she said, *steamy-hot.* I heard her chatting with some of the other girls. Said he made her scream when they... you know. And she called him *a fright machine scarier than hell.*" He grimaced. "I think being scared turned her on. How twisted is that? And now you can see what it got her." He spit on the ground. "Catch the bastard who did this. She didn't deserve to die."

"Nobody does." Combs spoke reflexively, then put up a hand of apology. "She mention a name?" It wouldn't be real, whatever name he'd told her. But they still might track him or connect the name to other crimes.

Delong tucked in his chins. "I heard her talk to him on her cell phone. He asked her to do something, I don't know what. I think that's where she got the extra cash." He pursed his lips. "But he used a fake name. She laughed about it, said she didn't care, cuz the name fit: Casper Fright."

Gonzales answered on the first ring. "I got a lead on the black-market insulin. At least three groups of kids traveled to Mexico over the past few weeks. I did a nationwide search and got reports about calls from concerned parents from Texas, New Mexico, even upstate New York relaying very similar stories from their kids."

Combs grunted. "It's spring break all month long. Different schools have staggered schedules, and they come from all over the country. Lots of high school and college kids partying down on the Gulf." Thank goodness his kids weren't old enough yet, although Melinda already campaigned to go. He shuddered.

"Yeah, well, the organizers used that to their benefit. They pitched a story about helping diabetics who couldn't afford prescriptions in the states by picking up discounted meds over the border. See, the price of insulin in the states keeps going up. It's a fraction of the cost in Canada or Mexico."

"Doesn't insurance pay for that?" Combs paid his share of premiums without fail. After what had happened to his ex-wife, he couldn't risk not having health coverage for himself and his kids. "Of course... not everyone has insurance."

"Right. And there're different types of diabetes, and brands of insulin. Some get pills, others require injections. That can add up. And it's not like you take one pill or one shot a day." He paused. "My aunt died of complications from diabetes twenty years ago. Lost her feet first, and her sight. Awful disease. They've got better ways to monitor blood sugar now."

Like with an alert dog? He'd prefer the electronic monitor systems he saw advertised these days, but guessed some people would prefer a fido fix. "Sorry about your aunt."

Gonzales paused. "Thanks. Makes it more personal, ya know?" He cleared his throat. "Kids come off parents' insurance at age 26, and some of them don't have jobs to fund the jacked-up price increase. So they ration insulin, try to make it stretch out."

Combs breathed in. "Isn't that dangerous?"

"Yep. Can be deadly. So that's why folks cross the border, north or south. And why some enterprising jerk with a purple cap enlisted spring-break kids." He cleared his throat again. "Kids from two of the groups offered a description that fit Quinn Donovan. And one of them said Sebastian Viejo brought in someone with a service dog."

Checkmate. "We need to find her." He looked back at the trailer, where the ME was following the covered body to the waiting ambulance. "Wouldn't customs stop them from coming back into the country?"

"Technically, sure—you're not supposed to do that. But the border guys shrug it off if people bring in a two or three-month supply of insulin. So our enterprising genius took kids to half a dozen pharmacies, and each one bought a couple months' worth." He snorted. "The kids I talked to swore they didn't even ask to get paid. They did it to help. And they all turned the insulin over to somebody else." He paused. "You can imagine how their parents feel. Scared to death they'll be prosecuted as drug mules."

"But is it safe? The insulin, I mean." Combs understood the cost issue, but wasn't sure he'd trust unregulated product from across the border.

"Same brand, same product as in the states. But there are some fakes out there, too, so you have to choose a reputable pharmacy. There are some lists on the internet put together by concerned citizens and others." He took a breath. "Also, insulin degrades quickly if not refrigerated appropriately. Maybe that's what happened with Rudolph. He used the Mexico product and..." He made a raspberry sound.

Combs tightened his lips. He'd feel crazy-angry if someone enticed his kids to bring in contraband. "We've got another wrinkle, Gonzales, with Clarabelle."

He groaned. "It's already so damned wrinkled Botox couldn't save us. What you got?"

"According to her boss from Hog Heaven... you remember the BBQ place, right?"

"How could I forget? What'd he say?"

"She recently came into some money from somebody she called Casper Fright." He rolled his eyes.

A long pause. "I really am not in the mood, Combs."

"Neither am I. Not making it up." He could imagine the bantam-size detective pacing back and forth. "That's the name he gave Clarabelle. And get this. She's not diabetic."

"But that's why the Larson kid met up with…." Gonzales's voice faded as he pulled the phone away and cursed in creative, elegant style. "She set up Hank Larson. Why?"

Combs answered through gritted teeth. "That's the question of the day." His phone buzzed, and he looked at the text, his nose wrinkled like something smelled bad. "Hold on, Gonzales." Why would Doc Eugene text him?

>**Running late. Macy will be fine with a slight delay.**
<**??? Something wrong with the cat?**

He waited impatiently for the veterinarian's reply. September handled all the pet stuff. He really didn't have time for this.

>**Sept asked me to give meds, said she might not make it home in time.**

With a muffled curse, he disconnected from Gonzales and dialed September's cell.

Chapter 42 - SHADOW

Shadow could barely contain his excitement. Arnold drove the big truck and September rode beside him up front in the passenger seat. There wasn't room for Shadow—he wanted to sit on September's lap—but she'd asked him to "kennel up" in the back.

The truck bed, enclosed with waffled metal walls, let the wind whip inside. So many smells! Shadow's tail couldn't stop wagging. The truck bounced along the road, so a good-dog had to brace his paws to keep from being thrown from side to side. Every few minutes, September looked back at him through the cab window. Her wrinkled brow shouted her worry for him, or maybe something else. But Shadow couldn't help enjoying the adventure. So many smells!

He sniffed the hair-coated blanket next to the cab window. Another dog used to rest here. Shadow wouldn't want to share this space with a strange dog. But he felt comforted that Arnold liked dogs enough to make a special place for good-dogs to ride.

Before Shadow had jumped into the truck for the adventure, Arnold moved a heavy box from the front seat, and September loaded up his tracking bag. At the thought, Shadow's wags grew wider and faster. He loved sniffing out the missing. Maybe he'd find Arnold's missing dog! He sniffed the blanket again, to cement the other dog's identity in his memory. Female. Short fur.

He nosed the tracking bag, detecting the ever-present smell of treats. September always kept treats in the bag, both for him and for the lost animals they found. Different animals liked different tastes and smells, too, so she kept an assortment. Shadow particularly enjoyed tracking down lost cats, because cats got the best treats. They smelled extra strong and tasted fine. Maybe Arnold's dog liked cat treats, too, and they'd both get some. Wouldn't that be grand?

Many more objects filled the back of the truck. Some of them Shadow knew without sniffing too closely. Others seemed strange, and a few were downright scary. But it was a good-dog's job to be prepared. He had to protect September. So Shadow needed to explore everything about this truck, to help her when they stopped.

He carefully stood and pawed slowly down one side of the truck. Bags of dirt—why did people put dirt in bags?—sat in a pile on one side. September didn't like for him and Kinsler to dig in the garden, but he'd seen Arnold using a shovel to do just that. Sometimes people puzzled Shadow.

Several tools hung on hooks on the wall above the bags of soil. He didn't know what they did, but the metal ends gleamed sharp and smelled of oil. Shadow carefully touched his nose to one that had fallen into the bed of the truck.

Maybe September would teach him the names of the tools? Shadow loved playing the show-me game. He already knew the names of so many objects, important things like *ball*, and *book*. Like *rope* and *gun*. He'd seen September handle the gun, and that made his tummy hurt. And Shadow whined. He didn't like the gun, but he respected it. And as long as September held the gun, that was fine. He knew that Combs also carried one of the scary things, and that worried him some. But not as much as when strangers pointed guns at good-dogs, or at September. He lifted his lips at the thought.

He'd like to play the show-me game with the tools and not think about guns. This morning, he'd learned to name the tiny dancing light of a *red-dot*. He'd seen Macy play chase-the-red-dot before, and felt happy he could play *red-dot* now, too.

But September wasn't ready to play games with Shadow. She sat next to Arnold in the front, and a glass window separated them. He sighed and again sniffed the tool, jittering on the floor of the truck bed. The shiny sharp end smelled of fresh-cut branches. So maybe Arnold used the sharps to trim and shape growing things. He'd seen the big man laboring to knock down one of the old prickly bushes in the back of their house. He pawed the tool, feeling smart and accomplished. He didn't know the name, but he knew what it did.

On the other side of the truck sat plastic canisters of liquid. He smelled oil in one, gas in another, and recognized the odor from the loud noisy machines that cut the grass short in their front yard. But another big square container with an attached long tube held a mysterious strong chemical odor. It made his eyes water. Shadow sneezed and sneezed again. He didn't like that smell. Shadow wondered why Arnold kept nasty-smelling stuff in canisters in his truck?

He sneezed again and shook himself. Shadow congratulated himself he'd not lost his balance in the rumbling truck. They'd traveled a long way, but the truck hadn't slowed down. Shadow whined. He'd really like to sit beside September, and hear her tell him "good dog" and stroke his face. He didn't feel right, not like himself, unless they were together.

When he saw the pair of leather gloves peeking out of one of Arnold's bags, he reflexively grabbed one. It wasn't September's, and didn't smell like her. But in a pinch, any chew toy would do. Shadow settled on the stranger dog's bed, held the glove between his paws, and gnawed. And waited for the truck to stop, and September to tell a good-dog what he should do.

Chapter 43 - SEPTEMBER

S eptember swayed in the passenger seat and looked surreptitiously at Arnold. He had offered no objection when she'd invited herself for the ride-along, not even when she loaded up Shadow into the back. She half-turned to check on her furry partner. She placed a palm against the glass, and the big black shepherd mirrored the action with his own paw.

Her phone rang again; she silenced the call and sighed. That made three calls from Combs in the past ten minutes, plus an angry, worried text. Why had Doc Eugene said anything? He acted as protective as Combs did. While she appreciated the care, sometimes it smothered her, and she knew neither would approve of her trip to help Teddy. But right now, after what Teddy said about Combs keeping her watched, she didn't trust herself to keep a civil tongue. Besides, he might have already sent an armed babysitter after her. She fumed.

"You ought to take the call." Arnold didn't look at her, but his lips twitched in a barely suppressed smile. He continued to focus on the road, while his big hands kept the steering wheel steady. "I don't think your caller took the hint. Or you could turn the phone off."

"I can't turn it off, I'm expecting another call." She blew out an exasperated breath. "I don't want to argue with him."

"Your fiancé?"

She nodded.

"Did you tell him you planned to run off with the gardener?" He turned toward her with a wide grin, but at her expression, his face fell. "Hey, just kidding. C'mon, lighten up. Am I really that bad? Besides, you're my sister-in-law. Were, anyway."

September rubbed both hands over her face. "Sorry, Arnold, I don't mean to be so testy. It's been a day from hell. Everything's gone wrong."

He grunted. "Some weeks it's Monday all week long." When she turned to stare at Shadow again, he added, "He'll be fine. Kami loved riding back there." He nodded at the St. Jude medal hanging from the mirror. "Belonged to her. I thought she had cancer, and turned out to be arthritis instead and she made it another two years. She was a German Shorthair Pointer, with only half an ear on one side. I miss her." He glanced in the mirror at the back of the truck. "Lots of wonderful smells, and nothing dangerous for a dog to eat. I make sure of that." He sighed. "I sure miss Kami. But I'm not ready yet."

September sighed and turn back around. "I know, they leave a hole in your heart." She remembered her first dog, and the familiar hurt cut deep. Shadow had healed the raw edges of that hurt, and made his own special place in her heart. "Shadow rides in the back seat of my car, too. But we don't have glass between us. It feels different." Her phone rang again, and she groaned.

"Answer the phone, September. It'll just get worse putting it off. Whatever it is." He looked at her. "Want me to pull over and give you some privacy?"

They had many more miles to go, and little time to spare. "No, keep going. Does this truck go any faster?" She raised her eyebrows. "Oh, but thank you again. I really appreciate the ride, Arnold." She hadn't told him anything about her errand, and wouldn't. She didn't want to put anyone else at risk.

September took a deep breath and accepted Combs's call.

"Where are you? And what's this about being gone overnight?"

That's not what she'd told Doc Eugene. "I'll be home, but it might be late. I'm riding with Arnold Stonebridge down to Brenham to look at roses for the garden." *Go with the truth, or as much of it as you can. And keep your temper!*

"Oh." A long pause. "Can I talk to him for a minute?" Testy.

Her jaw tightened. "Sure." She held out the phone to Arnold. "He'd like a word."

Arnold took the phone, not slowing while he talked. "Hey Detective Combs. I know it's unexpected and all, but we spent a lot of time going over the garden plans today and —" He paused, listening. "Yes, she asked, and I didn't have any problem. Shadow's riding shotgun in the back. It's about three hours there and three back. I already put in the rose order so unless September vetoes, it's just a pick up." He listened, nodded, and handed the phone back to September. Arnold whispered, "He's pissed."

"Why didn't you tell me about the visit? I had to hear from Doc Eugene, and he made it sound like—"

"You know what a worrywart Doc is. I should have told you, but knew you were buried with your case. Also, Teddy ran into some, uhm, family problems with Leslie and Sylvia, his grandkids, so we may meet up with them. And besides, with your safety surveillance, I figured you already knew." Her neck and face heated, unable to prevent the hurt and anger. "Why didn't you tell *me*, or even ask me, Combs?"

He stuttered, then steadied his voice. "I should have. I'm sorry. But I pulled 'em off last night. Nobody's on your tail, I promise. I just wanted to keep anyone from coming after you again."

She turned away from Arnold to look out the passenger window to collect her thoughts. *Nobody followed her, so she and Teddy were on their own.* She didn't know whether to feel relieved or fearful that backup had disappeared. Through gritted teeth, she said, "Please don't worry about me. I'll be home later tonight." She prayed she hadn't lied. The reality of the situation caught her breath, and she dropped her voice. "You really pissed me off. But I love you, Jeff." She disconnected before he could say anything.

Arnold shifted in his seat and cleared his throat. She glanced over and was startled by his scowl. "What?"

"You lied to him. And to me. What's going on, September?" His wide shoulders hunched over the wheel. "I don't want to get between you and the Detective. That's not good business. Besides, I like the guy."

"Oh don't be silly." But she owed him a better explanation. "You're right. I didn't tell either of you everything. But that's because I don't know what's going on. Not really. And, I don't want you to get dragged into this, either."

"Might've thought of that before you hitched a ride." He grumbled, but clearly looked intrigued. "You planned to burn rubber out at your house, if you'd had gas. And not to check out roses in Brenham. Where were you going?"

"Just stop." She pursed her lips, considering. People she cared about always got hurt when they got too close. However well-intentioned, she didn't need Arnold going to the police. At least, not yet. She'd promised herself that when the time was right, she'd call in the cavalry. "Okay, here's what I know. My friend Teddy called me. He was supposed to pick up his grandkids on the Gulf, but they changed it to one of the painted churches. You know them?"

Arnold's brow smoothed. "Those historic church tours? Yeah, did that back in high school with my Sunday school group." He nodded with understanding. "There's one not too far from Brenham. So you planned to head south, anyway? Meet up with this Teddy fellow?"

She breathed with relief. "Exactly. Teddy called, said he'd had family problems, and asked if I could help." *That was the truth. Just not the whole truth.* She hoped it would suffice. "He's waiting for me at the rest stop on I35, two miles south of Salado."

A half smile lifted his lips. "Makes sense. That's only an hour away. So why didn't you tell Detective Combs?"

Her mouth dropped open. She searched for something to say when her email pinged. She glanced down, expecting something from Combs. Or maybe Doc Eugene. "Nikki!"

"Who's Nikki?" Arnold kept driving.

In the back, Shadow barked, then barked loudly again. September held up her hand and pressed the palm flat on the window. He knew when her heart rate changed. Shadow always knew…

Quickly, she read Nikki's message, and viewed the several attached images. "Good girl," she whispered, impressed by the girl's thinking. Cell phone idiosyncrasies had delayed delivery of the pictures, but better late than never. Nikki didn't know where they were, but sent pictures they could track. Even more importantly, she described her captors. September forwarded the entire message to Teddy and prayed he could work his magic to figure out where to find the girls.

The truck slowed and pulled over to the side of the road, stopping with a jerk. Arnold clicked on hazard lights and turned to September. "Why'd we stop?" She eyed the man's massive hands. He'd played college football, and might as well be a weight lifter, based on the heavy supplies Arnold routinely lugged around for his business. She glanced at the time on her phone, knowing once Teddy got her message and identified the church, he'd leave without her. "I'm sort of on a schedule here." Her nerves thrummed.

He glared. "I might look like some dumb jock, but I ranked second in my class for my business degree, and have a Master's in horticulture from Texas A&M. You lie to me one more time and we turn around."

"Arnold, please." She licked her lips.

"Who's Nikki? She sent you something important. And what's up with this Teddy person?" He crossed his arms. "We're not going anywhere, September. Not until you tell me what's going on."

Chapter 44 - COMBS

Combs pulled up to the house on Rabbit Run Road and frowned. September hadn't closed the gate. He sighed and swung his car into the circle drive. They'd agreed to keep the ornate green gates closed when home, and especially while gone. That wouldn't stop, but would slow, potential intruders. Without the correct code, the gate had to be opened from inside the house. He engaged the gate close and watched it swing shut as the automatic garage door opened for him to drive in.

September had relaxed her instinct to constantly look over her shoulder. The front door no longer boasted half a dozen locks—she felt satisfied with three.

He liked to think his presence had something to do with her new-found confidence. But Combs worried she'd gone too far the other way. After the stressful day they'd both had, disappointment welled in his chest that they couldn't be together, mend some hurt feelings. Combs knew trust came hard for her, though. She'd only survived her horrible years of imprisonment by keeping secrets and hiding the truth. She'd emerged damaged, but alive, and as her emotional scars healed, September opened up her heart. To him.

He wanted her to trust him. And Combs wanted to trust September. He had his own scars to heal. To make a life together, they both had to do better.

Combs pulled his car in next to September's. *Right. She'd*

probably left the gate remote in the car when she left in Arnold's truck. He pinched the bridge of his nose, feeling a headache building. Roses. She wanted more roses. Fine.

He had to cut her some slack. Cut them both some slack. Hell, his own marriage hadn't been a bed of roses. Combs's work consumed him, and his then-wife looked elsewhere for what she needed. What his kids needed. That hurt, but he had to own up to it. But now, with his ex-wife in hospice, he couldn't ever risk losing his family again. He'd promised September, his kids, and himself, to be home more. To work assigned shifts. Take vacations. Have a life. Find a balance between work and family. A man didn't get many chances for happiness. September's delight made him happy, so if a fantasy wedding rocked her world, he'd support the notion. "But how many freakin' roses does a person need?" He shook his head, but had to smile.

Climbing out of his car, he noticed the back cargo door of September's vehicle was ajar. She must have been in a hurry when she left. He opened it wider so when he slammed it, the latch would catch. He cocked his head, noting the empty spot where she kept a duffel bag with Shadow's gear for their tracking assignments. He closed the door and rubbed the back of his neck. She'd left the glove box open, too. The headache hadn't taken over yet, but he needed some OTC to prevent a full-blown migraine. Combs thumbed the remote and headed to the house.

The case ate at him. And since September wasn't here, no harm in keeping working on it. He walked to the door, jingling keys as he went. Might be nice to have the house to himself. He needed a shower, a change of clothes. And a drink. He should call his kids, too, and check with Aunt Ethel. He smiled. Uncle Stan would keep 'em in line. After a shower, maybe he'd run over there, raise a few with his mentor. The retired cop had a wealth of experience and always offered wonderful insight into a current case.

Combs quickly entered and disarmed the alarm. Macy appeared, meowing with a muffled plaintive sound. The beeping drew the cat to the door like kids to dirt. September always warned him to watch that Macy didn't door-dash. "Weird cat. Nice cat. What've you got this time, Macy?"

The big sable and white thief loved to swipe and carry objects around the house; pencils, dirty socks, stuffed toys. Today, Macy carried a wad of yellow paper. "Pilfering September's office supplies again?" He loved paper products. Once, he shredded a multi-pack of toilet paper, which left drifts of confetti all over.

Macy *meerowed* again, and dropped the wad, paw-batting it across the entry before pouncing on it. He bit the paper and lifted his prize high, trotting ahead of Combs into the kitchen, his plume-like tail straight up over his back.

Before Combs could pour a drink, the gate intercom buzzed. Puzzled, he hurried to answer, then remembered Doc Eugene's message. Sure enough, he spied the veterinarian's panel truck and buzzed him in.

Combs met him at the door, drink in hand. "You want one? It's been a day."

Doc Eugene declined. "I need to drive home after this, and wouldn't want to be stopped by Heartland's finest." He peered around the room. "Macy around? You know, September should teach you how to pill her animals. I might not always be available." He shoved his glasses up the bridge of his nose. "Macy's easy."

Barking a short laugh, Combs lead the way back into the kitchen. "Not happening. She has the touch for the critters. And trained cat or not, my luck I'd do something wrong and get bit. By September."

The veterinarian laughed. "And *her* bite's probably worse than *Macy's*." He looked around the kitchen. "As I recall, she keeps his prescription in one of the kitchen drawers." Combs pointed next to the tall refrigerator, and Doc Eugene found the small bottle. "Macy, come. Pill time, kitty."

With a chirrup of anticipation, the big Maine Coon padded across the room to the veterinarian's side and dropped the yellow wad. The veterinarian picked up the paper and set it on the counter. "We'll play fetch after your pill." He tapped the counter, and the cat obligingly leaped up and from there to the top of the refrigerator. Macy licked his whiskers as the veterinarian selected a couple of treats from the nearby canister before he shook out a tiny pill. "Pill time. Open." Macy took the pill then hooked a paw around the man's hand to pull it closer when he offered the treats.

Combs watched, as always, in awe at how well September's animals behaved. He used to put Kinsler in a half-Nelson to give him his monthly flea medication, and had gladly relinquished the chore to his fiancée. He sipped his drink, watching the doctor scratch the cat's chin, then answered his cell when it jangled.

"Aunt Ethel?" He grinned. She still used a land line. "I planned to call soon. Have the barbarians torn down the house yet?"

Doc Eugene picked up the wad of paper, held it out to the cat before gently tossing it across the kitchen floor. He grinned when Macy launched himself from on high, dashed to get the ball, and proudly carried it back.

"Dad, it's me. Aunt Ethel doesn't know I'm calling. She took away my phone, said I was obsessing." Melinda's worried whisper clearly carried over the line.

The cat carried the paper ball back to the veterinarian, sat in front of him, and pawed his leg.

"Obsessing over what? Too much social media again?" Combs pinched his nose again. "Her rules this week, honey. We discussed this."

"Daddy, you don't understand. This is important." Her words came fast, voice rising. "It's how I stay connected to my friends, especially the kids from the barn last year. You remember Nikki?"

He straightened abruptly. His drink sloshed. Combs carefully set it on the stained glass table. "What about Nikki Larson?"

Doc Eugene, bent to take the wadded ball from Macy, looked up sharply. The cat tugged back, and the paper unwound.

"Nikki posted a selfie a little while ago on this secret forum. She goes by Nikki-Kitty, but it's her. Nobody else has white-blond hair like that. Anyway, she's with two other girls, named Leslie and Sylvia. Dad, it's a cry for help. She posted the DWR code, twice!" She finished with a breathless flourish. "That's the highest level!"

The veterinarian straightened and unfolded the paper ball. He smoothed it on the countertop. "Detective, look at this."

Combs waved him quiet. "Melinda, what the heck is DWR?"

Doc Eugene brought over the paper. "It's a list for her trip. Why'd she take her gun and extra ammunition?"

Combs grabbed the paper and scanned it quickly. His breath quickened when he read the names of Leslie and Sylvia. *Teddy's grandkids.* She'd said Teddy planned a trip with them.

Typical September understatement.

Melinda no longer whispered. "DWR one time means *do what's right*. But the second one means *danger Will Robinson*. That's from some really old TV show. I looked it up. But on the forum, it's code for 911."

Chapter 45 - NIKKI

Nikki pulled her charger out of the backpack and plugged the tablet into the outlet underneath the tiny desk. After contacting the super-secret kids forum, she needed all the juice possible to put into play everything that Kid Kewl described. It wouldn't do for the battery to crap out in the middle of everything. She took a bite of the granola bar the sisters had shared. All of them had missed lunch, not that they had much of an appetite.

The tablet had a camera and a mic and everything. She just needed to figure out how to access multiple channels for the live feed, and he'd do the rest.

She worried about Quinn and her gun. Knowing kung fu and drop-kicking bad guys in the throat only worked sometimes. The scary man could reach out with his special *camera*—she made a face, knew it was a gun, she wasn't a stoopid-head kid anymore.

An email arrived with a soft *ding* and Nikki quickly muted the tablet. She didn't want Quinn or Mr. Fright to hear and confiscate her tablet like they took the other girls' phones. Sylvia and Leslie sat in the corner, arms around each other, acting totally helpless and weepy.

"Hey. I finally got a message back from September." She whispered, remembering how sound carried in the church. She hoped this tiny office had better insulation. She beckoned the girls closer. They squeezed together under the desk and together read September's note.

"Grandpa's going to save us!" Leslie clamped a hand over Sylvia's mouth, even though the words were quiet. Grabbing a pad of paper and pencil from the desk, Sylvia wrote, *Gramps is bad-ass.*

Nikki hoped so. September said she'd sent everything to Mr. Williams.

Leslie took the pencil to write. *She called cops?*

Nikki shrugged. September's email hadn't said, only that Mr. Williams would find the girls based on Nikki's church pictures. That could take hours. By then, who knows what might happen to them. Besides, the man in the tower had plans for when Mr. Williams got here. She didn't think the girl's grandpa had much chance against a gun. And no matter what she said, Nikki didn't trust Quinn to protect anyone. Quinn lied. About everything. But they could even the odds with her—Kid Kewl's—plan, get help sooner rather than later, and maybe catch the bad guy.

Nikki took a turn with the pencil. *We need lots of distractions.* She scribbled down the details Kid Kewl suggested. She watched the girls' faces as they read her note. Once she had the last piece, he'd get the word out to the police.

She wrote a reply message to September; the sisters read over her shoulder. Within less than a minute, a reply came back with the missing piece. Nikki grinned, and fist-bumped each of the sisters. "She's got us covered. September sent me the login for her YouTube channel."

Chapter 46 - SEPTEMBER

September shifted in the passenger seat as Arnold's truck rolled into the Bell County Southbound rest area and up to Teddy's RV.

"Thanks for the ride." She swung out of the cab, walked around to the rear and collected the dog's gear. Shadow bounded out as she turned to Arnold, who had also exited the vehicle. "Please, please, Arnold, don't do anything dumb."

His eyebrows rose. "Did that just come out of your mouth?"

"Leave while you can. But give us time to get the girls before you call the police."

"You can't call the police." Teddy heard the last words as he got out of Nellie Nova, neglecting to latch the door in his distress. "Who's this? Not a cop! September, you'll get my girls killed!"

Lefty wriggled through the door, leash trailing across the asphalt as he followed Teddy. Shadow immediately placed himself between September and the strange dog, bristling.

"Shadow, *wait. Settle.*" At September's whip-crack command, both dogs sank to the ground. She dropped Shadow's bag inside the RV, turned to Teddy and hugged him. "I got here as soon as I could. Theodore Williams, meet Arnold Stonebridge."

The men eyed each other, taking each other's measure. At a plaintive meow, Teddy broke eye contact to latch the RV door and prevent his cat's escape. When he turned back, Arnold held out a rough paw, and they reluctantly shook hands. Teddy cocked his head at the much bigger man. "Does he know?"

"Enough. And I don't like it, you dragging her into this. Or me." When Teddy would have argued, Arnold interrupted. "I'll have the cops on speed-dial, and hit it as soon as I sniff major trouble. But since I'm here, let me help."

Teddy stared up at Arnold but finally nodded. "I don't have time to argue." He looked around the deserted rest area and pointed to the building. "I need brain food, and nobody's here at the moment, so let's confab inside."

The trio, along with the two dogs, moved to the limestone building. September noted the massive window, shaped like a wagon wheel. They entered the lobby and her mouth dropped at the sight of the interactive grist mill display. Teddy walked directly to the vending area and fed several dollars into various machines. When an attendant crossed toward them, eyes on the two dogs, Teddy called hoarsely, "They're both service dogs. Okay?"

The woman held up both hands, palms out, and backed away, giving the group privacy.

Teddy looked ready to explode. He punched the vending machine, then collected his purchases. Tearing open a Milky Way bar, Teddy took a bite and talked around the sticky mouthful. "As soon as you sent Nikki's pictures of the church, I found it. It's not on the regular tour route, not even an active congregation anymore. Pretty remote, and farther north than I expected, in a tiny town called Freedom. That's why I wanted to meet here, it's only about twenty minutes away." He bit again and chewed. "If I hadn't known you were coming, I'd be there by now." He swallowed hard, and returned to the vending machine for a high energy drink.

"Just show up? That's your plan?" Arnold stuck both hands in his pockets, rocking back and forth.

"They told me to show up, and don't tell the cops if I wanted my girls back. And to bring September." He popped the rest of the bar in his mouth and swallowed. "I don't like it, but I don't have a choice." He wadded the wrapper, popped open the beverage, and gulped three swallows. Teddy set down the can, tore open another candy bar, and stuck two more in his jacket pocket.

"There are always choices." Arnold crossed his arms. "You always do as you're told?"

Teddy balled his fists. "What the hell do you know about—"

"Stop it!" September shushed them both, conscious of the attendant clearly eavesdropping. "Listen to me. You've not heard from them yet, have you?"

He shook his head and took off his glasses to clean them. "They said to wait for a text with directions. I got tired of waiting."

"So they won't expect us until they summon you." Arnold nodded, a calculating look in his eyes.

"Surprise works to our advantage. Right?" September looked from one man to the other.

Reluctant nods.

"Teddy, they took your girls to get to you, and through you, to me." When Arnold spoke, she talked over questions. "We don't know why, and that doesn't matter. But they couldn't reach me in Heartland. Combs made sure of that." With shock, she realized his precautions had probably kept her alive. "Now we know I'm the one they want. That's how we keep the girls safe. No arguments." Her fierce expression stopped any further dissent.

Arnold cleared his throat. "So Teddy shows up early. That's a surprise so they throw up their hands and say 'ya got me, here's the kids?' What's keeping them from hurting him? Or the girls?"

"He's a fast talker." She half smiled at him, and patted Teddy's arm. "You don't know him, but Teddy could sell ice cubes to polar bears. So he tells them I'm delayed—traffic or something. Teddy, you keep them talking, distracted, focused on you. Nikki, Sylvia, and Leslie make a ruckus to add to the confusion." She held up a hand to stop Teddy's denial. "The girls came up with this on their own. I can't control it, and neither can you." The YouTube gambit reminded her of a similar ruse she'd used with her old Blackberry and a radio call-in program.

"No. The police train to handle hostage situations." Arnold shook his head. "We can tell them everything. They come in silently, and I don't know, infiltrate or..."

"And get my granddaughters killed. Not negotiable." Teddy crossed his arms, his face red. "I look old and decrepit but like September said, I've talked myself out of worse situations. Too much at stake here. I'd rather take my chances on my own balls, than some hot-head rookie cop out of the back country trying to play hero." His face flushed, and she could see his pulse in his temple.

September put a hand on both men's arms. "Nikki has that covered. I'm not sure how, but that little girl has connections." She explained the child's plan with her tablet. "Nikki says there are only two bad guys. Quinn Donovan—"

"—that's the motorcycle girl that dumped Lefty." Teddy glanced down at the quiet dog, and he wagged at the sound of the name.

"Right. And the other man she called Casper Fright. An obvious alias, but Teddy might sleuth something more on him." September turned to Arnold. "He's got skills, Arnold. That's his business. Information, finding what's hidden, sort of an internet detective."

"Oh hell, September, no need to be polite. I'm a hacker, pure and simple. And I'll never forgive myself if what I've done with my life ends up hurting my girls." Teddy's voice caught. He stumbled and grabbed September's arm.

Arnold supported Teddy's other arm, and they led him back outside toward their vehicles. "So your plan means Teddy drives to the church to surprise the bad guys. He keeps one of them busy, while the girls make a ruckus to distract the other one. Meanwhile, September sneaks into the church somehow, and snap, whammy, abracadabra, she bravely swaps herself and Teddy safely spirits the girls away? Oh, and you're relying on Nikki—how old is she?"

"I don't know. Maybe eleven?" September shrugged. "She's very bright, works for Doc Eugene." Shadow pressed against her side. Lefty sat nearby, watching with interest.

Arnold laughed without humor and shook his head. "You're relying on the tech skill of a middle schooler to call in the cops before the bad guys do the dirty on September. They'll have guns. They probably have reinforcements. No offense, but in this Marine vet's opinion, y'all are dumber than a coal bucket."

She bristled. "It's my choice. I've got to do what's right. And I've got a gun Teddy can carry."

He rolled his eyes. "You think they'll let him keep it?"

Teddy just looked beaten. "You got a better idea?"

Arnold grinned. "As a matter of fact, I do."

Chapter 47 - TEDDY

As they reached the vehicles, Teddy saw September's face had paled to match the white trim on the RV. Shadow bumped her hand again, and she leaned down to press her forehead to his. "Baby-dog, better *take-a-break* before we hit the road again." He licked her cheek and bounded to the designated grassy spot. Lefty whined. "You too. Go *take-a-break*." She saw Arnold stare. "Lefty's part of this. We'll explain later. No time now. What's your idea?"

Teddy scowled and eyed the bigger man. "Look, I know you got dragged into this, and any other time, I'd say no. If you're a veteran, thanks for your service." He paused, mind whirling. "But we can't afford to turn down help." Quinn Donovan and her kind played for keeps; they had training, money, and influence pulling the strings—just like now. In what world could a gardener, even a veteran with skills, out-play those hidden puppet-masters? "Why should you risk helping us?"

Arnold's mouth tightened into a thin line. "When Victor Grant came to town, he left bodies behind, including my brother, Aaron."

"Victor's dead." September shuddered. Shadow nudged her hand. But her satisfaction rang loud and clear in the two words.

"He's dead now, sure. But somebody else pulled the strings." Arnold's face flushed, and he scrubbed his eyes. "Did you know that my brother fell while walking Kami? Not her fault. I'd picked up Aaron for the day to give your brother Mark a break, and the two of them slipped out. Aaron broke his leg just above the ankle. Kami bore his weight and helped him hobble back to the house. She barked and barked until I came." He breathed heavily. "She stayed with him, brought her stuffed toys to make him smile. Not too long after that, my brother died, and Kami... every time we put on her harness for a walk, she looked for him."

September put a hand on his arm, and he shook it off.

"Does it make sense that the universe is out to get you, September? You're like a whack-a-mole—the more you dodge, the more some bad-ass keeps whacking—and my brother got in the way. Pulling a trigger would have been more merciful." His voice shook. "I watched him die over months and months. At the end, he didn't know me, or your brother Mark. Didn't know Kami. I don't care about justice. I want vengeance." He breathed hard. "Either I'm part of the plan, or I call the cops right now."

Teddy frowned. "I'm all ears."

Arnold pointed at his truck. "I like the idea of a distraction. We've got two vehicles. Teddy shows up in his RV and says you're on your way. How? In my rig?" He opened the back. "That's not a distraction or a sneaky arrival. You roll up in this, everybody hears and sees you." Arnold pulled out a rolled-up ball of fabric, and shook it out, revealing stained dingy-white coveralls.

September eyed them dubiously. "I don't understand."

Teddy shook his head. "I need them to see and recognize me. Besides, those won't fit me."

Ignoring them, Arnold reached further into the truck bed. He dragged out a plastic backpack sprayer and a combination ventilator-mask. "Not you. Me. I wear this." He grinned. "They expect Teddy. They won't expect some random gardener making rounds to spray the church landscaping."

"But what—"

"How does that—"

September and Teddy protested over top of each other.

"Hear me out. I agree, your plan requires a distraction. I'm your man." He gestured to the suit and equipment. "You two drive up in the RV, but September stays hidden. Teddy meets the bad guys for his verbal tap dance."

Teddy nodded. "They still haven't sent the address, so that'll discombobulate 'em from the get-go." He could tell the Donovan girl September was stuck in traffic. Then September could sneak out of Nellie Nova and find his girls. "I can give September a signal when the time's right."

"They'll be watching for me." September hunched her shoulders. "They'll shoot as soon as I step out of the RV."

Arnold held up a hand. "That's where I come in. At Teddy's signal, I'll drive up all obvious as stink on a skunk. We'll have to play some by ear once we see the layout. But if Teddy parks to one side of the door, I can swing the truck close and block the view for you to get into the church." He turned back to Teddy. "You're the internet genius. Can you get us pictures ahead of time? There may be more than one entrance. If you keep one entertained, the other can't watch all the doors."

"Or windows." September rocked nervously from foot to foot.

"No windows." Teddy shook his head. "Stained glass won't open. Nikki sent pictures from inside the church, and I've got pictures of the outside." He looked at September. "I like it. That gives you some cover, better protection."

September hugged herself. "So does my gun." At Arnold's incredulous look, she added, "Combs insisted. I took a class."

"You ever shot anybody?" Arnold raised his eyebrows when she shook her head. "Didn't think so. Doing it takes a lot more than thinking it."

"I have. Not something I brag about." Teddy whispered. "You're not the only veteran, Arnold." He relished their surprise. "If the plan works, September won't even see the kidnappers. Let me carry. They won't expect a doddering old man to have a gun." He demonstrated limping a few steps, squinting through his glasses like he couldn't see well.

"A pro leaves nothing to chance. They'll search you, old man or not."

"Why won't they shoot you, Arnold?" September touched his arm. "You'll make a big target in that get-up."

"We're all targets." Arnold grinned. "I'm counting on that. Even a pro won't consider me a threat."

Teddy wanted more explanation, but time pressed on. They

needed to go, now. Sooner the better. "What signal should we use? A text?"

September nodded. "Set the text now, so it comes to all of us. I'll let Nikki know so she won't freak over Arnold's spaceman get-up." She took a big breath. "She'll already be broadcasting, Arnold. Soon as that happens, the police will come—"

Teddy felt his heart race. "—and sharing on social media means anyone in the area could show up. Like a flash mob."

"Which risks more people getting hurt." September turned to Teddy. "I still think we should trust the police to do their job."

"No!" His stomach turned over. All the candy made him queasy. "If you've got cold feet, at least don't stop me. Or us. You still with me on this, Arnold?"

The big man nodded. He and Teddy exchanged cell phone numbers.

"I need a rope, if you've got it. And some kind of tape. Masking tape or electrical, something like that?" Arnold looked first at Teddy then at September.

September turned away, resigned. "I've got some gaffer's tape and an extra tracking line in Shadow's bag. It's only about twenty feet, though."

"That's plenty."

September waited for him to unlock the RV. "Shadow. Lefty. Come-a-pup, let's go!"

The two dogs, resting companionably next to each other, sprang up. They raced, mouthing each other along the way. Teddy worried how they'd get along stuck together in the RV as he opened the door. He'd leave the animal stuff to September. His dry mouth made him want to cough. At the thought, he took another slug of the energy drink, then tossed the can in a receptacle before he climbed into the driver's seat. Meriwether reclined in the passenger seat. The dogs ignored the cat.

Teddy waited impatiently, until September collected the leather line and tape, and handed it out the door to Arnold. She didn't ask why he needed it, and he didn't say.

"It'll take me about ten minutes to get into my gear, and slosh together bug juice I've wanted to get rid of. Not lethal, but it'll do the job. I'll follow you, Teddy, and wait for your signal to come on in."

Teddy watched the man climb in the back of his truck. Arnold pulled up a section of the truck bed lining and dumped it onto the pavement. He pulled off long lengths of tape, cutting them with his teeth, and stuck them on the side of his truck in readiness for—something. The man looked like a football player, and Teddy hoped Arnold's imposing size would help with whatever happened next.

September moved to the back of the vehicle with Shadow and Lefty as Teddy started the RV. "You said twenty minutes, Teddy?"

He took off his glasses, polishing them on his shirttail. "I could make it in ten, with no traffic, but we need to give Arnold time to suit up. Open the laptop, and you'll see the pictures surrounding the church. Send to Arnold, too." He wished September would give him her gun. He might get a chance to pop Donovan. His shoulders fell, though, realizing if he hurt one, the other would go after his granddaughters.

"There's no way out. Is there, September?" He put the RV in gear. "Thank you for helping me." He spoke past the lump in his throat. He considered her almost a daughter. Having to choose between September and his granddaughters was tearing his heart in two.

"I'm sorry. Arnold's right. I wish I knew what I did to piss them off." She paused, and he heard her typing on the keyboard. "Done. Also sent Nikki the update."

When an email notification came in she added, "Nikki says they're fine so far, holed up in a second-floor office. Donovan's partner took a long gun, maybe an automatic, and tripod up to the bell tower." She shivered. "We'll be easy pickings from there."

He agreed, but tightened his jaw. Meriwether meowed and leaped back onto the dashboard. Teddy reached up to stroke the cat's cheek. "He's a wonderful cat. Promise me you'll find someone to love him as much as I do…"

"Stop. Just shut up, Teddy." September nearly yelled the denial. "Strap on your winning attitude, Mr. Bad-Ass Hacker. Don't give up before we've even tried." She walked forward, swaying in the moving vehicle, and hugged his neck. "We've been through lots together, and always came out the other side. Right?" She hugged him again. "Right? You've got a road trip to South Bend to enjoy with the girls. So let's do this."

Shadow woofed, and Lefty joined in the happy bark-athon. Teddy patted September's hand. For some reason, he felt terribly hungry, and gobbled down another of the candy bars. He guessed the extra energy would come in handy.

A few minutes later he slowed to a stop. "Problem. They don't want surprises." Teddy pointed to a chain stretched across the private drive, barring access to the church. "I can't off-road in Nellie—although it looks like other vehicles did—we'd get stuck going into the roadside ditch. Guess we hoof it."

September smiled grimly. She fished in the pocket of her windbreaker. "Used these this morning on a pesky stick Lia's pup tried to swallow." She produced a pair of cable cutters. "They ought to do the trick." Quickly, she slid out of the door. Using one hand, the tool cut the chain like butter, and she climbed back into the vehicle. She pocketed the cutters, tethered Lefty to the leg of the built-in table, and urged Shadow to follow her into the tiny toilet space.

Teddy waited until September closed the door before he pulled through the makeshift barrier and drove to the quaint church's parking lot. A familiar-looking motorcycle slouched in the shade of a massive tree that sprawled higher than the roof of the stone building. On the other side of the lot, a black sedan—looked like a rental—rested near front steps and arching wooden double doors.

Swallowing hard, Teddy chose a parking spot in the middle of the lot, leaving room for Arnold's truck to park between Nellie Nova and the church, to hide September when she disembarked. *It's going to work, it's got to work. Please God, let this work.* He hadn't attended church since his wife's funeral and hadn't prayed since God turned a deaf ear to saving her. But Teddy prayed now, silently, fervently—bargaining, pitching, offering anything he could think of in exchange for Leslie and Sylvia's safety. And Nikki's, of course.

He opened the door, stepped out, and let it swing back to latch. Teddy adjusted his glasses, let his shoulders sag and posture droop, then slowly shuffled to the front door of the Gothic revival church. He became the gnarly old man they expected, and hopefully underestimated. Over the years, he'd learned a few tricks that came in handy, even without a gun at hand. Although tempted to look up at the bell tower high overhead, he didn't want

Donovan's partner to suspect he knew anything about their plans. With a deep breath, he hitched himself up the steps and opened the door.

Painted light filled the narthex, spilling from the massive stained glass windows lining each side of the nave. It made him feel dizzy. And thirsty. His mouth tasted like dusty cardboard, and he wished he hadn't tossed the rest of the energy drink. The wooden pews sat out of order, some splintered and needing oil. Blood-red cushions had faded over time, and Teddy suspected they'd eject insects or other wildlife should he sit on them. But the painted statuary, and a blue star-studded arching ceiling, paint peeling here and there, spoke of past glories.

The church felt deserted. Had he come to the right place? He hesitated to call out. Maybe he could hunt down the girls before Donovan and her partner discovered his presence.

He looked around for stairs. September said they'd holed up in a second-floor office. Teddy moved more quickly down the center aisle, foregoing the old-man gimp to weave between the pews. His heart pounded a drumbeat inside his head, though, and his hands trembled. Above the altar hung an ornate cross, and more gilded panels and wall tapestries decorated the chancel. He eyed the fancy painted doors on each side and guessed they led to the sacristy, or maybe a storage area for vestments. The stairs to the second-floor office must be there.

He hurried forward. Before he reached the left-hand door, the narthex door behind him squeaked open.

Teddy froze, anticipating a bullet in his back. His clothes stuck to his body. He felt sweat trickle down his back and run into his eyes.

Galloping paw-thuds made him flinch. Lefty skidded to a stop beside him, barking with excitement and nose-boinking him repeatedly. *What the hell?* The door to the RV must not have latched, so Lefty had squirmed out. The big three-legged dog moved better running than in the odd bunny-hop slow gait.

"Shush, quiet. Quit it!" He hissed at the dog. What was Lefty doing, anyway?

The door in front of him opened. A thin figure in form-fitting athletic gear stood silhouetted in the meager light. "Teddy

Williams." She held a gun pointed at his middle. "Thanks for coming, even before my associate messaged you. Knew I could count on you."

Teddy squinted. "Where have you been? I worried about you, ya know. And what are you doing here?" Charlie Cider, the kid he'd rescued last Christmas in South Bend. His lips tingled, and another dizzy spell made the room spin.

"Call me Quinn Donovan." She took a step closer, jamming the gun in his ribs. When she whispered in his ear, her lips next to his skin tickled. But the words chilled his soul.

"Do everything I say if you want the kids to live."

Chapter 48 - QUINN

Q uinn backed away from the old man. He'd saved a
terrified little girl, but Charlie Cider died—and gave
birth to Quinn Donovan—the instant she pulled the
trigger on Mr. Bleak. On that day, Quinn promised herself she'd
never again be a victim. No, she'd exact vengeance upon the guilty
who victimized the innocent. She'd needed help to arrange Bleak's
death, though, and now paid the price.

She understood the rules. Do the job and don't question your
betters. Break the rules and suffer the consequences, like Tanner
Rudolf and Sebastian Viejo.

Teddy held up a hand, started to speak, but she scowled and
put a finger to her lips. Mr. Fright wanted Quinn to follow the rules
like a good girl.

Too late for that.

"Sit down, Mr. Williams." She motioned with her gun toward
the first pew. He sat, and dust motes rose to glitter in the light
streaming through the still-open church door. Tanner Rudolph's
dog hopped up on the seat next to him. "You're early. You
couldn't wait for instructions? Just as resourceful as I remember."
She spoke clearly, so the kids and her erstwhile colleague would
hear.

Do they deserve consequences if they didn't know the rules?

"Where are my granddaughters? If you've hurt them——"

"Spare me the dramatics. They're fine. For now." What the hell had this old man done to be used for bait? And what had the bait done to piss off her employer?

She'd been a clueless kid, bounced from place to place as her family dodged the law, and punished repeatedly for breaking mysterious rules that constantly changed. She learned to hide, lie and steal, to ride motorcycles and hot-wire cars and so much more. To know when to fight, and when to lie there and take it, just to survive. *Eye for an eye.* Granny taught hard lessons. Quinn's jaw tightened. She felt her pulse thrum in her temple. Thanks to her new employer's recent training, she had even better skills now. To fight. To run.

To hide.

The wholesome kids upstairs had no concept of such choices. Thoughts of breaking rules titillated them if it helped innocent victims.

But because of Fright's manipulation, the sisters didn't know they'd broken Quinn's rules when they didn't deliver the product as required. Nikki only wanted to save her brother.

She'd been proud of this operation, felt accomplished when they approved her brainchild. But it had never been about moving the insulin. No, it had been about hooking this man, Teddy Williams, the one person who'd ever been kind to her.

Quinn knew how the story ended.

"What's it doing?" She tipped her head, watching the mutt. She left it at the shelter, as directed. How'd it turn up here? It kept nose poking Teddy in the arm. He tried to hold still, wincing with each bruising boink. She leaned forward, keeping the gun trained on him, and whispered, urgency in her soft words. "Are you a wicked man, Teddy Williams? What bad things have you done? You saved me once. Why should I save you now?"

She heard footsteps clattering down the stairs and straightened as Casper Fright burst through the deacon's door. He skidded to a stop and looked between Quinn and Teddy with the dog. "What's that dog doing here?"

"My dog, he's just a pet, belongs to my girls. Don't hurt him. Me. Us." Teddy roused from his bemused expression. His voice wavered. Sweat poured down his face. He put one arm around the dog and hugged it close, and it licked the old man's face, sniffing and licking at his lips.

"Disgusting." Fright unsheathed a knife and stroked the blade, caressing it like a lover.

Quinn raised an eyebrow. She breathed deep, slow breaths to calm herself. He'd left his *special gun* upstairs, probably set up with a scope for long distance targets. Good. She knew how to deal with knives.

"Did you think to search him?"

Quinn shook her head. "Haven't had time." If Teddy had brought a gun, he'd be dead in thirty seconds.

"Stand up, old man." Mr. Fright waited impatiently for him to struggle to his feet. Quinn did as expected: said nothing, and kept her gun on Teddy.

"I did everything you asked." He continued the old-man act, quavery voice, unsteady gait, trembling hands held aloft. "I didn't call the police. I just want to see my granddaughters. Please?"

"You're in no position to make demands." Finding no gun, Mr. Fright shoved him backward, and Teddy half fell into the pew. Lefty whined and scooted close to him again. "You know the deal. Three for one. Where is she?"

She? *Who?* Quinn cocked her head. A new wrinkle.

"On the way. I promise, she'll be here." Teddy babbled. "I couldn't tell her the truth. Who would agree to that? To trade yourself for three kids you don't even know?" He wrung his trembling hands and stuck one in a pocket.

"How long? Delays get you killed. You stand between me and my target. But I'll let you pick which kid dies while we wait."

Teddy juggled his phone out of the pocket. "No, wait-wait-wait, I'll tell her to hurry. Please, just wait. I promise, she's on the way." He pushed a button.

Mr. Fright batted the phone out of his hand, and it spun across the sanctuary floor. "If that went to the cops—"

"Not the cops, no-no-no, please don't hurt them." He sank sideways in the pew, sobbing, face white, whole body trembling. "She'll be here, then you can let the kids go. You will, right? You'll do that?" He whimpered. "God, I feel so sick…"

Quinn couldn't decide if Teddy was putting on an act, or had aged twenty years in the past few months.

"Clock's ticking, Grandpa." Mr. Fright turned to Quinn. "Go bring one of them down." He grinned at Teddy.

"Which one?" She didn't hesitate. Quinn wanted to walk out of here alive.

"I don't care. How about that little one with white hair, probably easiest to handle?" He watched Teddy's facial expression, eager to see how the man reacted. "The other two are his grandkids, right? So grandpa, you got a reprieve. I'll kill that little one to prove I'm serious. Maybe that'll persuade September to hurry up."

Quinn didn't like the idea of blood ruining all the bright painting in the quaint little church. She didn't believe in God. But watching Casper Fright at work proved the devil was alive and doing well, and needed no more sacrifices. She'd follow his directions, watch for the right opportunity, and she might still get out of here without innocent blood on her soul.

She trotted across the chancel to the other deacon's door with stairs leading directly to the tiny office. Nikki wouldn't fight her. Not if Quinn convinced her to listen to reason.

Lefty whined and nudged Teddy. The man slumped in place, eyes half closed, unresponsive. Lefty barked, but the man wouldn't rouse. He gently nosed Teddy's face, sniffing at his lips.

The dog stood up, carefully shook himself, and hopped off the pew. He looked around, spied the man's phone, and raced to retrieve it. Lefty whined again, looked back at Teddy, and then down at the phone. He nose-poked the surface. He nosed it again, scooting it across the floor, until it lit up. Lefty cocked his head, watching with excitement.

"9-1-1, what's your emergency?"

Lefty barked three times, paused, and repeated the three barks. He ran back to Teddy and pushed his front half into the man's lap.

Chapter 49 - SEPTEMBER

S he had to tell Combs. Had to!
September cradled her head in her arms, sitting on
the lid-down toilet, waiting for Teddy's text signal. She'd
controlled her impulse to stop Lefty when he managed to get loose
and follow Teddy out. Too many secrets, enough already! How
could she keep this from him? She'd felt betrayed by his secrets—
how could she turn around and do the same? No matter what
Teddy wanted, she had to trust the police.

No, scratch that. She had to trust her fiancé. Without trust,
they had no future. Sure, the YouTube feed would alert the
authorities. But he had to know now, before it was too late. It had
to come from her.

Before she could change her mind, September sent a text to
Combs.

**<At church in Wintergreen, ransom demand re: Teddy's
grandkids**

She took a breath, typed in the church's address. He didn't
need to know that *she* was the ransom payment. Maybe he'd have a
better answer.

**<I'd do the same for Melinda, for Willie. No choice,
doing it for the kids.**

Almost immediately, his text came back.

>**Wait. Police on way.**

She choked back a sob. Overlapping his message came Teddy's text:

>**Go Time**

Combs was hours away. It was up to her, to Teddy, Arnold, and their plan. She sent a final text:

<**Ck my YouTube live feed. Jeff, luv you forever**

She silenced her phone and took a deep breath before exiting the RV toilet. "No, Shadow, you need to wait for me." Arnold had got the same text alert. He'd be here any minute.

Shadow whined. She hated leaving him behind. He'd helped her in the past, but not as an attack dog. Going into the church meant she might not survive. She made that choice for herself, had to do everything possible to rescue the girls dragged into this mess. Shadow would follow her into hell and back. And she'd do anything to protect him. But she couldn't risk that distracting her from focusing on saving the girls.

"Baby-dog, you stay here. I'll need you more than ever after this." She couldn't risk him giving her away. She hugged him and bent low to scramble to the RV's front door.

The door ajar explained why she didn't see Lefty anywhere. But Meriwether yawned and stretched, sunning himself on the dashboard.

Arnold's truck trundled down the road. September looked at the church, noting the open door. If Arnold positioned his truck correctly, she could walk right into the church without being seen.

He swung into the lot and paused beside the RV, shielding it from the church's view. September climbed out. "Shadow, wait!" She stroked his cheek, then made sure the door latched. And she closed her ears to his yelp of despair.

Before Quinn made it through the deacon's door to the stairs, an engine growled outside. She saw a massive vehicle with green lettering on the doors. "Incoming," she called. "Some gardening service. What do you want me to do?"

Fright's eyes glittered. "Might be our little friend September." His eyes didn't move from Teddy.

Hurrying to the open chancel door, she squinted at the approaching truck. "Don't see a woman. It's some big dude in the driver's seat."

"Then get rid of him. Do your job. The woman will show up eventually, and I'll take her out as she leaves her car." He nodded at Teddy slumped in the pew. "Kill him. Then go kill the kids." He whirled, disappeared through the door, and she heard him climbing the stairs.

Sighing, Quinn crossed to Teddy. She shooed the dog off the pew and sat beside him. "You don't look so good." His eyes welled with tears, making snail tracks down each furrowed, sweaty cheek. "You're not a bad man, are you Teddy?"

His lip trembled, and he tried to speak, but couldn't.

"Shush, it's okay," she whispered, suddenly recognizing his symptoms as ones she'd experienced herself. She'd lost her baby as a result, and learned more than she ever wanted to know about diabetes. "That's why the dog keeps poking you. I didn't know you were diabetic." She raised her voice, so that both Mr. Fright and the girls heard. What they did as a result would decide Teddy's fate. "No need to waste a bullet. He'll be dead in an hour without help." She patted him on the hand, then whispered again, "That girl Nikki, she's got tricks up her sleeves. So do your girls. Hang in there, Grandpa."

She strode to the front door and pushed it the rest of the way open, sticking the gun temporarily in her waistband at the small of her back. The truck slowed as it drew abreast Teddy's RV as if deciding to park, and instead puttered along until it stopped right next to the church.

A big lumberjack-looking man with close cropped sandy hair climbed out. He wore white coveralls, with green stains on the knees and dirt coloring the cuffs. "Hey there, how y'all doing?" He slammed the truck door, nodded at her, and lumbered to the bed of the vehicle.

"What are you doing?" She eyed her motorcycle, parked under the low branches of the nearby tree. What she wouldn't give to climb aboard and ride away without looking back. Quinn stiffened her spine. *Finish the job, then move on.* She'd chosen this life when she accepted her benefactor's help. No do-overs in this business.

"What's it look like?" He shrugged a liquid-filled backpack over his shoulders, pulled on a ventilator-mask and gloves, then adjusted the wand-sprayer in one hand.

"You can't be here. The church... there's an event and you can't be here." She didn't want to kill him. But she would, if he wouldn't listen to reason.

"I got my job to do. Shouldn't take long." He pushed by her, walking with long strides toward the side of the building. He pointed the sprayer wand at the flower beds and kept walking. She followed him around the corner of the building.

Chapter 50 - TIGGER

Tigger half-dozed in a cubbyhole at the top of the spiral staircase. A breeze ruffled his fur backward, his tummy rumbled, and his hind legs throbbed. The snacks he'd gobbled from the baggy helped, but the pain came in waves. He panted, wanting a drink, and a hidey-hole more than anything else.

Instinct demanded Tigger hide. Hide himself away from all perceived threats until he healed. He couldn't protect himself, couldn't run away, had barely had strength to climb the many stairs. But from a high perch, he could watch for danger. Make himself small. Stay silent until the threat disappeared.

The strange man climbed back up the narrow stairs, his shoulders so broad he had to turn sideways to navigate them. He'd left behind something that smelled oily-scary—like Quinn's gun—on the small wooden floor, propped up on a stand. He didn't like Quinn's gun, but he loved and trusted Quinn, so that made hers okay.

The man clambered into the tiny space. Tigger shrank back against the wall. If he didn't move, the man wouldn't see him.

The scary stranger played with the gun, pointing it here and there as he stared out across the view. He shifted again, and this time, one of his shoes pressed against Tigger's tender bandaged paws.

Screaming, Tigger launched himself at his attacker, healthy front paws clawing across the man's torso.

Arnold never acknowledged September. He just slowed to a crawl so that she could keep pace with his truck. He pulled close to the building and got out. September hugged the side of his truck, pulling out her gun when she heard the girl's voice.

Quinn Donovan.

She admired Arnold's matter-of-fact demeanor. She peered beneath the truck, and saw two pairs of legs—his in white coveralls, and a girl in form-fitting leggings—move away. Arnold led Donovan from the front door to give her a chance to slip inside.

A scream split the air.

September gasped. One of the girls? Voice too low for that. A man. It came from overhead. She dashed for the church door, gun in hand.

Donovan whirled, saw September. She pulled her own gun.

Moving with the grace of an orchestra conductor, Arnold brandished the sprayer's wand, aimed, and let fly with the juice. It hit Donovan square in the face.

The air filled with the choking smell of garlic.

Screaming, Donovan clawed her face with one hand, eyes squinted closed. She pointed the gun with the other. Three shots. Two hit Arnold square in the chest.

He toppled. The chemical continued to spew.

Crying in disbelief, September ran into the church, slammed the door, and threw the lock.

The man's cries of surprise ratcheted up Tigger's arousal. The stranger abruptly stood, trying to shake Tigger off his back. He kicked the gun. It fell down the metal stairs, clattering and echoing so loud it hurt Tigger's ears.

Tigger climbed higher. Elevation meant safety! He clawed up the man's shoulders, biting at his neck before he saw a swinging velvet-padded rope.

He grappled for purchase. Paw over paw, Tigger pulled himself up the rope.

The old church bell pealed, clanging with each swing of the cat's eighteen-pound weight. Tigger reached the wooden stock directly above the bell, clambered aboard, and rode the rise-and-fall until it slowed to a stop. Tigger curled himself into a tight ball. And stayed alert for more danger, waiting for Quinn to return to him.

Chapter 51 - SHADOW

Shadow raced up and down the length of the RV, stopping at each window, pawing and crying for September to turn around. Let him out. It was a good-dog's job to stay with his person. To protect her!

She'd taken her gun. That meant danger. She shouldn't be alone. He looked around Teddy's big car. The cat blinked at him and flicked his tail. Lefty was gone.

Why did Lefty get to go but September left Shadow behind? Whimpering, Shadow again paced window to window, to figure out what to do. He watched September bend low and walk beside the big truck that belonged to the gardener. Maybe Teddy took Lefty into the building.

He woofed softly, tail raised in excitement, when Arnold climbed out of his truck wearing funny white clothes. His head cocked when the big man shrugged on the backpack and waved the stick around. A girl came from inside the building. She left the door open and talked to Arnold. Shadow wagged hard when he saw September ready herself to run inside.

His ears slicked back at the stranger's scream of pain and anger. The girl with Arnold whirled and pointed a gun at September.

Shadow roared! He punched the window. Guns hurt good-dogs and their people. He had to stop the girl, protect September. Out, he had to get out, out, OUT!

A big noise clanged overhead, again and again. It hurt a good-dog's ears. Shadow yelped and flinched at each bonging sound. The big cat on the dashboard hissed and slunk to the floor, finding shadowy places to hide.

Bounding into the front seat, Shadow nosed that window, too. He pawed the door. Sometimes when he did that in September's car, the window scrolled down. Whining, he clawed at the panel on the passenger side, and then pushed into the driver's seat. It smelled good, like Teddy.

Pop! Pop-Pop!

He knew the sound of a gun. He redoubled his efforts, whimpering, when more screams split the air. Shadow also heard sirens in the distance. They made him want to howl along, but he had business to finish.

Shadow focused, needing to puzzle out his escape. He ignored the motorcycle when it roared to life. Instead, he carefully sniffed each button and lever on Teddy's door panel. He couldn't manage the handle that cracked open the door. But Shadow found Teddy's scent on another button, in a different location than those in September's car.

The motorcycle ran a short distance and stopped. Shadow glanced up and lifted his lips in a silent snarl at the girl with the gun. She bent over a car and hit the tires with something, and the car settled like a dog taking a nap. Then she rolled her motorcycle toward the RV.

His snarl grew into a full-throated growl. He wanted to bite, make this scary stranger run away. His ears slicked to the back and spittle flew to dot the glass between them. She had pointed a gun at September. *Danger!*

She ignored him and bent low to do something to the RV tires.

So he poked the Teddy-scented button on the door panel. The window rolled down. The girl looked up at him, eyes bright red and raining wet. Shadow leaped out of Teddy's window, straight at the motorcycle girl.

Chapter 52 - NIKKI

When the church bell clanged, Nikki nearly jumped out of her skin. She yanked the tablet's charger out of the wall socket and scrambled from under the desk. She now wore the sweater she'd packed, the better to hide a surprise, if they needed it. Nikki and the girls had been whispering into the mic, narrating to an invisible live-stream audience. But now she needed actual visuals.

Outside, gunshots followed the overhead cacophony. Nikki dashed to the tiny window and propped the tablet atop the AC unit to record the drama. "She's running away! See? See? On her motorcycle, and outta here!" Nikki's elation made her want to jump up and down. *One down, one to go.*

The other girls crowded close. "That's Grandpa's RV! I told you I heard him." Leslie poked her sister. "Oh-oh-oh, look, look! A black dog jumped out. It chased the motorcycle." Leslie's voice shook.

Nikki grinned. "That's Shadow, September's dog. I told you about him." She loved cats more than anything, but she had a soft spot for the big shepherd. September let her give him treats when he visited the clinic. Seeing Shadow meant September couldn't be far away.

Nikki moved the tablet, panning through the small window, but couldn't get a good angle to see past a big truck. The door into the small office burst open. All three girls screamed and shrank back together.

Mr. Fright, face bloody from claws, strode inside. He pointed a scary looking gun. "Move. Downstairs. Now."

Nikki gulped, but held up the tablet. "Smile for your close-up." She flung it at him, and in the same move, dove to the floor. Reflexively, she hugged and hid her face against the Buc-ee's beaver toy fallen from her bag.

He roared, batting the tablet out of the air, and followed with a blast from the gun. Plaster from the wall powdered, and the AC window unit shuddered. The accordion-pleats holding it in place tattered in the onslaught. The sisters screamed and clung to each other.

Mr. Fright yelled, enunciating each word clearly. "September Day, those are warning shots. I've got the kids. If you care about them at all, come out now." His narrowed eyes stared at Nikki, aiming the gun at her face. "You girls do exactly what I say, or you all die. Blondie, here gets it first."

Chapter 53 - SHADOW

Shadow raced after the motorcycle for only moments before more gunshots stopped him. He spun and thundered up to the building, swerving for a moment to check out the white body on the ground. Arnold didn't move. The air reeked.

He sneezed, and raced up the stone steps to the door. September's scent clung to the pathway, and her hand left trace on the door handle. Shadow scratched at the threshold, whined and scratched again. He stood on his hind legs and mouthed the handle. But the door wouldn't open. He barked, and barked again. She was inside! Shadow called for her to let him in, let a good-dog protect his person.

But nobody came.

Whirling, Shadow abandoned the door. He'd look for other ways in. Their house had a back door and maybe this place did, too. Or a window like on Teddy's car that he could open.

Trotting with purpose, Shadow passed by one massive tall window after another, dodging around overgrown shrubs and an immense tree. He jumped up to look through the windows, but couldn't see past the dark thick colored glass. Shadow ran all the way around the building, panting with frustration and excitement, but couldn't find a way inside.

A man's harsh voice yelled from high overhead, shouting September's name. Was she there? Was that why she couldn't open the front door? Shadow ran until he could stare up at the tiny window, different from those within a good-dog's nose-reach. Shadow sniffed the air and cocked his head, sifting for any clue that might tell him what to do.

Motion drew his attention, and Shadow's panting mouth snapped shut. High above, in the uppermost branches of the tree, a squirrel chittered at him. It scampered away, leaping from limb to limb, before launching itself onto the high pitched roof and disappearing.

Shadow bounded toward the trunk of the massive tree, placing front paws against its girth. He woofed under his breath. Squirrels teased good-dogs by staying high above, out of reach. But Shadow knew how to climb a tree. If he could leap up to reach that lowest limb, he'd climb to the high window and reach September.

Backing away for a running start, Shadow hurled himself up the trunk of the massive tree.

September winced at the man's threat to hurt the kids. He'd show up any moment, likely with the girls at gunpoint. Looking around the ornate sanctuary, she saw no place to hide, even if she'd wanted to.

A soft moan near the altar drew her attention, then Lefty barked three times. The sound echoed. She kept her gun ready as she trotted down the nave, hunching her shoulders as if God might strike her dead for bringing firearms into this holy place. "Teddy!"

He'd fallen sideways on the seat, legs splayed before him. She saw no obvious injury. September shook him, and he moaned again, and blinked. "Feel awful. Head pounding, blurry vision, gut hurts like hell. Are my girls okay?" He noticed her gun and offered a lopsided grin. "You were right, they searched me."

Teddy's disorientation worried her. He sounded drunk and he looked gray. What had they done to him? "Teddy. Teddy! Listen to me, he's coming downstairs." She shook him again and noted how her words echoed in the high-ceilinged space. Just as she'd heard his words, the man holding the girls hostage would hear anything she said. So, without speaking further, September pressed her gun into Teddy's hand. They had already searched him. "Hang on, Teddy. Use it. For your girls!" Teddy needed to shoot as soon as Mr. Fright appeared through the door.

But which door? Nikki's email said they'd holed up in an upstairs office. One of the arched doors on each side of the altar must lead to the stairwell.

She heard the clattering of footsteps on stairs on the left side—you couldn't pay kids to walk quietly—so September dashed to the right-hand door and slipped inside. She didn't have to make it easy for Mr. Fright. The three girls spilled out of the opposite door. Mr. Fright held a gun to Nikki's head.

Shadow balanced on a tree limb high above the parking lot. The squirrel chattered at him from the roof above him, but he ignored the evil creature. He focused on the small window, now within reach.

A metal box filled most of the lower portion, except for a section on each side that seemed to hold it in place. A ragged, torn portion offered a glimpse into the room.

Pawing forward, Shadow balanced on the dipping limb to stretch his neck and sniff. He detected no trace of September. But the familiar scent of Nikki made his tail wag.

He tentatively grasped the ragged edge of the material. Foam, like the inside of one of his bear-toys. He tugged, and it pulled away. Within seconds, Shadow opened a space wide enough for a good-dog to wiggle through.

His nose dropped to the floor. He read the spore with eager whiffering. September asked him to track Nikki before. So he followed the neon-bright trail out of the office and down the twisty stairs. At the bottom of the stairs, his head came up. Nikki's trail led one way. But September's scent came from the other direction. With quiet paws, Shadow wove through the jumble of storage containers to reach her.

Chapter 54 - SEPTEMBER

S eptember peered through the crack of the door. Teddy still held her gun, shielded by his body and out of view of Mr. Fright. But she didn't know if he'd be able to do anything.

"I know you're here." Mr. Fright laughed harshly. "Come out, now. I'm honored to be your executioner. I had so much in mind for you, but once again you've disrupted plans. Five seconds before I start killing kids."

The girls' faces, eyes wide and lips trembling, offered a glimpse of their personal hells. The sisters stared at Teddy, tears rolling down their cheeks. "Is he dead? Grandpa?" Nikki hugged a beaver toy like a teddy bear, very much a frightened little girl.

Mr. Fright urged the girls further into the sanctuary, closer to Teddy. One hand clamped hard around the back of Nikki's neck, and the other moved his gun back and forth, the barrel sniffing for prey. "Five...four..."

When a cold nose touched her wrist, September nearly screamed. She met Shadow's eyes, and half smiled at his excited wags, so clearly proud of himself. September held a finger up to her lips, signaling silence, and he wagged harder and licked her other hand. Cautiously, she stepped into the doorway, revealing her profile only before retreating out of sight.

He stopped his countdown. "You have a gun. Don't lie. Throw it out, now."

Gun. She saw Teddy blink, but then his eyes again fell closed. The girls looked terrified. "I left my *gun* in the car." She took a big breath, touched Shadow on his neck to catch his attention. September stepped out of the door into full view, but Shadow remained hidden. She grabbed one of the many tall brass stands, a cross affixed to the top, and held it like a talisman. "Who are you? Why me, what have I ever done to you?"

"Not me. You did it to Wong. And I don't know, or care how or why. I just follow orders." He nodded at the cross and sneered. "That's no protection." Mr. Fright kept his grip on Nikki but swung the gun barrel at September.

Shadow knew the word for gun. But the long-barreled monster Mr. Fright held looked nothing like the pistols he'd seen. Dogs could generalize a particular word, but in this situation, September couldn't take the chance. Lives were at stake.

September licked her lips, and spoke emphatically to Shadow. "Let's play *show-me*. This is *cross*." September's voice echoed strong and righteous in the old, elegant church. Mr. Fright frowned, confusion evident, but kept his aim steady. He tightened his grip on Nikki's neck and the girl squealed.

With her other hand September pulled out her keys with Macy's laser toy. She swirled the red-dot on the floor in front of Shadow to get his attention. "This is *red-dot*." She swooped the laser pointer across the room, swirling it in a tight circle on Mr. Fright's gun, pointing like a wrathful old world prophet. "Shadow, *show-me red-dot!*"

Like an avenging angel, Shadow exploded into view and dashed across the nave, and with unerring aim knocked away Mr. Fright's gun.

He roared when the gun spun away. It landed on a distant pew cushion with a soft "poof" of ancient dust.

"Wait, Shadow!" September ran to retrieve Fright's gun.

Teddy roused, pushed himself up on one arm, and aimed September's gun. "Sonofabitch, threatened my girls!" He pulled the trigger, twice. But both shots went wild.

Mr. Fright pulled Nikki closer still, and kicked to fend off Shadow's teeth. "Out of my way. I'll break her neck."

"Now!" Nikki screamed. Her hands came out from under her

oversized sweater.

Insulin pens appeared in each girl's fist. Together, they stabbed Mr. Fright until he let Nikki go.

He bared his teeth, gold tooth glinting like an adder's fang, when he shoved the girls away. The sisters scrambled to Teddy's side. Nikki backed away, stumbling until she fetched up against the altar and stood in place, frozen, watching with wide eyes.

Whirling, the man dashed toward September, ignoring Shadow's snarling snaps at his ankles. September scrambled backward. She swung the brass cross, whipping it before her in an arc to keep him at bay.

He caught it with one hand. Wrenched it away. It clanged against wooden pews in its flight. Mr. Fright fell upon her, pinning September down on one of the pews. He kicked repeatedly; one shoe caught Shadow and September shuddered when the dog yelped in pain.

Mr. Fright's hot, powerful hands encircled September's neck. His thumbs pressed hard against her throat.

Panicked, she grabbed at his wrists. She pulled. His breath heated her face. She wanted to scream. Had no breath. Pried at his fingers, beat his arms, clutched his hair. Her world became the man's crazed eyes, rictus grin, and his thumbs in her throat. His gold tooth sparkled. Pain, so much pain. No breath! No strength! She'd die, he'd kill the others, and she'd never know why...

She couldn't overcome his superior strength. Black sparklies danced before her eyes. Faintly, she heard kid screams. Nikki's halo of hair swirled when the girl jumped on Mr. Fright's back, pummeling him with some kind of stuffed toy. He shrugged her off.

September had seconds left. It took all she had to relax. She blinked, let her eyes flutter closed, feigning unconsciousness. Fell limp. Let both hands fall away. He continued throttling her, not noticing as she felt for the hard outline in her pocket. Struggling, September grappled the plastic handle, pulling it free. No sharp edge on the small tool meant stabbing or beating at him wouldn't work. He pressed harder, body arching away from hers with the effort. With all she had, September opened the tool wide, and snaked the bolt cutter jaws first up between their bodies, cutting open her own flesh as she shoved it beneath his murderous thumbs. He ignored the intrusion, intent on her demise. With all her remaining strength, using both hands, September pressed the powerful spring-loaded handles closed.

A muted "snick" sounded, and the world stopped when he released her. A glass-shattering scream tore the air. Mr. Fright's blood-gouting hand recoiled.

She gasped when he staggered away, his remaining intact hand gripped the maimed fist. He stumbled toward the door as distant sirens grew closer, fumbled the lock open, and staggered from the church.

"Grandpa? Grandpa, wake up!" The sisters hovered over him, but couldn't rouse him. "Call 9-1-1, he's really sick."

Nikki stood by herself, hands fallen to each side. The warrior-child had finally run out of gas. She trembled. Hiccups shook her slight body.

September struggled upright, still sucking air like a parched rose sucks water. She opened her arms, and Nikki stiffly walked into the embrace. Her voice cracked, but she forced the words out, to calm and comfort the distraught child. "I got you, you're so dang brave, Nikki. I'm proud of you."

The little girl stared up at September, almost like she didn't recognize her. Her lower lip trembled.

Massaging her sore throat, September croaked again. "It's okay, we're all okay. You don't have to be strong anymore. You saved us, Nikki. We're safe." September hugged her hard, and abruptly, Nikki's stiff posture relaxed into shivering sobs. "That's right, sweetie, cry it out, get it all out." They sank to the old wooden pew. Shadow bounded up, whining and reaching in to slurp first September's face and then Nikki's.

The little girl's half laugh edged toward hysteria. She turned her head away from his. "Shadow saved us." She reached out a hand to him. "I wish I had some treats." She looked around, and stooped to pick up the beaver toy. "Maybe this?" It had Hank's bloody handprint on it. Shadow wouldn't mind, but Nikki didn't want the toy anymore.

September saw Shadow nose something on the cushion beside them. Bile rose. Acid in her damaged throat. "Leave it," she told him. The police would collect the severed thumb, and identify the real name of Casper Fright.

Shadow backed away from the grisly find, and instead gently took the stuffed toy from Nikki's hand. He sighed, and leaned against September's side.

A figure filled the entry door. September flinched. Who?... A ghostly figure in soiled white coveralls stumbled into the church.

"Arnold! I thought you were dead." Shadow leaped up, dropped the toy, and barked with excitement before reclaiming the prize.

The big man unzipped the front of his coveralls, poking two fingers in the holes left by Quinn's gun shots. Arnold thumped his chest, and metal echoed. "Help me get this off. Between the pizza stone and truck bed liner, I'm carrying an extra thirty or forty pounds, but it did the trick." Shadow's tracking line laced over Arnold's shoulders to suspend the taped-together protection.

As the sirens pulled into the church lot September helped Arnold shrug off the body armor. "Did you call the police?" Hell, her throat felt like she'd swallowed glass.

He shook his head. "I was out cold until minutes ago. I woke up just as a scary guy ran out. Somebody slashed the tires on the sedan and my truck, and the motorcycle's gone. So he took Teddy's RV."

Chapter 55 - KALI

K ali puffed slowly on a cigar, feeling pleased with the progress of her project. Taking out one of her many bought-and-paid-for judges last year had been a necessary evil, but caused temporary delays. She'd worked for and planned this for years. Success would cement her power. Beyond local or even state level, she'd have control of anything she wished.

Even a small chance of a derailment couldn't be allowed. She paced the room, checking the special phone repeatedly as she awaited the expected update from Casper Fright. She smiled, enjoying the taste of the smoke, and anticipating the special rewards she'd bestow upon him for removing the threat. She liked the man's whimsical choice of a church for the execution. "Answered prayers, for me," she whispered.

September Day had no idea of the power she held, and now would never learn the truth. Her demise would send a message to Kali's many enemies. They'd think twice before questioning her authority ever again.

The phone rang and she snatched it up. She wanted all of the details, wanted to relish hearing the blow-by-blow. "Tell me."

He panted, and she smiled, imagining the results of his efforts. Her smile faded when the panting gasps continued. "Well?" In the background she heard sirens, and her nostrils flared. "You failed." She wanted to throw the phone, but instead clenched it in her fist until sharp green-painted nails drew blood.

"Not over yet, just delayed." His words slurred like a drunkard, and she heard wind and tires-on-highway sounds. "Will circle back later to finish the job."

"No!" *Why won't she die?* Her own chest heaved with emotion.

"It was the girl, Quinn Donovan, who betrayed you. She disabled my car, tipped off the kids. *She* gave them *your name!*" She detected a singularly unattractive whine in his voice.

Her pulse galloped, and a red haze colored her vision. The Donovan girl didn't know her name.

Casper Fright had admitted to his own betrayal.

Kali would deal with Quinn later. She had tracking devices implanted into her minions for just such an occasion, as Mr. Fright knew very well. He also knew the consequences of failure.

When he continued making excuses, she disconnected the call, pulled out the SIM card, and destroyed it. She used another clean phone to give directions to intercept Casper Fright and deliver the payment his performance deserved.

As for September Day, Kali made an executive decision. She'd finally scratch that itch herself. Time to get her own hands dirty.

Chapter 56 - SEPTEMBER—A Week Later

September viewed the garden with delight. Green and damp earth smelled fresh and clean, a promise of rebirth she couldn't wait to see unfold. Arnold's plan had transformed the place, even before the roses bloomed. "Yes, put them over by the fence, Melinda. Willie, watch your dog. You don't want Kinsler dashing out the gate."

Combs and Willie were lugging roses from Arnold's truck. She turned to him, wrinkling her brow. "Are you sure you feel up to this?"

Arnold grinned, and flexed his arms. "Still hurts to raise them too high, but the doctor said I got away with bruises. No broken ribs, and not even a scratch. He just doesn't want me lifting anything for another week." He waved a hand around the area. "Great idea to have a rose planting party. And free kid labor."

Willie dropped one of the pots and black soil spilled out. September made a face. "Free doesn't meant perfect, I'm afraid."

Combs followed his son, and straightened the tipped-over plant. "Attention to detail, please." He cocked an eyebrow at September. "He needs to listen to you. Don't let him get away with half-ass-ery." Combs carefully set down the two plants he'd carried.

She crossed her arms, hugging herself. It had been a lovely day. Bright blue skies, sun warming the air to a delightful 65 degrees, and the smell of fresh dirt. But September didn't want to push Melinda or Willie too far and spoil the mood.

Melinda pushed hair out of her eyes with dirty gloves, and left a smear on her cheek. "Dad, we need more holes." She'd volunteered to plant a rose in each spot Arnold had marked with a little flag. Thanks to his earlier groundwork, the usually stone-hard Texas soil seemed to welcome the attention.

"Yes ma'am." Crossing to his daughter, Combs planted a kiss on top of her curly red hair, and picked up the shovel again. "How many did you order?" He looked at September, cracking his knuckles. "I'm working up an appetite." He wiggled his eyebrows.

She blushed, and smiled back. When she'd got home from the church debacle, they'd made up, and had a long talk, peppered with apologies, assurances, and tears on both sides. Combs promised more transparency. And she agreed to self-defense training and Combs's increased security—until they figured out how to stop her relentless enemy. Still, September couldn't shake her guilt, with so many friends in danger because of her. "We have fixings for lots of homemade pizza, courtesy of Arnold's metal pizza stone. Complete with bullet dimples."

Combs whistled, and glanced at Arnold before attacking the next hole. "Pretty nifty DIY body armor. Where'd you learn that trick?"

"From my military days. Sometimes you make do with what you got. Just lucky Donovan shot a 9mm instead of AK47 rounds from that Mutant rifle that Mr. Spooky Guy carried. Those would've gone through." Arnold looked uncomfortable, and changed the subject. "Hey Willie, we'll need a couple people to muscle those big fifteen-gallon roses from the truck. Just bring the smaller ones." He looked over at September. "We can wrestle 'em off the truck, and plant them later."

"Oh, there's plenty of time. The wedding isn't until this summer." She'd had her fill of churches. They'd decided to hold both the wedding and the reception in the garden.

Kinsler zoomed around the place, yapping with happy excitement. Shadow watched, whining, but the big black dog stayed close to September's side. "Baby-dog, I'm fine. Go play. Play with Kinsler. But you two stay out of trouble." She laughed when he play-bowed to her, and then dashed after the much smaller dog with delighted woofs.

"Kinsler's not a trouble-maker. He's a hero dog, you know." Willie reappeared, with another two roses. He plopped them down, again spilling black soil.

"The roses need that dirt, Willie. You don't want to short change them." She kept her tone pleasant and neutral. How did you talk to kids, anyway? She always worried she'd say something wrong and start a battle.

"Okay." He knelt and used both hands to scoop the dirt up and dump it back into the pot.

Her mouth dropped open. He hadn't argued.

Combs grinned at her and winked. *He must have talked to them.*

"How's Teddy doing?" Arnold asked as September knelt in the dirt next to Melinda.

"Teddy's fine. The doctors told him all his symptoms came from stress. And eating all that junk food." The man seemed addicted to Milky Way bars and energy drinks. "He's still waiting to get Nellie Nova back from the police." Mr. Fright had abandoned the RV not very far down the road. The police found Meriwether snoozing on the dashboard, his paws bloody—someone else's blood, not his own. "Teddy has promised to improve his diet. Said he has to be an example to Leslie and Sylvia. Oh, and they're both grounded for the foreseeable future."

"So's Hank." Melinda grabbed the next rose, tipped it sideways to loosen the root ball, and caught it in a gloved hand when it slid out. "They're lucky to be alive. Right Dad?" She looked at Combs sideways. "I'd never go off like that on a spring break. Nope, I'd follow the rules." She batted her eyes, then loosened the dirt around the rose, and dumped it into the hole he'd dug.

Combs tightened his lips. "Damn straight. That's *if* you ever went south for spring break, and that's doubtful." He shoveled dirt aside for the next hole. "Those kids only got a slap on the wrist."

"Oh Dad. Can't you take a joke?" She stood up, brushing dirt off her jeans. "I don't want to go to south Texas anyway."

"She wants to stay here with Hanky-poo!" Willie sing-songed the allegation. "She's always live-streaming with him. Probably wants to lip-lock with 'im. Gag-a-maggot, that's gross."

"I'm gonna kill you, Willie!" Melinda whirled and chased after her brother, scooping up a dirt clod in one gloved fist. Kinsler broke away from his tag game with Shadow to dash after the kids.

Arnold laughed, and shook his head. "Were we ever that

young? Hey, whatever happened to Lefty. Did he really call 9-1-1?"

September nodded as Shadow pranced up to her. "I trained him to do that. Every phone's different, but he figured out what to do." She smiled sadly. "Teddy wanted to adopt Lefty for his grandkids, but it was best Lefty returned to Tanner Rudolph's family. They want to place Lefty with someone who really needs him. Special dogs need to be with special people." She pressed her forehead against Shadow's neck, grateful he always knew when to disobey. Just as a guide dog refused a command to lead his partner into traffic, a service dog's selective disobedience kept human partners safe. Sometimes dogs knew better.

Combs leaned on the shovel and mopped his brow with the back of one hand. "Apparently, the insulin that Rudolph used was expired. You can't always count on the stuff from overseas. That's why he died."

"Did you find out anything more about Quinn Donovan?" September grabbed the next rose, tipped it out of the bucket, and gently placed it into the hole. Grabbing handfuls of mounded dirt shoveled from the hole, September scooped most of it back around the roots. Shadow reached out, tested the loose soil, and mimicked her, tentatively paw-raking the dirt. "Teddy swears she's the same girl he helped last Christmas."

"No sign of either Charlene 'Charlie' Cider or Quinn Donovan. We found her motorcycle, so she's traveling another way." Combs shrugged. "Her prints aren't in the system."

September scooted on her knees to the next hole. When Shadow pawed the area again, he tipped his head to one side and looked at her, asking permission. She patted the marked place, and told him, "It's okay, baby-dog. You can dig. Shadow, dig."

Kinsler raced to join him. Soon, the two dogs kicked up dirt in companionable silence. She intended to add a sand box to the garden design as a legal doggy digging outlet. That way, Kinsler would leave her roses alone.

"Doc Eugene's got Donovan's cat. She called the cat Tigger, but he thinks it's the same animal as Sherlock, the white Maine Coon cat Charlie took." September brushed dirt off her jeans. "Donovan, or somebody, shaved down the cat's fur and colored it. Doc says Nikki did a great job with first aid and that he's responding well to the treatments." Her eyes widened. "I'd never heard of using tilapia skin as a temporary graft. It apparently reduces pain, too."

"Fish? That's bizarre." Arnold wrinkled his nose. "Wouldn't that stink? I thought cats eat fish?"

September shrugged. "Good questions. I'm sure Doc Eugene figured out a way to make that work. Nikki wants to adopt the cat once he's well."

Combs offered a hand to help September to her feet. "Nikki did a great job with the live-stream, too. Frustrating as hell for me to watch while y'all fought off the bad guys." He pulled September close. "We agreed, right? No more Lone Ranger stuff."

"No argument there!" She leaned into his kiss. "Nikki had back-end help with the live-stream. But she's not talking."

Melinda sauntered back to the digging area and leaned against Combs's other side. He looked at her. "Don't suppose you'd know anything about Nikki's techie friends?"

The girl shrugged, lips thin, and looked away.

Combs watched Shadow's digging efforts. He hugged September's waist. "He can have my job." Willie raced to join in, and the adults stood back watching the excavation fun.

Arnold checked the stock of plants. "Only two left."

"I'll get them." Melinda ran to collect the last pair. She plopped them down and kneeled beside her brother. "Your turn to plant. Don't destroy them, Willie. Just tip them onto your hand, and lower—don't dump 'em—into the hole." She looked up at September. "He can be such a kid sometimes."

September hid a smile. The two dogs and both kids would need baths. But for now, the fun they shared trumped clean fur or clothes.

"Thanks for all the help." Arnold hooked up the hose to the drip irrigation line. "I'd give y'all a big fat discount, if I hadn't already done so. Appreciated the new set of tires, too."

"Least we could do." September wasn't sure why Nellie Nova's tires were spared, allowing Casper Fright to escape. He had no record, either, and only targeted her at the behest of someone else that September somehow wronged. Maybe she'd misheard, but she didn't know what she'd done. September wished she knew what.

Combs gave September another hug and released her. "We'll finish up out here. Why don't you start the pizza?" He glanced at Melinda, and she nodded and led the way back into the house. Shadow saw September leaving and rushed to join her.

"You're a mess, baby-dog. Shake." He did. "Paws." Shadow scrubbed first his front paws and then the rear paws, but he still carried clumps of dirt. The humans would also track, and they could sweep the slate floor. September shut the pet doors to keep the dirt contained. "Where's bear-toy?" His ears pricked, and he cocked his head side to side, before dashing across the room to pounce on the stuffed beaver toy from Nikki. Shadow settled down on his stuffed bed in the corner, stuffie between his paws, and suckled. From top of the refrigerator, Macy watched with interest.

"He's weird, sucking like that. Kinsler just rips toys apart." Melinda hurried to run water in the sink. September joined her. They took turns soaping the dirt from their hands and arms. Neither spoke.

September turned on the oven to preheat. Arnold's pizza steel, cleaned, seasoned, and ready, rested on the countertop. She opened the oven door, reached to carry it to the stove, and nearly dropped it. Without a word, Melinda rushed forward and caught the other side. Together, they placed the nearly twenty-pound steel on the oven rack. September smiled thanks, but Melinda looked away.

Sighing, September set the pizza dough on the kitchen island. She gathered fixings from the refrigerator, dodging Macy-cat's paws each time she opened and closed the door. Pizza sauce, mozzarella cheese, fresh mushrooms, fresh basil and spinach, pepperoni, sausage, and jalapeno peppers for those who liked them. Together, they created four pizzas with different toppings.

Melinda made a face at the peppers.

"How about we put those on only one of the pizzas?"

Melinda smiled. "Good idea." She added shyly, "I've been meaning to thank you."

September's eyebrows raised. "For what?"

"Well… Willie's kinda right. I like Hank. He's a good guy. Even Dad says so, and he never likes the boys I do." She blushed. "If you hadn't got him to the hospital, Hank might have died."

"Oh. Well, I'm glad I could help." September struggled with how to respond. "Melinda, can I ask a favor?"

"Okay, I guess." She busied herself with the food.

September hesitated. *What the hell, not much can make things worse.* "You know I've not been around kids much. Little kids, like Willie, I mean."

"Yeah?" Suspicious.

"And I didn't babysit or anything growing up. So I'm out of my depth."

"I kind of noticed." Melinda snorted, glanced at her quickly then away. "No offense."

Shrugging, September agreed. "It's true. And I need help. You know I love your dad, more than anything."

"Obviously." Melinda didn't look at her.

"And I don't want to mess up. Not with Willie. Or… with you." Her words tumbled faster. "I know I'm not, and can never be, your mom, but I need to be your parent. I mean, after the wedding and all. If you'll let me." September grimaced. That was wrong. No choices there. She would be the kids' step-mom, for better or worse.

The oven beeped. "Ready to put them in." Melinda didn't look at September, just pulled open the door, and placed the first pie on the metal pan. She set the timer.

"Oh hell, Melinda, I'm trying. Can you meet me halfway? What I really want to ask—"

The girl rounded on her, hands on hips, red hair flying. A dare in her voice, ready to slap it down. "What? Ask already!"

"Will you be one of my bridesmaids?"

Melinda's jaw dropped. Then a smile transformed her ready-to-snark expression into one of joy. "Really?" she squealed. "Yes, yes, YES!" She wheeled, started for the door, and then ran back and hugged September hard. "You're the most kick-ass step-mom ever!" She raced out the door, yelling the news to her father.

Bemused, September followed more slowly, and Shadow joined her, the new beaver toy still clutched in his jaws. They watched Willie toss a Frisbee for the terrier to chase.

Shadow whined. He pawed the door and looked up at September.

"I know, that's your Frisbee. He's okay, Shadow. We're a family now, we need to share."

The big black dog leaped up to place muddy paws on her shoulders and slurp her face. She stroked his face and opened the door. She laughed when Shadow grabbed up his new bear-toy and raced out the door, offering it up for a joyous game with Willie and Kinsler.

Chapter 57 – NIKKI—Three weeks later

Nikki couldn't wait to introduce Hope-kitty to Tigger. She'd talked to September for tips, because she wanted the cats to get along and become best friends. After helping to take care of the cat at the vet clinic, she'd fallen in love with the big boy. His paws already looked better, and the short, patchy fur—solid white, not the fake gray and black tabby markings—had grown. Oh, she'd had to convince Mom, but it hadn't been hard. Mom still hovered over Hank, worrying every time he blinked.

Hank had got all smitten (she liked that word) over Melinda Combs. Mom liked her because she was almost fifteen, close to Hank's age, and a cop's kid. So when Mom let Hank pick her up today after his Saturday job, and Melinda rode in the front seat, Nikki didn't tease or threaten to tell Mom about them. Sure, Hank stayed grounded, but they weren't going anywhere. Mom wouldn't be home from her new job for hours. Nikki just smiled when they sat out in the car together, while she lugged Tigger's carrier inside.

Hope-kitty sat at the top of the stairs. When she saw Nikki, she mewed as she walked down the steps, but abruptly stopped and hissed.

"Don't be scared. He's a new friend." Nikki latched the front door. "September said he needs to have his own room for a while until you get used to each other. So no peeking." Nikki turned the front of the carrier sideways, so the cats couldn't see each other.

She lugged the carrier through the kitchen to the laundry room. Nikki had already set up a separate litter box and food bowls, so that Tigger had everything he needed. Hope-kitty had been a barn cat with other felines, and Tigger used to live in a cattery with other Maine Coons. So September said maybe they'd accept each other more quickly.

Nikki crossed her fingers. She hated the thought of Tigger stuck in the laundry room for weeks or months if they didn't get along. Closing the laundry room door behind her, Nikki set down Tigger's carrier and opened the door for him to exit. He stuck his head out, delicately sniffing, then quickly strode out into the room. She grinned when he leaped gracefully atop the washer and checked out the food and water bowl on the counter nearby.

The laundry door squeaked open. Her eyes widened at Tigger's reaction. The big cat stared at the door, fur bristling with concern. But then he meowed, a plaintive cry, and Nikki looked over her shoulder.

Quinn Donovan shut the door and leaned against it, a backpack slung over her shoulder. She dropped the bag, said his name, and held out her arms. Tigger launched himself at the girl.

Nikki, mouth open and heart a trip-hammer, backed against the counter. Tigger's purr sounded motor-boat loud in the small room. "I... we, I mean, the veterinarian took care of him. He's all better now." *If I scream, there's no one to hear.*

"I can see that." Quinn pressed her face into the cat's fur, murmuring to him. "I had to see for myself." She looked up. "Thank you. He's all I have."

Swallowing hard, Nikki crossed her arms and steeled herself. "Are you... gonna kill me now?" Her eyes welled.

Laughing softly, Quinn shook her head. "Why would I do that? You saved my best friend." She crossed to Nikki, put one hand on her shoulder and squeezed. "But if you tell anyone I was here—"

"No, I won't say nothing. Anything, I mean." Her mouth felt so dry. She licked her lips. "You taking Tigger with you?" She'd have to make up a story about how the cat got away. September and Doc Eugene would think her careless and stupid. Her lip trembled.

Quinn sighed and nuzzled the cat. "Take care of Tigger." She stroked the cat's fur. "Wish I could take him with me. Maybe after I finish my next job. But not now. It's too dangerous for both of us." She carefully set Tigger back on the counter, dug in her pocket, and deposited jerky treats into one bowl. Tigger eagerly ate a treat, but kept returning to Quinn for pets.

Nikki felt her breathing slow. Maybe Quinn wouldn't hurt her after all.

"Promise you'll take care of him."

"I promise. I swear."

"You'd better." She pulled open the door.

"Hey, you left your bag." Nikki took a half step, wincing when Hope-kitty slunk inside past Quinn's legs. *Oh my gosh, if the cats start fighting and Quinn hurts Hope...!*

"Keep the bag." Quinn glanced over her shoulder. "Funds inside to take care of Tigger, so there's no excuse. And I heard you needed a new tablet." She put a finger to her lips. "Tell no one. Keep Tigger safe. I'll be watching."

She closed the door behind her, and Nikki nearly collapsed with relief.

Tigger hopped down from the washing machine and trotted to the closed door. He pawed at the opening, crying for Quinn. She might be a bad guy, but Tigger loved her.

Hope-kitty slunk closer, sniffing the much bigger cat. Nikki held her breath, praying the cats wouldn't hurt each other.

When Tigger cried again, a piteous meow filled with grief, Hope drew closer still. She sniffed his flank. And then his neck. And finally, Hope-kitty stroked herself the length of the big cat's body. Her purr joined his cat-song, in a lullaby that eased Nikki's heart and, she prayed, would soothe the big cat's sorrow, until Quinn returned.

~Look for DARE OR DIE coming soon!~

FACT, FICTION, & ACKNOWLEDGMENTS

Thank you for reading WIN OR LOSE, and I hope you enjoyed this sixth book in the September & Shadow thriller series. Thank you for coming along with me on the adventure. There never would have been Thrillers With Bite without you, dear reader, adopting these books. (Can you hear my purrs and woofs of delight?)

After publishing 35+ nonfiction pet books, research fuels my curiosity. While in fiction I get to make up crappiocca, as September would say, much of my inspiration comes from news stories, past and present—the weirder, the better. For me, and I hope for you, the story becomes more engaging when built not just on "what if" but "it happened." So in each book, I like to include a Cliff's Notes version of what's real and what's made up.

As with the other books in the series, much of WIN OR LOSE arises from science, especially dog and cat behavior and learning theory, the benefits of service dogs, and the devastation and reality of those suffering from diabetes. By definition, thrillers include murder and mayhem, but as an animal advocate professional, I make a conscious choice to not show a pet's death in any of my books. All bets are off with the human characters, though.

I rely on a vast number of veterinarians, behaviorists, consultants, trainers, and pet-centric writers and readers, and rescue organizations that share their incredible resources and support to make my stories as believable as possible. Find out more information at IAABC.org, APDT.com, DWAA.org and CatWriters.com.

FACT: The *show-me* game is real, created by trainer Kayce Cover as a vocabulary exercise used with a variety of animals, which my own dog loves to play. See
http://kaycecover.synalia.com

FICTION: Pet viewpoint chapters are pure speculation, although I would love to read dog and cat minds. However, I make every attempt to base animal characters' motivations and actions on canine and feline body language, scent discrimination, and the science behind the human-animal bond.

FACT: Yes, some dogs climb trees. I've never seen a German Shepherd climb a tree, but Shadow (my idea of a super dog!) certainly would give it a try. After all, most dogs would want to catch that evil squirrel! Here's a fun video of one tree-climbing pooch: https://youtu.be/3A1H4JFsSnY

FICTION: While cats certainly climb with dexterity, and a healthy Maine Coon undoubtedly could scale the bell rope in the story, an injured feline in pain probably wouldn't attempt it. Oh, I'm sure given the right circumstances the aggression and/or fear could overcome the pain. For the purposes of the story, Tigger bravely did just that. The bell in this story, modest by some standards, works similarly to the one described here: https://www.bellringingcentral.co.uk/brccontent/artofringing/index.html

FACT: Real-life pets inspired some of the pet characters in WIN OR LOSE. I've held a "Name That Dog/Name That Cat" contest for each of the novels in the series. This most recent contest resulted in 104 cat name nominations with nearly 400 votes for the winning name. And 150 dog name suggestions with 2300+ votes for the winning dog name.

Congratulations to Crystal Stewart for nominating the winning kitty, Tigger! She says that Tigger is a grey striped tabby cat. "You need to earn the cat's trust but once she trusts you, Tigger is very protective and loving."

Congratulations to Linda Stinnett for the winning dog, Lefty. Lefty is an alumni of Great Pyrenees Rescue Society (GPRS) based out of Spring TX and Linda volunteers for that group. When he was a very young pup, Lefty came to the Humane Society in Twin Falls, ID with a badly broken leg and an infection that was resisting multiple rounds of antibiotics. The infection finally went into the bone and it was either take the leg, or lose the dog. Linda picked him up, supposedly to foster as he healed, and became a foster failure and kept him. Once his leg was gone, he turned into a playful puppy and she says he never missed his leg.

The contest was so hotly contested that I also included the runner up winners. The kitty Stormageddon (Storm) was nominated by Eileen Hays. Storm hid out in the front room about a week and a half, where the other cats were fed, before they ever saw her. "Every now and then we would hear a soft mewing, and finally saw her at the food bowl one night." She hid behind the hutch, then under a sleeper-sofa, and wouldn't come out. A live trap caught her, and the vet said Storm had barely been weaned. "We have no idea how she managed to get to our house and make her way inside. She quickly settled in and rules the roost!" And yes, Stormageddon likes to nurse on earlobes.

Kami the dog was nominated by Nancy Huber, is a rescue from Nancy's local Humane Society, and arrived ten years ago to be socialized with her other dogs. "She was the naughtiest pack dog I've ever had and now the best single dog I've ever had." When Nancy fell and broke her leg while walking Kami, the dog bore her weight so she could get back to the house. "She brought me one after the other of her stuffed animal toys until the living room was an obstacle course. She never left my side, following carefully behind my scooter, then walker and crutches and boot and brace. After six months recovery and physical therapy we are walking again, and she is so happy. She still stops and waits at each step until I say go." Kami wears a St. Jude medal with her dog tags, after being erroneously diagnosed with cancer—later confirmed to be arthritis by vet oncologist. She gets bi-monthly osteoarthritis infusions and is doing just great. Truly a miracle as I don't know how I'd replace her."

THANK YOU to everyone who participated in the contest and to all the winners. I think they all deserve treats. Maybe even pizza!

FACT: Only dogs and guide horses for the blind are service animals trained to perform a specific function for their human partner. They become the ears for the deaf, eyes for the blind, support for other-abled partners, and alert animals for health and physically challenged individuals, including diabetics. Diabetic alert dogs detect differences in blood sugar through the scent of their partner's breath, sweat, or other factors. A friend's daughter trained her own service dogs, using saliva on cotton balls to teach the scent discrimination. Today, highly effective electronic monitoring systems work wonders, but dogs may have advantages. Some people report dogs are more accurate than electronics that can malfunction.

FACT: We routinely train dogs to call 911. In the past, large button phones made training such things easier, and service dogs in particular routinely call for help. Today, cell phones with touch screens make "accidental" canine calls possible. With a simple nose-or-paw-touch, dogs activate the "emergency" system (search online for some fun stories). Researchers also have studied the ability of dogs to be trained and reliably communicate with emergency personnel with touch-screen technology. Read about one study here. http://clintzeagler.com/a12-byrne.pdf

FACT: People can suffer from transient diabetes. Pregnancy can cause this, as with Quinn/Charlie's situation, which sadly resulted in her losing her baby. Extreme stress, poor diet, and more also can prompt an episode similar to Teddy's situation. Who can argue with a grandpa's extreme fear and stress over his grandkids' kidnapping?

FACT: The cost of insulin has skyrocketed over the past few years, leaving many individuals without insurance no choice other than to seek alternatives. One friend told me, "We went from paying $50 per vial of insulin for the first seven years to suddenly paying $600 per vial to paying thousands. The real problem is young adults dying shortly after their 26th birthday. Why? Because at age 26, they fall off their parent's insurance and they start the very dangerous process of rationing insulin because they can no longer afford it. It's a very serious problem." People needing lower cost insulin travel to Canada or Mexico, and indeed, the authorities often look the other way for bringing in small amounts for personal use.

FICTION: Some folks have traveled and purchased insulin on behalf of others. But as for Quinn's altruistic scheme, I made that up.

FACT: Specific protocols now exist for emergency calls dealing with potential child endangerment. I based September's call about Nikki's abduction on this information. Learn more at this site: https://iaedjournal.org/child-abduction/

FACT: The painted churches of Texas are real. In the late 1800s and first half of the 1900s, German, Czech, Polish, and Ukrainian immigrants arrived by ship to the port of Galveston, Texas. They built and decorated churches to honor and keep alive their culture and memories of distant hometowns. They settled in the Texas hill country in towns reminiscent of European towns, like Fredericksburg, Schulenburg, Moravia, and Praha (Prague). Today, many of these restored churches continue to serve their communities.

Refer to these links for pictures and videos of actual painted churches: https://www.youtube.com/results?search_query=painted+churches+of+texas+ https://travelingturpins.com/the-painted-churches-of-texas/

FICTION: I made up the name and description of the church and its location of Freedom, Texas, to better fit the story requirements.

FACT: DIY armor works — but please don't experiment with this at home! I based Arnold's safety material on this YouTube test of such a product that employed untempered steel married to a thick horse's stall mat. You'll learn a bit more about Mr. Fright's "Mutant" gun in this video, too: https://www.youtube.com/watch?v=uj1cm8WUGfg&t=59s

In researching where to find such things, it became clear that Arnold would have similar mats in the bed of his truck. And that "pizza steel" widely available for baking scrumptious meals also fit the bill.

FACT: There are motorcycle-riding pets, and gear designed for keeping them safe. More commonly, dogs ride on the backs of bikes, but more and more "Adventure Cats" now join their humans during fun outings. Check out https://www.adventurecats.org/

FACT: The degloving injury happens too often, mostly from drag-accidents when dogs fall from trucks. And yes, the sugar bandage also works, as do tilapia (fish) skin grafts. Veterinarians always have the best options for appropriately treating any animal illness or injury, so as Nikki says, "First aid is only FIRST aid—see the vet!"

For those wanting more context, read this veterinary article about some options for degloving injuries (graphic images, so be aware!):
https://todaysveterinarypractice.com/unique-therapies-for-difficult-wounds/
And here's another fun article about using fish skin:
https://www.akc.org/expert-advice/news/fish-skin-bandages-heal-canine-burn-victims/

FACT: Texas famously has gorgeous roses available, and you may have heard of Tyler, Texas roses. I know this because at one time, we surrounded our "Rosemont" home with over 700 roses. Today, we're updating our garden, just like September. We get our roses from Antique Rose Emporium https://antiqueroseemporium.com in Brenham, Texas, and you can choose from hundreds of varieties of roses.

FACT: Malathion, an organophosphate insecticide, controls bugs like mosquitoes, and spider mites that affect roses. It's highly toxic to bees and other beneficial insects, though, and mostly used in agriculture. It also smells like garlic. When exposed to high doses, like being sprayed in the face by an irate gardener, it can irritate the eyes, cause vomiting, weakness, muscle tremors, and more. The liver and kidneys usually neutralize and eliminate the toxin within a day or two, so Quinn would recover quickly. Learn more here: http://npic.orst.edu/factsheets/malagen.html

FACT: I wish that rosette disease was fiction. Over the past several years, it infected and killed nearly all of our roses. Perhaps only twenty of the original 700 plants survived, hence, the redesign and planting of new beauties. Learn more about this awful scourge here: https://newgarden.com/newsletter-articles/the-latest-on-rose-rosette-disease

FICTION: There's no such place as Four Paws Shelter or Wintergreen, Texas, and I fudged on some things for sake of the plot. But I based most of the policies of the shelter in the story on a composite of other real-life rescues and shelters, like this one in San Antonio: https://www.sanantonio.gov/Animal-Care/What-We-Do-Services/Reclaim-Your-Pet

FACT: The idea of a dog chewing through an AC unit sounds ludicrous and must be fiction, right? When I worked as a veterinary technician, more than one dog did just that. The clinic, located in an old house in Lexington, Kentucky, had an upstairs used for storage. A young German Shepherd broke out of his kennel, opened the door to the front reception area, and the door to the stairs. On the second floor, he chewed through the accordion folds, and got out onto the roof of the clinic. A pizza restaurant across the street called the veterinarian late at night, with what she at first believed was a crank call—"You have a dog on your roof." The dog jumped off the roof, and by the time the staff arrived to look for him, he was sitting (grinning proudly) at the front door. Oh, and later, another shepherd from the same family did the same thing—only he chewed through the AC on the ground floor. I think the dogs shared notes.

FACT: This book would not have happened without an incredible support team of friends, family and accomplished colleagues. Cool Gus Publishing, Jennifer Talty and Bob Mayer made these thrillers with "dog viewpoint" a reality when many in the publishing industry howled at the notion. Special thanks to my editor Nicola Aquino of Spit & Polish Editing, and first readers Kristi Brashier, Gail La Bruno, Frank Steele, and BJ Thompson for your eagle eyes, spot-on comments and unflagging encouragement and support. Wags and purrs to my Triple-A Team (Amy's Audacious Allies) for all your help sharing the word about all my books. Youse guyz rock!

I continued to be indebted to the International Thriller Writers organization, which launched my fiction career by welcoming me into the Debut Authors Program. Wow, just look, now I have six books in a series! The authors, readers and industry mavens who make up this organization are some of the most generous and supportive people I have ever met. Long live the bunny slippers with teeth (and the rhinestone #1-Bitch Pin).

Finally, I am grateful to all the cats and dogs I've met over the years who have shared my heart and often my pillow. Shadow-Pup the Kelpie and Karma-Kat inspire me daily. And the pets who live on in my heart continue to bring happy memories.

I never would have been a reader and now a writer if not for my fantastic parents Phil and Mary Monteith, who instilled in me a love of the written word, and never looked askance when my stuffed animals and invisible wolf friend told fantastical stories.

And of course, my deepest thanks to my husband Mahmoud, who continues to support my writing passion, even when he doesn't always understand it.

I love hearing from you! Please drop me a line at my blog https://AmyShojai.com or my website https://shojai.com where you can subscribe to my PET PEEVES newsletter (and maybe win some pet books!). Follow me on twitter @amyshojai and like me on Facebook: http://www.facebook.com/amyshojai.cabc.

ABOUT THE AUTHOR

Amy Shojai is a certified animal behavior consultant, and the award-winning author of more than 35 bestselling pet books that cover furry babies to old fogies, first aid to natural healing, and behavior/training to Chicken Soupicity. She has been featured as an expert in hundreds of print venues including The Wall Street Journal, New York Times, Reader's Digest, and Family Circle, as well as television networks such as CNN, and Animal Planet's DOGS 101 and CATS 101. Amy brings her unique pet-centric viewpoint to public appearances. She is also a playwright and co-author of STRAYS, THE MUSICAL and the author of the critically acclaimed THRILLERS WITH BITE pet-centric thriller series. Stay up to date with new books and appearances by visiting Shojai.com to subscribe to Amy's Pets Peeves newsletter.

Made in the USA
Coppell, TX
20 November 2024

40150469R00144